ONE WILL: THREE WIVES

One Will: Three Wives

A novel
by

EDITH TARBESCU

Adelaide Books
New York / Lisbon
2020

ONE WILL: THREE WIVES

A novel

By Edith Tarbescu

Published by Adelaide Books, New York / Lisbon
adelaidebooks.org

Editor-in-Chief
Stevan V. Nikolic

For any information, please address Adelaide Books

at info@adelaidebooks.org

or write to:

Adelaide Books
244 Fifth Ave. Suite D27
New York, NY, 10001

ISBN: 978-1-953510-82-2

Printed in the United States of America

For my daughters:

Renata Tarbescu-Dany and Michelle Truly

Acknowledgements

A special thanks to Gail Brooks, Police Officer Gerald Clark, 20th precinct, New York City, Maria Espinosa, Marylou Garbin, Sybil Nassau, Gabe Robinson, free-lance editor, formerly editor at Harper. And special thanks to Stevan Nikolic, Editor-in-Chief, Adelaide Books.

Chapter 1

Detective Cheri Marsh was accustomed to being pushed, jostled, and shoved. She was also used to the sounds of New York: tires screeching, horns blowing, and eardrum bursting construction. As she waited in line at the deli counter the woman behind her reeked of garlic. The man next to her smelled of cigarette smoke. It was dark outside and she could see people rushing to buses, subways, restaurants, bars. She planned to finish up at work, pick up her car with her gym bag inside and spend a couple of hours working out. She often told friends, "I don't miss Montana anymore," but that wasn't entirely true. She missed the mountains and the clean air. After she left Billings, Montana for Manhattan her grandmother told her, "Don't forget who you are and where you come from." She was too busy most of the time to think about who she was.

The woman in front of her couldn't decide what to order. The garlic lady was breathing down her neck and Mr. Tobacco was gulping mouthfuls of air next to her. While the deli kept filling up a woman in back shouted, "Let's go."

As Cheri inched forward she stopped thinking about Montana and thought about food. After finally ordering black coffee and two pastries, she made her way outside. She noticed the cloud-filled sky and took a deep breath. It smelled like snow. Wending her way through the crowds, she realized she wasn't a newbie anymore and elbowed a few stragglers out of her way.

Standing in front of the 20th precinct on West 82nd Street, Cheri inhaled deeply. Most people were home from work by now. She and her partner still had work to do.

She passed the Snapple machine in the lobby, the receptionist behind a glass partition and the elevator before she ran up three flights of stairs to the detectives' squad room. It sounded like Grand Central Terminal: phones ringing, people arguing, detectives barking orders but Cheri stayed focused on her computer. She only looked up when she heard, "Bullshit, you're kidding me." That's when she noticed her partner, James, making his way through the maze. She shouted "O'Brien, where were you?"

"I decided to make a food run." He caught her eye and smiled. She managed a half-assed smile but he didn't seem to notice. She handed him a bag from the deli on Broadway. He pulled out a flaky, still-warm apple turnover. "My favorite. Thanks."

"Figured you needed this after your bout with the flu." He was only an inch taller than her, but his broad shoulders made him appear bigger than five-ten. His dark hair was his best feature. While they were dating Cheri teased him about having a Samson complex. Now, she tried to avoid looking at him. But she always knew when he was near, his after-shave cologne was a give-away.

They finished at the same time and walked out together. "Have a good one," he said.

"You, too." She turned and walked away, determined not to look back.

She was at the gym less than ten minutes when her cell rang. She picked it up on the first ring and recognized the Captain's voice. "Work," he grunted. "You have to take over a case from McClure and Casey."

She was tempted to say, Now? Instead she said, "Yes, sir. But what's the story with the other team?"

"They'll explain. Call your partner. Here's the address, tell him where to meet you. And get moving."

She alerted James then ran down a flight of stairs, picked up her precinct pool car, a white Chevy Impala, and drove straight to the crime scene.

As soon as she jumped out of the car she spotted her partner. James was standing inside the perimeter of the yellow police tape in a huddle with Detectives McClure and Casey along with a couple of cops in uniform. Techs were working the scene nearby. Crowds of onlookers were craning their necks, trying to take photos with Smartphones as the policemen kept ordering them to step back. The crowd kept pressing forward, calling out questions. Cheri noticed a reporter from the Daily News, but she didn't respond when he called her name.

"Looks like we're playing sloppy seconds," James whispered.

Cheri nodded. She noticed the Forensics' team and the Coroner's team at work on the body. She recognized some of those people but didn't stop to interrupt them. Flashbulbs were popping as Detective Bill McClure pointed to the body on the ground. "Either suicide or a homicide. Fifth floor, balcony."

James scanned the side of the building then faced the outgoing detectives. "That height is definitely a ball breaker. Fill us in."

"We will," said McClure. "Meanwhile, I want you to know that everything's been bagged and tagged. We're handing over a clean case."

"We didn't ask to get taken off the case," said Casey. "We got fucked on account of me." He let out a whoosh of air and moved closer to Marsh and O'Brien. "After we discovered the vic's last name, it rang a bell but not right away. Plus, his name isn't uncommon in New York: Rabinowitz."

Cheri nodded. "Who's the vic?"

"A hedge fund manager. My wife works at his brokerage firm, back office. Conflict of interest according to the captain when I told him about my wife's job."

"Luck of the Irish," said James.

"Yeah," said Casey.

"Any witnesses?" asked Cheri.

McClure shrugged. "Not so far. We canvassed the buildings across the street, nobody saw or heard anything. We were specifically interested in the person who lives in the apartment across from the vic. We went over there little while ago, heard noise inside so we kept banging on the door. No response. Could've been a radio or TV turned on to deter burglars. Name of the woman who owns the condo is Helen Powers. A widow. Lives alone. Got that info from a neighbor."

"We'll get on it," said Cheri. She and James turned and looked at the body lying on the ground. As she stared at the mix of dried blood and brains spilled on the sidewalk, she wondered if the vic jumped or was pushed. Her gut feeling told her he was shoved. She was learning to trust her instincts but she needed more than a hunch to call it homicide.

"All the stuff in the apartment's been bagged," said Casey. "Forensics is still checking for fingerprints."

Marsh and O'Brien watched as the coroner's team wearing latex gloves carefully turned the body over, exposing more dried blood. "If he was going to take a flyer," she told James, "why was he all dressed up? Expensive leather shoes, fancy suit, gold cufflinks." She bent closer and noticed that he was still wearing a gold and silver Rolex so probably wasn't a robbery. She made notes then told the people working the crime scene that she and O'Brien were going upstairs to check out the apartment.

She faced McClure and Casey. "After we check out the possible witness across the street, we'll notify next of kin."

"That part's tricky," said McClure. "There was a will in the top drawer of the desk with a note: If anything happens to me, notify my attorney. He will sort it out with my wife and two ex-wives. There was a name and numbers for his attorney. We called his cell earlier. According to him, one of the wives lives on the Upper East Side. The other one lives at 18 Gramercy Park."

McClure handed her the pad with the names and addresses jotted down. "Third wife lives in Rio."

"As in Rio de Janeiro?"

Detective Casey winked at her. "You got it."

McClure handed over the keys to the victim's apartment. "Any questions, call."

"Will do," said James.

"Let's check out the apartment upstairs," said Cheri.

They took the elevator to the fifth floor and Cheri opened the door to a huge, at least for New York, living room with big windows and a balcony at the other end of the room. As soon as they entered the room, she eyed the furniture: white leather couches, a well-stocked bar, an antique desk. No paintings, no personal photographs.

They each pulled on a pair of latex gloves and started going through the evidence that had been bagged and tagged by Detectives McClure and Casey. Not only were there bags of pot but also cocaine and a silver spoon for sniffing. "No ordinary spoon for a hedge fund manager," said Cheri. She checked the name on the back of the spoon, but it didn't mean anything to her.

James sniffed the coke. "Good stuff," he murmured.

"Put it back," she said jokingly, then added, "But if it's that good we could sell it on the street."

He laughed as she continued going through sealed evidence bags. "Hey, look at this." She handed him a business card that read: ESCORT SERVICE on one side and MASSEUSE on the other, then told him that the note from McClure said this was found on top of the desk in the room leading to the balcony.

James whistled loud. "We'll interview the woman from the escort service as soon as possible. Anything else of interest in that evidence bag?"

She took her time going through the bags one by one sifting through everything. When she was on the next to last bag she shouted, "James, c'mere." She held out her hand. "Take a look at this."

"It's a receipt. But what's it for?" he asked.

Her face turned red with excitement. "It's for a custom-made suit. Ready for pick up next week."

James took the receipt from her and studied it. "Jeez, the guy really had big bucks." He thought for a second. "But a guy doesn't order a thirty-eight hundred dollar suit if he's planning to kill himself."

Cheri nodded. "You got it. The case has all the markings of a homicide now." She shook her head and chuckled. "We should call it the Custom-Made Suit Case from now on."

James looked at her and smiled. From the look in his eyes, she was glad he appreciated her tight jeans and blue turtleneck.

"More luck of the Irish with this receipt," he said. "Guard it carefully."

"I'm gonna sleep with it."

McClure and Casey stuck their heads in the door. "One more thing," said Casey. "We checked out the security camera in the lobby. The tape is missing."

"Did you talk to the superintendent?" asked Cheri.

"Yup," said McClure. "Just before you arrived on the scene."

"What did he say?" asked James.

"Said, that's Nueva York."

"Might have been tampered with," said McClure.

"Gotcha," said James. "We'll check it out."

"How about fingerprints?" asked Cheri. "Any prints?"

McClure turned and looked at her. "It's early, but so far only those of the deceased, a middle-age man named Benjamin Rabinowitz, partner in a hedge firm according to his business card. You'll get the examiner's full report when it's ready, could take time. They usually do."

"Outer door found open or locked?" asked Cheri.

Detective Casey turned away from the window and said, "The police on the scene found the door locked. Looks like you can secure it from the inside if you're leaving. You don't need a key."

Cheri nodded as she faced her partner. "If he wasn't pushed, maybe he was pretending to be Spiderman."

James nodded. "Anything can happen in New York."

McClure told them that he and Casey were leaving and the four detectives shook hands. "Jeez, I hate to leave this case," said Casey, turning to leave. "Going to be a whopper."

As Cheri continued looking through the evidence bags, she found the copy of the will and held it up to show her partner."

"One will, three wives," said James, reading the note from McClure attached to it. "Hope the guy made tons of money."

"You ever hear of a poor hedge fund manager?"

He laughed then raised his arm and sneezed into his elbow. "Excuse me."

She took a step back. "Hope you're over the flu."

"I'm over it but still a little shaky."

Cheri nodded as she untied her pony tail and let her hair hang loose. When she first told James she was part Native-American he said, "You're pulling my leg." She finally showed him pictures from a family reunion. Half her relatives looked German-American like her father. The other half looked Assiniboine like her mother's family in Montana. She inherited the Germanic genes: blonde hair with blue almond shaped eyes.

She looked at the pad of paper again. "Casey or McClure jotted down the names and addresses of the wives for us."

James smiled as he ran his fingers through his hair. "Wonder why one of the wives lives in Rio."

"We ought to fly down there to interview her," said Cheri.

James raised his eyebrows. "The Captain's not going to spring for a trip to Samba-ville. We'll have the Rio Leos talk to her first. If she becomes a person of interest, we might make the trip. Meanwhile, I'll visit one of the women. You talk to the other one. That okay with you?"

"I like checking out expensive cribs. We should also drive down to Wall Street and talk to the dead man's partner at the hedge fund as soon as we can. But you're the boss."

He sneezed into his elbow again. "I agree. We also need to find out about the three wives: motives, alibis..." He popped a cough drop in his mouth.

She nodded. "Everybody can use extra dough, but money wouldn't be the only motive. You heard of revenge, haven't you?" Luckily, he didn't appear to take it personally. Jesus what was wrong with her? She kept putting her foot in her mouth lately.

He rubbed his jaw thoughtfully. "Just had a funny thought, maybe the guy on the balcony was an actor doing publicity for a show before someone saw him and didn't like his act. Speaking of the theater, I have an in with a scalper. He can get me two seats center orchestra, any show you want. to see." Wearing a pair of latex gloves, he continued going through the plastic evidence bags, not looking at Cheri while he spoke.

She didn't look at him, either. "I'm kind of busy these days," she said, trying to sound as casual as possible then quickly added, "Can I get back to you?"

"Sure, no problem. Sorry to digress. We have to talk to the lawyer and get the date of the latest will and find out which of the women stands to inherit the whole enchilada. Three wives?" James repeated. "Randy bastard. Probably deserved to take a flyer over a balcony."

"A flyer as in murdered," said Cheri. She pulled a Kleenex out of her jeans pocket and rubbed her eyes. They felt dry from the cold air. "About the theater tickets, I appreciate you asking. I am seeing somebody. Besides, those tickets would be expensive."

She reminded herself to use will power or she'd find herself in the same fix. She and James weren't living together at the time, but they were becoming serious, especially after three years. Besides she believed in "Duty First" as if it was one of the Ten Commandments. She also had to be careful. As a former actor, she knew the inside of the unemployment office.

"The police in Rio been alerted yet?" he asked.

Cheri turned to look at her partner. "Casey told me he spoke to them earlier, said we should get a call back from them." She stared at a picture of the dead man lying on the ground. The photo was gruesome. Five stories weren't high but even with a helmet, sidewalks were capable of breaking more than a few bones. In the other photos, the guy was covered with a white sheet. She continued thinking about the victim. "A Wall Street wheeler-dealer," she said, facing James. "I bet more than a few people wanted to see this dude laid out in concrete. "Maybe a drug dealer took him out," she added. "Brokers are big users."

"Really? That's news to me," he said with a smirk as he studied the names and addresses of the wives. He turned and looked out of the window. "Looks like snow. We better get moving " He glanced at the pad with the wives' names again. I'll notify Kati. You give Leslie the news. We'll talk to Brazil later or tomorrow. First, we should try to interview the person across the street. It's getting late, maybe somebody's home by now."

"It's a deal," said Cheri. "Let's lock up first." She pulled a woolen beret out of one of her coat pockets and a pair of woolen gloves out of the other.

When they got downstairs they found the coroner's team and the forensics team still at work. "We'll be transporting the body to the morgue soon," the coroner told Cheri. "That's what the crowd is waiting for, then they'll disperse. I swear New Yorkers are hungry for blood."

"You have our cell numbers," said Cheri. ""We're going across the street, hope to talk to a potential witness." As O'Brien and Marsh turned to cross the street, she got a blast of cold air coming off the Hudson River. One of her favorite walks in New York when it isn't bitter cold, was along the embankment between the West Side Highway and the river. During the summer she loved watching sailboats meander upriver, along with barges and power boats.

They stopped in front of the apartment building across the street and looked up. "This is it," said Cheri. "Not sure this woman will be of much help. Look at the distance between this building and the vic's apartment across the street. You'd need binoculars."

"We'll see," said James.

The lobby wasn't lavish but it was nicely furnished with comfortable chairs and gilt framed mirrors. Everything was chained so nobody could walk out with the furniture. Typical New York, thought Cheri. Bars, chains, alarms. They need guard dogs instead. Maybe she should train Dobermans or German Shepherds. It could be a lucrative second job. Nah, she thought. She didn't have time.

James pressed the button for the fifth floor. "Guess you heard, her name's Helen Powers," he said, as they stepped out of the elevator.

"Got it," said Cheri.

They knocked several times before a woman's voice called "Who is it?"

"Detective Marsh," said Cheri. She flashed her gold badge through a crack in the door. The safety latch was still secure.

"What is it?"

"A few questions for you."

The woman who opened the door appeared to be in her mid-fifties. A cardio practitioner, thought Cheri, as she scanned the woman's trim body dressed in a gray and white striped turtleneck with white woolen slacks.

"This is Detective O'Brien," she said. "We want to ask you a few questions.

Helen Powers led them into the living room while Cheri checked out the bright green walls. If she ever painted an apartment, she'd remember this color It reminded her of Granny Smith apples.

Helen sat erect on an old white sofa that was fading from the sun. A white rug under the coffee table gave the room a feeling of floating in space.

"We won't take up much time," said James.

Helen smiled at James. She's obviously charmed by this tall detective with black hair and dark eyes, thought Cheri. Everybody is charmed by James and his dimples.

"As you probably know by now, there was an incident across the street. We're here to talk to you about what happened on that balcony across the street," he said. "Can you tell us what you saw, if anything."

Helen sat back and twisted a thin gold wedding ring back and forth. "Not much," she said at last.

Cheri leaned forward and said softly, "just tell us what you remember."

The woman looked down at her lap, then cleared her throat. "I think l saw two people out on that balcony. I'm not sure."

"Go on," said Cheri. "Two men? Two women? One of each?"

"One appeared to be a man in a suit. And there was somebody with him. That person was less clear."

"Was he, or she, shorter or taller than the man in the suit."

She shook her head. "I was only out there for a minute, wanted to check the weather before I went to dinner."

Cheri nodded, trying to loosen Helen up, get her talking. "In the time you were outside, did there appear to be a physical struggle between the two people?"

"I couldn't tell."

"Were they arguing?"

"That's possible."

"What gave you that idea?"

"Their body language. The man kept raising his hand at the person with him. He kept doing that as if they might have been arguing."

"Were they far apart or close together?"

"Couldn't be too far apart," said Helen Powers. "Small balcony."

"Good point," said James. "You're very observant."

Cheri followed up by asking, "Was the other person wearing a coat?"

"I couldn't tell."

"A dress?" asked James.

Helen bit her lip and concentrated. "It could have been, but I can't swear to that. Too dark, too far even with street lights."

"I notice you're not wearing glasses," said Cheri. "Do you ever wear them?"

"Only for reading."

She made a mental note of that before James asked, "Then what happened?"

"I watched for a moment then imagined my late husband telling me, Come inside, Helen. Don't be a busy-body, so I came back in and closed the drapes. I also had something on the stove."

"I assume you didn't go back out to see if anything had changed," said James.

"No, I didn't go out on the balcony until I heard sirens. That's when I looked down and saw a row of police cars and an ambulance. I was curious so I took the elevator downstairs and found the area cordoned off with yellow tape. You know, like on TV"

James nodded. "Go on." Helen's eyes darted back and forth from James to Cheri. "Wish I could tell you more." She glanced at a family photograph on the mantle, then looked at James again. "My husband died recently, so this isn't easy for me."

"Sorry to hear that," said James. "Just a couple more questions and we'll leave you alone. You still think they appeared to be arguing?"

"I believe so. But I figured it was a domestic dispute and none of my business."

James stood up and said softly, "Can we step out on the balcony?"

"Sure." Helen led the way, then opened a pair of drapes.

While the three of them stood outside and looked at the apartment directly across the street, Cheri pulled out a Nikon SLR digital camera with a zoom lens and took a series of black and white photographs.

"Do you remember what time you saw the two people out there?" she asked.

"No. I don't wear a watch. I use a Smartphone, but I didn't have it with me, don't carry it everywhere."

"Was it dusk when you first went outside?"

"I can't remember." She stopped. "I'm sorry. I did look at the clock on my stove later. It was around five o'clock, I think."

After they stepped back into the living room the detectives thanked Helen, left their business cards and asked her to call if she thought of anything else. "I'll do all I can to help," she said. "Maybe I'll remember more."

"We understand," said Cheri. "This isn't easy."

Helen cleared her throat before asking, "Do you think anybody on that balcony could have seen me?"

"No," said James. "If the dead man was pushed, the perp wasn't looking across the street." After they stepped into the elevator James said, "Did you notice the drapes?"

"No, what about them?"

"They were sheer, especially for New York. She might have seen more than she's telling. "Good point," said Cheri. "Now, she probably wishes she hadn't talked to us." When they reached the ground floor he stopped and looked around the lobby "Nice, huh?"

"Yeah, but I'm worried about our witness. She might not cooperate."

"We'll close this case, with or without her," said James. They stepped outside, pulled their jacket collars up and ducked their heads under the raised collars.

Cheri kept sniffling from the bitter cold as she pulled a Kleenex out of her pocket. "What's next?"

"The two wives here in New York, let's notify them."

"Sure," said Cheri, "but I don't mind notifying both of the wives. You were just sick."

"Nah," he said, pointing at the sky. "It's lousy out, traffic will be a bitch, especially if the weather gets worse." He looked at the notebook again. "The woman in Brazil is named Pepita, by the way." He clicked his tongue. "Three marriages. The guy never learned."

She smiled at him. "That reminds me of a line in a book I read: "Lord, make me chaste but not yet." He looked at her and winked.

"About Broadway," she said, wistfully. "Thanks for thinking of me."

"I always think of you."

Shit, they were getting too close for comfort. Take it slow, she told herself.

"So, who's the guy you're seeing? Anybody I know?"

She shook her head. "A playwright."

He kept looking down at the pavement while they walked. "You mentioned wanting to see Franco's show. I can get tickets to that. A limited run, don't forget."

"I read that." She didn't tell him how badly she wanted to see it. She also didn't tell him that her new guy has a show opening off-Broadway, no Hollywood names, not a money maker.

The theater had been her first love. She moved to New York to study acting at NYU. She decided to give it five years. If she didn't make it to Broadway by then, she would shift gears and enroll in the police academy. When she told people about Plan B, they looked surprised, but it made sense to her. There were a lot of detectives in her family. They loved the work, felt useful, they said.

"I'll definitely consider your offer," she added.

"We'll keep in touch via phone," he told her. "Be careful driving." He looked up at the sky. "Hope the snow holds off."

"Me, too. Talk to you later."

As she watched him pull a pair of black leather gloves out of his pocket, she realized she still cared for the bastard. She stopped walking and looked at him. "My gut tells me that one of Ben's wives killed him. We just have to figure out which one. Maybe we'll get a confession. We know how to make that happen."

"Not us," he mumbled. "We never play dirty."

She turned and waved. "I'm off to notify Leslie that her beloved husband died unless, of course, she already knows."

Chapter 2

As soon as Cheri stepped inside her car she turned on the CD player then quickly turned it off. The weather was too unpredictable. She adjusted the rear view mirror and pulled out into streaming traffic. Snow was starting to fall by then.

As she inched along in stop and go traffic she tried not to focus on the smell of exhaust fumes and decided James was right. Traffic was a bitch. Side streets were especially slow. It took her double the time to reach Gramercy Park, the only area she knew of in New York with a private park. It killed her to learn that if you lived in a condo across from the park you got a coveted key to a piece of greenery in the middle of tall apartment buildings. She started singing "New York, New York," then swerved to avoid a collision with a taxi.

By the time she pulled into a specially reserved parking space her nerves were shot. She pulled the visor down showing her NYPD sticker and locked the car door. After checking with the doorman she waited for the elevator. Only one other person was in the lobby, a silver-haired woman.

"I love your jacket," Cheri told the lady.

The woman smiled. "I bought it in Switzerland last week. Do you ski?"

"Of course, "said Cheri, reminded of the slopes in Montana where she had learned to ski.

"Then you should ski the Swiss Alps."

Cheri nodded as they stepped into the elevator. "I'll do that. Thanks for the tip." The elevator came to a stop. "This is my floor," Cheri added.

As she walked down the long hallway, she realized there weren't any cooking odors, then reminded herself that people don't cook in these fancy buildings. They eat in restaurants or buy gourmet take-out. She checked the apartment number, rang the bell and waited. No answer. She rang a second time.

A voice from inside the apartment called "Coming."

An attractive woman dressed in black pants and a white tee-shirt that said LIFE IS GOOD opened the door slightly but kept the safety chain locked.

"Leslie Rabinowitz?"

"Yes?"

"Detective Cheri Marsh." She flashed her gold shield and a picture I.D. "Can I come in? I have to talk to you." She waited while Leslie unhooked the chain.

"Yes?" Leslie said.

"I need to step inside."

"Sure, sorry..."

Cheri stepped into a huge foyer filled with framed photographs and abstract paintings. She waited until Leslie locked the door then said, "I regret to inform you that your husband Benjamin Rabinowitz died."

Leslie stared at the detective like a child who had been pulled out of the deep end of a pool. "An identification card in his wallet indicated you're his wife," said Cheri.

"What happened?"

"Would you like to sit down first?"

Leslie reached for a small wooden table and gripped it before leading the way into the living room. After setting in a corner of the sofa she whispered, "Tell me what happened." Cheri remained standing facing her. "Benjamin fell or was pushed off a balcony. We don't have all the details yet, but he didn't leave a note so we're ruling out suicide." She deliberately didn't mention the thirty-eight hundred dollar custom-made suit ready for pick-up.

"Does there have to be a note?"

"Usually is one."

Leslie lowered her head in her hands and sobbed. "Maybe a loose railing. I read about an accident like that recently. It was the landlord's fault."

"No mention of that in the report." She crossed her arms and took a deep breath.

"It had to be an accident," Leslie insisted. "Nobody would kill Ben. He was a great guy."

Cheri was tempted to tell her that even great guys get whacked. But this wasn't the time for a course in murder. As she moved closer she noted details about the woman seated on the edge of the sofa: mid-to-late forties, sharp cheek-bones, shoulder-length dirty-blonde hair, large hands, especially for somebody so short, not more than five-foot four, and strong forearms. A tennis pro? But it was Leslie's reaction to the news the detective wondered about. *Did Leslie spend the last few hours rehearsing?* She knew from past experience that even guilty people were capable of histrionics.

"I should point something out," said Leslie. "Ben and I were in the midst of a divorce. We were legally separated."

"An amicable divorce?

"Yes, very. We're still friends. I mean we were friends."

"Any children?"

"I have a daughter from my first marriage."

"Where is she? I'd like to talk to her."

Leslie hesitated. "My daughter lives in Park Slope, Brooklyn."

"I'll need her contact information." She handed Leslie a pad of paper and a pen.

"My daughter's leaving for vacation. She'll be away two or three weeks," she whispered as she jotted down her daughter's name and address.

"Let me know when she's back." While Cheri waited, she checked out a pair of cross-country skis in the entryway. She also noticed a cabinet filled with miniature carvings of birds and owls, and at the other end of the room an ebony baby grand piano with a music stand next to it for playing duets. Her gaze finally settled on a pair of binoculars on an antique desk in front of a large window overlooking Gramercy Park.

"I'm a bird watcher," said Leslie, indicating the binoculars. "I don't use them for anything else." Why so defensive? Cheri wondered. She nodded as she handed her a business card. "We'll need to interview you. Call the office for an appointment."

"Am I a suspect?"

"That's not why we have to interview you. Just routine."

"Where did it happen? I mean where did Ben fall?"

Cheri furrowed her brows and said, "If he fell... We don't know all the details yet. But he went over a balcony on West End Avenue."

Leslie looked up. "Not in his office on Wall Street or in the apartment he shared with his girlfriend, Kati?"

"Neither. Know about any places Ben visited on West End Avenue?"

Leslie rubbed the side of her nose as if she had to think about that. She either knows about it, or she doesn't, thought Cheri. What is this big act about West End Avenue? Leslie finally said, "I hardly ever go cross town except to concerts or the theater so I never travel that far west." She gave the detective a feeble smile, but Cheri didn't respond.

"That's it for now. Don't lose my card in case you think of anything."

The detective was following Leslie to the door when she stopped abruptly. "From our preliminary investigation there appears to be another wife with the same address as your husband. Was your husband a bigamist, by any chance?"

"Of course not. He was living with his girlfriend. They weren't married yet."

Cheri quickly followed that up. "So, he lived with his lady while they waited for his divorce to be final. But you never heard anything about an apartment on West End Avenue?"

"No, I never did."

"When you have time, think about anything he might have told you about West End Avenue," said Cheri. "Maybe something will come to you." She was staring at the scratches on Leslie's forearms when Leslie blurted out "A dog scratched me. Today was my morning to walk shelter dogs. One dog didn't like me putting a harness on him."

"Did you report it to anybody? The manager in charge of the shelter?"

She shook her head. "No, I didn't want to make a big deal out of it."

Cheri continued staring at the scratches on both arms. Some looked as if they might have bled. "Does that happen often with shelter dogs?"

"No, this was an older dog with issues."

"Where is this shelter for homeless dogs?"

"It's called Bideawee, it's located Midtown on the East Side..." She started to give the detective the address when

Cheri stopped her. "No need, I'll find it. Meanwhile, the investigation will be ongoing. I also noticed you were limping. That ankle looks ugly," she said, pointing. "Is it broken or just a bad sprain?"

"Just a bad sprain," said Leslie. "Happened when a dog pulled me."

"Same dog that scratched you?"

"Yes, as a matter of fact. He needs training."

"I see," said Cheri, staring at the swollen ankle. "Guess it wasn't a good day for you. First, a dog scratched you and then you injured your ankle. Did you get it x-rayed?"

Leslie swallowed hard. "No. It isn't broken," she insisted.

Cheri nodded. "Hope not. You still could have seen a doctor for pain meds."

"My doctor wouldn't have seen me for weeks. He's very busy."

Cheri stared at the swollen ankle. "They have emergency rooms in New York."

"I know," Leslie said, sounding sarcastic.

"I have your cell number. I'll be in touch," Cheri added, as she looked at Leslie's arms again. "Take care of those scratches, they look pretty deep, and take care of that ankle."

Lots of holes in her story, thought Cheri, as she walked back to the elevator. *Wonder if they'll hold up or leak like a sieve.*

Chapter 3

Cheri was driving back to the police station when her phone rang. "It's me," said James. "How'd you make out?"

"Not bad. I'll tell you when I see you. Where are you?"

"In a coffee shop on Lexington Avenue. Terrible accident. A detour so I stopped for coffee."

"Did you visit Kati?" Cheri asked.

"Not yet. I'm on my way. If I die in a car accident, promise me you won't let this case get cold."

"I promise, but maybe you ought to call it a day. How do you feel?"

"Lousy."

"This storm could turn into a biggie..."

"With white-out conditions," he added. "But I'd still like to notify Kati." He asked her to hold on a sec then asked if there was any news from forensics.

"Not yet."

"And Brazil?"

"No news. Rio is one hour ahead of New York, by the way. I Googled it," said Cheri."

"Great. I'll check back with you later. I'll probably be gone when you get back. to the office, but if you're hungry I have a stash of M&M's in my top drawer. It's gonna be a long night so take it slow and try to get some food before it's all over."

"Thanks, I'll probably stop for a quick bite. You should eat, too, You were just sick."

He was mumbling something about food when Cheri heard a burst of background noise. She figured the coffee shop was filling up with stranded motorists. "I'll try to make it back," he said, before he started coughing. "NO," she shouted. "Go home. I'll drive over to Kati and give her the news about her husband. I have the address."

"It's going to be bad on the highway."

"Hey, I'm from Montana. I'm used to snow. Be careful driving, I don't want to lose my partner."

There was static on the line and she couldn't understand his answer but she imagined him smiling.

Kati opened the door a crack but kept the safety latch secured. "Yes?"

Cheri held out her shield. "Ms. Rabinowitz?"

"Yes, but I didn't call the police."

"I know. I have to talk to you for a minute. Can I come in?"

Kati ushered her into a huge living room with vaulted ceilings, framed paintings, and exotic East Indian sculptures. Cheri took a deep breath and smelled fresh coffee. In a professional voice, she informed her that her husband, Benjamin Rabinowitz, either jumped or was pushed over a balcony."

"Oh, my God," Kati screamed. She reached for an antique table for support, almost knocking over an Oriental vase. Cheri grabbed Kati's upper arm to steady her, then told her there weren't many details yet. She deliberately didn't mention

Leslie. Time enough to investigate the dead man's living arrangements. But within minutes, Cheri noticed a big age difference between Kati and Ben. He was almost old enough to be her father. She had seen recent photographs of him in the apartment on West End Avenue.

Katie continued to hold onto the table. "Were drugs involved?" she whispered.

"No, why? Was your husband a heavy user?

She nodded "A long time ago."

Detective Marsh followed her into the living room. "Did you ever meet anybody who might have sold him drugs?"

"Nobody came here. But I took a few messages that sounded threatening."

"We'll look into that. Meanwhile, everything's still under investigation. So far, we're inclined to think it was homicide and not suicide." She deliberately didn't mention the custom-made suit to Kati, either.

"You can't mean my Ben. He was on a business trip last night. I spoke to him on the phone." Tears were streaming down her cheeks leaving smudges of black mascara beneath her eyes.

"Sorry, ma'am, he wasn't out of town. He was here in New York."

A Seal Point Siamese cat wandered into the room and rubbed against Cheri's slacks. She was allergic to cats, but she didn't say anything.

Kati took a deep breath, exhaled loudly then asked, "Can I say good-bye?"

"Yes, he's at the city morgue. I'd like you to go there with me now and identify the body."

"I have to change first, please. I'm still in my exercise clothes." She pointed to her shocking pink spandex pants with a matching long sleeve top.

"I'll meet you there in an hour. I'll give you the address before I leave. I have to warn you that he's not going to look pretty."

Kati nodded but didn't respond.

"What kind of relationship did you have with the deceased?"

"We were happily married." When prompted she said that his recent divorce had gone through. Leslie was officially Ben's ex. "Ben signed the divorce papers. He told me he did. He never lied to me." Lie number one, thought Cheri, but decided to let it go. Court records would reveal the dates of marriages and divorces. While Kati went to get a pen and paper for the address of the morgue, Cheri checked out the view overlooking the corner of Fifth Avenue and Seventy-Seventh Street and noticed that it was still snowing. While Kati jotted down the address of the morgue she glanced at Kati's left hand. A wedding ring comprised of sapphires and diamonds was small but most likely exorbitant.

"Just returned from an exercise class?" asked Cheri.

"I have a Black Belt in judo," said Kati, then hesitated as if she was sorry she had mentioned it.

"That should give you an advantage in some situations."

"I guess," she said, and turned away from Cheri's gaze.

"Just curious. That picture against the wall, your husband?"

"Yes."

"Are you an artist?"

"I'm an actor."

"Have a professional name?"

Kati hesitated as if it was a State secret. "I'm known as Katherine Lowe."

"Are you in a play now?"

"Yes, a one-woman play. It's opening soon." Cheri stood in front of her, arms folded across her waist. "By the way, your husband didn't fall from his office on Wall Street."

"Where was the accident?"

Cheri cleared her throat and said pointedly. "We don't know if it was an accident. We're inclined to think it wasn't. Until then, it's unclassified. Getting back to your question, it was in an apartment on West End Avenue. Know anything about an apartment he kept near the Hudson River?"

"I haven't any idea about that or what Ben was doing there?"

"Was your husband unfaithful by any chance?"

"Of course not. We were totally in love."

"If he was a player," said Cheri, "tell me because I'll find out anyway."

"He was totally devoted to me," said Kati with tears streaming down her face.

"Did your husband sleep here lately or did he crash at his bachelor pad on West End Avenue?"

Kati kept shaking her head. "He didn't have a bachelor pad. Maybe that was a second office."

"Then why did he keep it a secret?"

"I don't know." She was practically shouting by then.

"He seemed to have a lot of secrets," said Cheri. She handed Kati a card and reminded her that she would meet her in an hour at the morgue. "Be on time," she added.

Kati pointed to a leather jacket and a helmet on a chair. "I rode to my judo class earlier on my motorcycle. I'll take my bike to the morgue. Faster than the bus."

"Good idea. See you later."

An hour later, the two women met at the morgue. Kati was wearing black pants and a long-sleeve gray turtleneck. A leather biking jacket was flung over one arm.

"Are you ready for the viewing?" the attendant at the morgue asked Kati.

She covered her eyes with one hand. "In a minute, please." Seating herself next to the body which was covered with a white sheet, she looked at Cheri and asked, "Is it okay if I take a few minutes?

Before Cheri could answer, the attendant told Kati it would better for her sake to get it over with.

"Okay." Kati took a deep breath before standing up and looking at the body. "Yes, that's my husband," she whispered. The sheet was pulled back from Ben's smashed head and Kati practically fell into the chair after the brief viewing. "Can I leave now?" she asked.

Cheri nodded and said she would walk outside with her.

The two women shook hands outside of the morgue. Cheri walked to the unmarked police car parked on the corner while Kati walked a few block to her parked motorcycle.

As Cheri opened the car door she had a strong hunch that one of them killed Ben. But which of the two wives pushed her dearly beloved husband over the balcony? It's too soon, she told herself. She needed more information. She was anxious to keep her adrenaline pumping, but it was too late to go to Wall Street.

After checking in with James, he told her. "We'll go to Wall Street as soon as we can get there. I heard the roads are bad down there."

"Heard the same thing," she said. "I'm anxious to meet Ben's partner at the hedge fund. He might have some tips for us. I don't mean stocks, I mean who might have killed Ben."

Chapter 4

After parking, Cheri stomped her feet on the wet pavement outside the police station and rubbed her bare hands together, her gloves still in her pockets. She stopped by to get a computer file of suspected drug dealers on the Upper West Side. The sky was filled with clouds and it had turned bitter cold, the kind of Arctic winter she had only experienced back home. As she was locking the car door her cell rang. "Hey, Nana, good to hear from you." She pressed the phone to her ear as a truck rumbled past. "How're you feeling?"

Her grandmother kept talking until Cheri said, "Glad you called. I was thinking about you. Can you do me a favor? Send me a chart of our family tree." That's when she realized her body was shivering from the cold. "Why?... I'm finally getting interested in my roots." She had been interested in the family background before, but now that her grandmother was old and physically frail, she felt the need to learn as much as she could about the Native American side of her family.

She continued listening to her eighty year old grandmother, the one they all referred to as the feisty one, then said, "As soon as you're better, we'll take a trip to Montana. I'll book a non-stop flight out of LaGuardia. My treat." Her grandmother asked, "Why" and Cheri told her, "I want to visit the reservation again." After saying, "I love you, too," she blew a kiss into the phone and hung up.

As soon as she stepped into the squad room, she headed for her desk to access the computer file. The room was unusually quiet, only a few people working phones. After transferring the information she needed to her Smartphone she got ready to leave. One of her colleagues shouted, "Hey, that was quick."

"Yeah," she said. "Found what I needed."

As she pulled her hat and coat back on, she thought about her Nana's call. The only thing she knew about her mother's family was that a German-Jewish merchant traveling through Northern Montana married a seventeen year old Native-American girl–her great-grandmother. The DNA was so strong, all her relatives had killer cheekbones. Her grandmother regaled her with true stories. One involved a coffee shop in Billings, Montana with a sign in the window that read: "No dogs or Indians allowed." That still rankled her when she thought about it. Just then, her cell rang again. She stopped in front of the police station and answered.

"It's me," said James. "Be careful driving home. It's bad."

"I will, thanks."

He coughed into the phone and said, "The roads are a mess while our mayor is sitting on his ass. The Wall Street area is the biggest mess of all and expected to get worse."

"Hope it's better tomorrow," she said "Take care of your cough."

She pictured his dimples when he smiled and had to catch herself from blowing a kiss into the phone. Luckily, she stopped in time.

The windshield wipers were squeaking as they swept back and forth. That's when she realized it was turning into a full-blown blizzard.

Cold, hungry, and bedraggled, Cheri stepped into her apartment, locked the door and hung her wet jacket over the shower rack. Her kitchen still smelled of lavendar incense from the night before. After ransacking the refrigerator she made a goat cheese and cucumber sandwich on whole grain bread. She was safe in her cozy six-hundred square foot apartment. After growing up in a rambling house on the outskirts of Billings her small pad in Manhattan was an incentive to get promoted and move to a bigger place. At times like this she missed the open spaces of Montana. She also missed the smell of Indian fry bread and the sound of crows circling the mountains. *Pack it up and go home? No way.* She didn't make it to Broadway as an actress, but she was one hell of a detective. And she didn't miss making rounds or the constant rejections.

With that in mind, she turned on her laptop. She took huge bites of her sandwich while she scanned the Net. Benjamin Rabinowitz was featured in one of the headlines. "Successful Wall Street Stockbroker found dead. At last count he was married to his third wife." News travels fast these days, thought Cheri. She made it a point never to discuss a case with journalists. There was finite space in a print newspaper but it wasn't finite online and writers often filled it with rumors and gossip.

After sending e-mail to forensics and to the detectives in Rio de Janeiro, she changed into sweatpants and a short-sleeve t-shirt, popped a DVD in her player and began practicing kickboxing. Despite her miniscule living room she kicked like a woman possessed. When she recently told James she was gearing up for the New York Martial Arts Competition he looked at her with awe. Nobody ever looked at her like that, especially when she was dubbed Chunky Cheri or Chunky Cherry in high-school.

After showering, she checked her e-mail. Nothing from forensics or Brazil. Damn, she thought. No leads, but it's still early. She Googled Benjamin Rabinowitz and read about him online. Successful broker, big bucks, society dinners, fund-raisers. But she didn't want to turn him into a stereotype. And he wasn't. He helped out at a homeless shelter, volunteered at a school in Harlem teaching first-graders how to read and he donated a ton of money to cancer research in memory of his mother. There was also a DUI, later dropped, plus a domestic dispute charge, also dropped. The details in both cases were foggy. Her cell rang again and she picked it up on the first ring.

"Hi, it's me."

"Hey, Tom, how are you doing?

"Nervous about my show. Other than that, I'm fine. By the way, I'll leave a ticket for you at the box office for Opening Night."

She hesitated then said softly. "Don't think I can make it. This case I'm on is taking all my time. "He didn't say anything at first. "You saying you can't make it to opening night?"

"I'm saying I don't think I can make it. This is a homicide case I'm working on."

"What's bugging you all of a sudden?" he asked.

"Something's been bugging me for a long time. We always talk about your play, your actors, your opening night, your theater. I have a life, too. You never ask me about anything."

"You usually tell me, anyway."

"Sure, I tell you about my job, but it would be nice if you asked, even once in a while."

"I hate to end this conversation, but I have to get to a dress rehearsal."

"That's what I mean." She wanted to tell him, I have important work, too. Solving a crime is more important than an off-Off Broadway play that probably won't even get reviewed. Shows open and close all the time. But she restrained herself. Why hurt his feelings?

She held the phone close to her ear and thought about how to end it. A little voice told her, Do it. End the conversation and end the relationship.

"I'm too superstitious to say good luck," she told him. "Break a leg."

"Thanks. I'll leave a ticket for you for opening night. Hope you'll be there to celebrate with me."

"Doubt I'll make it."

Before hanging up he told her he hoped she'd be there to share a bottle of champagne with him. There was another awkward silence and she told him he better hurry if he wants to get to the dress rehearsal in time. That's when she realized how self absorbed he was. Everything revolved around him and his playwriting. She covered her eyes with one hand, feeling suddenly relieved. She knew along that she had gotten involved with him on the rebound after her affair with James ended.

Cheri called her best friend and neighbor, Caz. "I think I just broke off with Tom," she told her.

"You don't know if you did or not?"

"I guess I did, said I can't be there for him on opening night."

"Why'd you do that?

"I'm self absorbed but not like him, plus he has a small penis."

Caz laughed. "But you managed to overlook it."

"Yeah, it was easy to overlook. You're bad."

"You should get back together with James," said Caz. "I can tell you still care for him."

"I do, but I don't want to get hurt again." Cheri took a deep breath. "Just wanted to tell you the news. Want to meet for coffee on Saturday?"

"Sure. I'll be finished with my latest assignment. How are you otherwise? How's the kickboxing?"

"Great. Getting good at kicking ass. See you Saturday."

"Perfect. Hey," said Caz, "instead of waiting till Saturday, want to come over for a glass of wine? You could probably use it."

"You're on," said Cheri. "Be right there. "After locking the door, she walked down the hallway and rang the bell.

After Caz opened the door, Cheri realized how beautiful Caz is. She was Eurasian with jet black hair, beautiful skin and dark, almond shaped eyes.

"Entre vous. I just happen to have a good bottle of Chardonnay." She poured the wine into special crystal glasses with delicate stems. While they sat on stools at the kitchen counter drinking their wine, Cheri noticed how neat everything was except for Caz's desk in a corner of the living room. The photographs lining the walls were all taken by Caz. There was one of Central Park in full bloom, the fountain in the garden at the Museum of Modern Art, and a black and white picture of the Brooklyn Bridge taken from the Hudson River. She took a deep breath and smelled food "What smells so good?"

"Nothing special. I cooked stir fry shrimp with hot sauce. Too bad you didn't call earlier."

"That's okay," said Cheri. "I had my usual: stir-fried algae with seaweed and grasshoppers." She stopped laughing and looked at her friend. "You been sleeping okay lately? You look tired."

"I didn't want to steal your thunder," said Caz. "A lot of layoffs at work. I'm feeling insecure."

Cheri thought of all the times she felt insecure when she worked in the theater. "What's the problem?"

"Nobody's buying magazines or newspapers any more. Everything's online."

"I'm sorry to hear the news. I'll whip up something special for you on Saturday. It won't contain algae or seaweed, I promise."

"Okay, what is it?"

"Indian fry bread, my grandmother's recipe. When I was a kid and fell off my bike, my grandmother cooked a batch of magic Indian fry bread for me. You sure Saturday's good?"

Caz nodded. "Yup, I'll be here working."

After they set the time, Cheri told her friend, "Can't wait for you to taste Nana's fry bread. It'll give you the confidence to become a warrior. You'll kick butt and nothing will scare you again."

After returning to her apartment Cheri told herself, back to work, think about Tom tomorrow. She sent another e-mail to forensics then decided to check her mail early the next day. With the time difference between New York and Rio maybe there will be something of interest to report to James in the morning.

She couldn't stop thinking about Ben and the fact that he wasn't an ordinary man, and this wasn't going to be an ordinary case. She smiled as she thought about his two addresses and two wives then shook her head in disbelief. Was he a bigamist? But why would anybody do that? Maybe he was a Mormon, then reminded herself that Mormons live in Utah, not on the Upper East Side.

Before getting ready for bed she took off the Catholic medal she wore on a gold chain, a gift from her mother, even thought they weren't Catholic. Her mother bought it in an antique shop thinking it was East Indian. Cheri later discovered that it was the Virgen del Cobre, a medal worn by South American women to protect their husbands working in copper mines. After she learned what it symbolized she continued wearing it for protection, even under tee-shirts at the gym. She was superstitious like all the women in her family. Theater folks were superstitious, too. You never said "Good luck." You had to say, "Break a leg."

She laid the medal on her bureau, then went back to her computer and pulled up Benjamin's picture again. Good looking dude. But what about that place on West End Avenue? Did he keep that for buying drugs? For a mistress? What reason did hc havc for keeping a secret apartment? That question led to more possibilities until Cheri finally asked herself, Did Leslie and Kati know about the apartment and lie to her?

Chapter 5

After a few hours of work the following morning, Cheri gestured to James excitedly, "I just spoke to Ben's attorney. Seems Ben never divorced Pepita. And he didn't divorce Leslie before he married Kati."

"That means he's officially still married to Pepita." James looked as confused as she felt.

"Looks that way. There's more. It seems his estate will be in litigation for a long time. He's being sued by a ton of investors."

"For what?" asked James.

"Not sure. The attorney deliberately kept things foggy, said he had to be in court soon. I think he just tells me that to put me off. He doesn't know how persistent I am."

"He'll learn," said James.

Cheri smiled at a thought she had. "If Ben is being sued, maybe his partner at the hedge firm knows something about that."

"We'll check it out," he said. "And what about Ben's will?"

"Whatever wills he left are invalid. He kept revising his will and leaving his money to his wife. He had three of them. It'll take time to get things sorted out."

James ran his hand through his hair and let out a whoosh of air. "This is getting interesting."

"Here's the thing," said Cheri. "Ben's attorney has an appointment with Leslie and Kati later today. He's planning to tell them that Ben was a bigamist. And he's going to tell them what I told him. That we're now considering this case a homicide: No suicide note plus the custom-made suit." She turned to James and smiled. "Glad you called the tailor and confirmed that the suit will be ready for pick up tomorrow."

"Yeah, that was a goodie. But we should be the ones to tell the wives that it's now considered a homicide."

Cheri shrugged. "I gave the attorney the information and he asked if he could pass it along. I said sure. He'll tell them about the wills, too. Invalid means nobody's collecting any money until it's squared away in court. And I bet there will be appeals."

"There are going to be two very disappointed women," said James.

'Maybe three, if you count Pepita," said Cheri. "He was still married to her, don't forget." She leaned forward in her chair and looked at her partner. James looked especially good and he smelled good. A new cologne, she thought. It's distracting.

"You want to go talk to our Wall Street guy?" When she didn't respond, James said, "You didn't answer me."

"Just distracted for a moment."

"By what?"

She wanted to say you but said, "All the details in this case. And you're right. Three wives. We'll get all the details about the litigation from the attorney."

After checking the weather, they decided to leave. The roads were finally passable, especially around Wall Street where there had been excessive flooding.

James took the FDR Drive and exited at the South Street Seaport. Snow was still piled up near the curbs. "Driving here is a bitch," he complained. "This area wasn't designed for cars."

"I read about this area," said Cheri. "This was horse and wagon country. You know," she added. "I would have loved to live in New York when they had stables in Central Park."

"Did you ride in Montana?"

"Sure. I played cowboys and Indian. I always wanted to be a cowgirl." She laughed. "The Indians got killed too often in the West."

"Yeah, damn blot on our history," he said, stopping for a light.

"Actually, I was a hybrid," said Cheri. "I liked being the cowgirl, but I always wanted a bow and arrow."

He laughed. "You would." After navigating narrow, one-way streets and nearly getting lost, James finally parked. Cheri kept up a running commentary while they walked as if she were an official tour guide. "There's the New York Stock Exchange," she said, pointing. "18 Broad Street. It has a neo-Roman façade."

"How do you know so much?"

"Googled it."

"Yeah, figures," he grunted "But that won't help us solve the case."

"Never mind, I was just trying to be informative."

She knew he was testy. He hated driving around the financial district.

They found 90 Broad Street then had to go through security before they were allowed upstairs. After a frustrating wait, a young woman from Ben's office appeared and escorted them to the elevator. After getting off at the thirty-ninth floor they took a private elevator to the top floor. As they waited in the reception area someone brought them coffee on a tray. After another fifteen minutes another assistant escorted them down a carpeted hallway.

The meeting room was standard: long conference table, wooden chairs, and a breakfront filled with books. The coup d'etat was a view that most people would kill for. The entire fourth wall, floor to ceiling, was glass. The windows overlooked the East River with a view of the Brooklyn Bridge connecting two boroughs: Brooklyn and Manhattan.

Cheri let out a sigh. "This is gorgeous," she exclaimed, taking a seat facing the window.

Ben's partner, Perry Hartman, a man in his fifties who was seated opposite them winked at her. "Just got back from Santa Fe." He pointed to an impressive looking silver and turquoise bolo.

Cheri smiled approvingly at the bolo as well as a huge turquoise belt buckle and said she'd never been to the Southwest—maybe some day. Meanwhile she and Detective O'Brien might be going to Rio. James gave her a sideways glance and she quickly added, "Wishful thinking."

"Gorgeous city," said Perry. "Rio is one of my favorites, especially during Carnival."

The detectives nodded as Cheri pulled a tape recorder off her belt. "Hope you don't mind. I'm going to record this."

"Not at all. You think Ben jumped?" Perry asked.

"Not sure," said James. "That's what we're investigating but we're leaning toward homicide. No suicide note." Cheri noticed that James deliberately left out the part about the custom-made suit.

Perry shook his head and muttered something under his breath. All Cheri heard was "Damn shame." Then he spoke up, louder than before. "Ben was one of the most respected investment bankers you'll find."

"Respected, huh?" she asked. "Well liked also?"

"I'd say so."

Cheri wondered, Why so fast to say he just got back from Santa Fe? Establishing an alibi? She had a habit of jumping the gun but she also relied on what she called her Native-American DNA.

"Tell us about Ben," said James. "I assume from this conference room that this firm is successful."

"Very successful. We have over sixty people working here, plus offices in London, Paris, and Prague."

Cheri leaned toward him. "Did you say Prague? According to Ben's lawyer, Ben was there recently."

"Right, he traveled there on business. Ben was a workaholic, but he knew how to have a good time. He was a skier, deep-sea diver, and a wonderful cook. Great with clients, knew how to talk to people. And I don't have to tell you that women loved him."

Not all, thought Cheri. One woman most likely murdered him. She smiled as she noted Perry's watch with small turquoise stones surrounding the face. He spent some serious bucks in Santa Fe. Odd, there weren't any paintings on the walls of the conference room. But the view. Nothing could match that. If I ever have an orgasm without sex, she thought, it would be in this room, looking at that view.

James made sure the tape recorder was working then cleared his throat. "Tell me something, did Ben have any enemies within this firm?"

"Not that I know of. But you know Wall Street. Our firm just completed a billion dollar deal so somebody might have gotten jealous. Ben and I started this company during the go-go days. Real estate was booming and the stock market was flying. We held our own during the recession, especially with our overseas offices."

"Are you aware of the fact that Ben was being sued by some investors?"

"Don't know anything about that," Perry answered.

Cheri picked up the questioning? "Any hanky-panky going on in this office, like insider trading? We won't snitch. We don't work for the Security and Exchange Commission."

Perry's face turned red as he slammed his hand on the desk. "We run a clean shop here. We get information from our analysts. We don't use insider trading."

"You might as well tell us about any litigation," said James. "That won't stay hidden for long."

"I said I don't..." Perry broke off abruptly and checked his watch. "I'm sorry, but I have an important client coming to see me in five minutes. The man's visiting from China, traveled here just to have this meeting. Not much more I can tell you, anyway. As far as I know, Ben was well liked." He paused before saying, pointedly, "Except by his present wife, Kati. "They were seeing a marriage counselor. Heard she's a prima-donna, his wife-the actress. I would talk to her if I were you. She's opening in a new play on Broadway, couldn't have gotten the part without Ben's investment in the show. I'm not saying she isn't talented." He stopped abruptly again and James said, "I know, you have a meeting."

"She opening off-Broadway, not on Broadway," said Cheri, correcting him. "and it's actor, not actress anymore."

"Have it your way. Anyway, feel free to call me. I'll be glad to help. Ben wasn't just my business partner. He was like a brother to me."

A brother, huh? Cheri thought about Cain and Abel.

"Sounds good," said James. "We'll be in touch. Before we go, was Ben a big drug user?"

Perry looked from one to the other. "I wouldn't say big. Everybody in our business uses drugs, relieves stress. But Ben wasn't an addict. And he didn't owe a dealer money if that's what you're getting at. He would have told me if he was scared of somebody."

After shaking hands and exchanging business cards, Perry escorted them to the elevator and waved. A short, balding man in a field of turquoise, thought Cheri, as the elevator doors closed.

The FDR Drive uptown was stop and go. They went over their interview with Perry and agreed that he was a person of interest. They also noted how anxious he was to implicate Kati in Ben's death.

"He's a jerk," said Cheri. "And he must think we're jerks."

James was quiet for a moment then said, "This case stinks of reckless people with tons of money." He honked at a taxi driver who cut in front of him, cursed him under his breath and got off the FDR Drive. As he waited on the corner for the light to change, he said, "I'm starving. Want to stop for an early dinner."

"I'd love to. I could also use a cup of coffee. Where to?"

He turned and smiled at her. "A surprise."

"But we can't stay long," she said. "Miles to go before we rest."

"I agree." He made a sharp right and continued straight ahead.

She studied his profile while he drove. At forty-five, his skin was only slightly lined around his eyes. The scar over his right eye where he had been grazed by a bullet while still a cop on the street had healed nicely. At the moment he was clean shaven. She liked him better this way and wondered if he shaved his mustache off for her.

After parking and walking a block, James led her into the ODEON Restaurant. The restaurant was nearly empty. It was too early for New Yorkers to be having dinner.

"My sister and brother-in-law brought me here for my birthday," he said after they were seated. "I hope you like it."

"I'm sure I will. Thanks." She was tempted to lean over and kiss him on the cheek but that was a no-no in public. If anybody saw them together, this had to look like a strictly working dinner."

"You remember the book *Bright Lights, City Lights?*" he asked. "This restaurant is pictured on the cover."

"No kidding," she said. After a quick detour into the world of literature, the waiter appeared to take their order. As he reached for a roll, James whispered to Cheri that the Rabinowitz case has the promise of a Trifecta: Big money, a Wall Street hedge fund, and three wives. Here's my plan," he continued. "We should take in Kati's show then talk to her afterwards. She'll be in good spirits after performing and we'll catch her off-guard. That way, we'll kill two birds with one arrow."

"One stone."

"Just making sure you're paying attention," he said.

"What am I going to do with you?

"Want me to tell you?"

"No, but your idea about seeing Kati's play sounds good."

"Y'know," he said, "That picture that Perry painted of Ben made it sound as if he walked on water. I should have told that jerk that his partner was a bigamist."

"He'll find out," said Cheri.

Seated close to the door, James complained about the noisy traffic then took advantage of that fact and moved closer to her. She felt shivers on her arm as their knees touched. He quickly moved away. That was one thing about James, she realized. He was always discreet in public.

They were ravenous, ate in a hurry and skipped dessert. She had pigged out on two hot rolls with butter which she regretted, then decided to do a longer workout at the gym.

On the drive back James said, "Forgot to ask, how's your Nana?"

"Think I told you she fell and broke her ankle, right?"

"You told me. How's she doing?"

"She moved up from a wheelchair to a walker, A nurse told me on the phone that she walks down the hall saying, "Move, feet, move."

James stopped for a light and turned to her. "You're just like her. Feisty."

"Thanks for the compliment." She studied his profile again in the light of an oncoming truck and added, "I'm planning to take her to our family's reservation in Montana when I can get away, maybe this summer. She'll be better by then and she's anxious to get out of that nursing home in Queens.

"I bet," said James.

Cheri nodded. "And I'm anxious to learn more about being an Indian princess before all the old people in my family die.

He smiled at her then turned back to concentrate on the traffic. "Going back to Montana will be good for both of you. He stopped for a light, then faced her again. "We should take a trip, also."

"Rio would be nice."

"Damn sure, but don't pack yet."

When they reached the 20th precinct James said, "Let's listen to parts of that tape." She followed him into the police station and set the tape recorder on the desk. The squad room was quieter than usual. But she knew that at any moment all hell might break loose.

"Here's the thing," said Cheri, after they listened to the first half of the tape. "I bet there were control issues between Perry and Ben. Two powerful men. Big bucks. Competition. Jealousy. I don't think they gave each other bro' hugs."

James laughed. "Probably not. We still need to get the rest of the picture. There's the third wife in Rio. We have to get a fix on her."

"Here's my theory, said Cheri. "Ben and his two wives in New York had a ménage a trois, then both women pushed Ben off the balcony."

James laughed. "This is New York. You never know."

As she hooked the tape recorder back on her belt, Cheri said, "Remember that Japanese film we saw years ago—*Rashomon*?"

"Sure. What about it?"

"There were three sides to the story: his, hers, and the story. Too bad we'll never hear Ben's side."

"Don't worry, we'll figure it out."

"I hope so. Meanwhile, I better go home and change or I'll be late for kickboxing."

"Have fun. Don't get stronger than me."

"Not a chance." She grabbed her purple jacket and matching beret. When she reached the door James said, "Don't forget, Detective Melo in Rio promised to call tomorrow after he interviews Pepita." He rubbed his forehead. "We also have an interview with Leslie tomorrow."

"I'm looking forward to that. Maybe she'll crack."

"Nah, doubt Leslie will crack," he said. "And I bet Pepita is like the other two: Smart and cagey. Ben Rabinowitz picked three tough broads."

Chapter 6

A policewoman ushered Leslie into a small, windowless interrogation room. There was one chair in back of the table, another two facing the door. Unknown to Leslie, a camera and microphone were attached to the ceiling above the perp's chair.

I'm Detective O'Brien," said James, stepping forward, and you know Detective Marsh."

Leslie nodded as she shifted uncomfortably in her chair and looked around. "This is all new to me. I've never even been in a police station before."

"Not a bad place," he said. "Lot of nice people hang out here."

Leslie stared at the metal bar to her left attached to the floor. It extended past her ankle to approximately calf height. "What's that?"

James smiled. "That's in case you have to be shackled."

Leslie nodded and sat up straighter, eyes riveted in front of her.

After turning on the tape recorder Cheri turned to Leslie. "How long were you married to Ben?" Leslie coughed a few times before answering. "Over fifteen years. We lived together for a while before making it official so I don't remember exactly."

"Cheri stood up and walked closer. "Did he have any enemies that you know of?" Leslie fiddled with an amber butterfly necklace on a gold chain. "He made and lost a lot of money for wealthy clients. Nobody likes to lose money. The stock market is a gamble, after all."

They ignored her comments about the market. "What about your finances?" James asked. "Are you financially stable?" Leslie rubbed her hands back and forth on a black cardigan and didn't answer immediately. Cheri caught a glimpse of James, arms folded across his chest, waiting for an answer. "I lost money with a money manager not long ago. Turned out he ran a Ponzi scheme. You probably read about it in the paper."

James picked up the questioning before they volleyed them back and forth in rapid fire. It was a technique they used to make the person in the hot seat feel hotter. "How much did you lose?" he asked.

"A lot."

"Did you have to sell paintings? Furniture?"

"No."

"Gold jewelry?" asked Cheri. Leslie stared wide-eyed as if the detective was clairvoyant. "I sold a few pieces of jewelry."

"How is the loss of that money affecting your current lifestyle?"

"I'm okay," she said quietly.

"You must be very frugal," said James. "Not easy, living in New York."

He nodded to Cheri who followed up by asking, "Do you work?" After Leslie nodded, Cheri asked, "What do you do?

"I give piano lessons. You probably noticed the piano in my apartment."

"Any other job?"

Leslie smiled. "No. I was hoping to become a concert pianist. I gave concerts in New York, including several at the Metropolitan Museum of Art."

"But you were married to a millionaire," said Cheri. "You didn't have to continue working so you..."

"I enjoyed playing in public," she said quickly. "I put my career on hold to travel with Ben. He liked having me with him."

James leaned across the table. "What about your divorce settlement?"

"I keep the condo. I can sell if I want to. We were working out the monetary details when Ben fell."

"Have to tell you things changed," said James. "We're calling Ben's death a homicide. We have a witness who came forward." That was a lie and Cheri knew it, but it seemed to work. Leslie gripped the arms of the chair after hearing about a witness. James didn't wait for Leslie to respond. He followed up by saying, "Big break in the case now with a witness."

"I imagine so," said Leslie.

"Were you counting on the money from Ben's life insurance?" She bolted upright and glared at the detectives. "I never knew how much he had in life insurance. We never talked about it."

"Never?"

"Ben was young and healthy. Why discuss death?"

Cheri stood up and resumed the questioning. "Husbands usually tell their wives the amount of a life insurance policy." She walked around the desk and stopped next to Leslie. "But he didn't tell you what his policy was worth?"

"No."

This time, Cheri eyed Leslie like a cat stalking her prey. "Too bad about the bigamy. You might have inherited all the life insurance if you didn't have to share it with another wife." Leslie kept nibbling on a cuticle until she finally gave up and shoved her hand in her pants pocket as she waited for the next question.

"You were never curious about the amount?" asked James.

"No. I wasn't waiting for him to die."

"But you expected a large inheritance, correct?"

"I told you, I didn't think about his death." Her face was turning red as Cheri asked,"What amount would you have expected? A million?"

"Five million?"

"More?

"I don't know," Leslie insisted. "I never thought about it."

"Fine," said Cheri. "But I think you should know that according to Ben's lawyer Ben left a large estate, including a life insurance policy, stocks, bonds and a collection of gold coins. Did you know about the stocks and bonds?"

"No, we never discussed stocks or the stock market. He said that he talked about it enough with clients and colleagues, didn't want to bring his work home with him."

Cheri stared at Leslie trying to get a fix on her, wondering why she was so nervous if she was innocent. "How did you feel when he left you for Kati?"

"He didn't leave me. It was a mutual decision." She pulled out a tissue and wiped her brow. For a moment, Cheri felt sorry for her, the older woman replaced by a newer model. Kati probably appeared exciting to Ben. A sexy young woman. Pink spandex outfits. A motorcycle. "Was Ben your first husband?" she asked.

"No, second. Told you I have a daughter from my first marriage." She wiped her face with a tissue again.

"You did," said Cheri. "Park Slope."

Leslie nodded.

"Too bad she's on vacation."

It was silent in the room until James asked Leslie if she'd like to take a break.

"Yes, I'd like to use the bathroom."

Cheri opened the door and pointed.

"Poor Mrs. Rabinowitz," said Cheri. "Once rich, now poor. Also very nervous."

"More than that," said James. "She's coming undone. Did you notice the fists on her lap and the strong forearms from playing the piano?"

"Sure did," said Cheri. "She's afraid of you, too. She was more comfortable with me until I asked how she felt when Ben left her for Kati."

"She looked as if she wanted to cry," said James. "She tried to cover up her emotions but it showed with her clenched fists."

"Ben betrayed her and she might have wanted revenge," said Cheri.

When Leslie returned from the bathroom Cheri barely gave her a chance to be seated before moving in close as if they were in a boxing ring. "Was Ben aware that you lost a lot of money?"

"Yes," she said, then stopped abruptly.

Detective Marsh hopped up on the edge of the desk, long legs dangling in a pair of Ugg boots. "So, you're staying in your condo?"

Leslie nodded.

James inched forward and studied her face. "You can afford it, even without the life insurance policy?"

Leslie bit her bottom lip. "For now."

"You're lucky," said James. Leslie shifted uncomfortably on the hard back chair. "Would you like a glass of water?" he asked.

She looked at him as if he suddenly became her savior. "Yes, I would," then quickly told him, "No thanks. Will this be over soon?"

He didn't answer but Cheri said, "Excuse us." She gestured for James to follow her into the other room.

"Let her go home and stew. We'll ask her about her alibi next time. She might be even more nervous then and flub her prepared answers." When they returned to the interrogation room James told Leslie, "That's all for now. We'll be in touch. In the meantime, we'd like to have you fingerprinted."

"Why?"

"To possibly eliminate you as a suspect."

Leslie nodded and headed toward the door. She stopped and turned around.

"Something you want to tell us?" asked Cheri. "We're not in a hurry."

"No."

They ushered her into a small area to wait for fingerprinting.

Later, while listening to the tape James asked Cheri, "What do you think?"

"I'd bet money she expected us to ask her about an alibi for the night Ben died. That took her by surprise. Maybe that's what she wanted to get out of the way when she stopped on her way out."

He nodded. "I agree. We kept her dangling. She probably went home and took a couple of Valium."

"She also struck me as a liar," said Cheri. "Did you notice her rubbing the side of her nose. That's a sign of a liar, especially about being able to afford that condo. And she didn't know the amount of the life insurance policy? Bullshit."

"We'll bring her back soon," he said. "For now, let her think she's home free. Meanwhile, we'll work with forensics.

And we'll keep in touch with Detective Melo in Rio. Pepita lives with a partner by the way. His name is Luis. The detective referred to him as Pepita's boy toy."

"Interesting," said Cheri. "Since Pepita was in Rio when Ben was murdered she might have paid a hit man to kill Ben, especially if she was still in his will and aware of the details. The lawyer didn't rule out the possibility she knew about the will. For now, he's trying to unravel the mess of one will, three wives. More than that, one of the wives might've murdered Ben."

Chapter 7

James was finishing up a phone conversation when Cheri entered. After setting a cup of coffee on her desk he gave her a thumbs up. "I was just on the phone with Detective Melo," he said. "There are a lot of holes in Luis' story. We might visit Ipanema Beach, after all. Or would you rather go during Carnival?"

Cheri laughed. "Either way sounds tempting."

"Only kidding about Carnival. We can't put this case on hold that long." He reached for the file on Ben Rabinowitz. According to the detective in Rio, Luis was in New York at the time Ben was murdered, said he'll know more soon."

"Very interesting. You betting on Luis being the murderer?"

"Not sure," said James. "But he's not looking good."

"I think it's one of the wives." Seating herself at her desk opposite his, she popped a Certs in her mouth. "Anything else happen while I was gone?"

He leaned forward. "I tried getting info about the missing tape in the lobby of Ben's high-rise. The camera was being repaired that day. According to the superintendent, Ben reported the camera broken, even insisted there must be a back-up camera but there wasn't any."

She smiled, pleased with the new development.

"There's more," said, James. "The super told me that a mysterious woman in a black hooded coat hung around the lobby on a few occasions before Ben was killed. The woman would enter the building, her hood pulled down covering most of her face, stand with her back to the camera as if she couldn't decide what to do, then leave. Of course, the camera didn't pick up the woman's face."

Cheri raised her eyebrows. "What about the day Ben died? Did the super see her that day?"

"No, said he was in and out most of the time."

Cheri thought for a second. "Maybe one or both of the wives owns that kind of coat. But if Our Lady of The Black Hooded Coat killed Ben, she's not going to admit to owning a coat like that."

"True," said James "We'll keep the coat in mind, but the mystery woman might not be connected to Ben. She could just be a weirdo. Lots of them in New York. For now, we have to find out who Ben was expecting and why he was so concerned about the broken camera."

"And," said Cheri, taking a sip of coffee, "if Ben suspected somebody wanted to bump him off, he wanted the perp to be identified on the security camera. We also have to concentrate on Ben's shady life, like why he had a secret apartment."

"I agree." James moved closer so nobody could hear him. "I'd still like to sit down with you outside of office hours and try to explain what happened. I miss you."

She shook her head. "I don't want to go over the same ground. Besides, you did explain. I need time."

"I'll give you all the time you want."

There was a loud cough and a policewoman called out, "Sorry to interrupt." She looked from James to Cheri and back to him. Cheri saw him mumble the word "shit" under his breath.

"No problem," he said. "What is it?"

"Tina Alvarez just arrived. She's the woman whose card was found on Ben's desk."

"The escort service," said James.

Cheri laughed. "Do we call her Madam Alvarez or just Tina?"

"Just plain Tina," he said.

"Give us five, then bring her in the interrogation room," said James.

Ten minutes later, a thirty-ish looking woman with café au lait skin and long black hair entered the room. Cheri's first impression was this lady looks strong. Strong enough to push a man over a balcony.

After James asked Tina's permission to record their conversation she nodded nervously and he started the questioning. "We found your card on Ben Rabinowitz's desk. There was also a note in his diary. Two o'clock. Tina Alvarez, here for massage. Is that correct?"

"Yes." She tugged at her skirt, attempting to cover her knees then raised one hand in the air. "I won't get in trouble for giving massages, will I? Nothing illegal. I have a license. And I have a Green Card."

After they assured her she wouldn't get in trouble, Cheri told her they had nothing to do with licenses. That was another department.

"I still have to be careful," she whispered. "This is just between us, si?" They nodded as she stared at the ceiling, obviously looking for cameras, or any other hidden device.

"No reason to be nervous," said Cheri. "We just want to ask you a few questions."

Tina crossed her legs, probably trying to hide her scarred calf under the other flawless leg. "I received a call," she began.

"A man by the name of Ben Rabinowitz asked for me special, heard I'm great masseuse and didn't want nobody else. 'I like Latin women,'" he said. "He gave me his address on West End Avenue. Ritzy building. I figured good tip."

James looked at Cheri and smiled. They were on the same wave-length: a legitimate masseuse who makes house calls and leaves a card that says, "Tina Martinez, Escort Service and under that, the word MASSEUSE?" She was good looking, clean, didn't appear to be a druggie. And except for a few old scars on her leg, there wasn't anything unusual about her.

Tina uncrossed her legs and tucked them under her chair. Cheri wondered why a woman with a scarred leg wore a short skirt instead of pants. "What time did he ask you to arrive?"

Tina thought for a second. "I don't remember."

"Did you get there on time?" asked Cheri.

"I'm always on time."

"What time did you leave?"

"I don't remember, but I was there a couple of hours."

Cheri moved closer to Tina. "Did anybody see you arrive or leave?"

"No, was quiet in the lobby. "Tina tugged on her skirt again.

"Where did you go after you left?"

"I went straight home," Tina said matter-of-factly. "No other appointments."

The detectives nodded. "Then what happened?" said Cheri.

Tina answered as if she had expected that question. "I stay at home, alone."

Cheri resumed in rapid fire sequence. "Who did you see next?"

"My daughter. She came home from her friend's house."

"Do you know that Ben died sometime after you left?"

She tugged harder on her skirt. "Yes, was on TV the next day. They said he fell from balcony."

"Were you on the balcony with him during your visit?"

Without skipping a beat, she said, "No, I didn't go on the balcony. Was too cold. I'm used to warm weather."

"So, you stayed inside the whole time?"

"Si..."

Cheri deliberately waited before asking the next question. "Did you by any chance have an argument with Benjamin about payment?"

Tina shook her head. "No, he paid me what I asked and said he would call me again. He told me he had sore back from sitting at his computer."

Cheri took a deep breath and nodded at James.

"While you were there, or as you were leaving, did you see anybody on the balcony?" he said.

She shook her head vigorously. "Nobody was in the apartment and nobody on the balcony that I know of. I came and went quietly. I swear to you, I don't look for trouble."

After thanking her, James told Tina not to leave the city "And don't talk to anybody about what you told us. We have reason to believe Ben was pushed off the balcony."

Tina's eyes opened wide. "Pushed? Who pushed him?"

"That's what we're trying to find out."

Tina started rubbing her hands together. "I hope the person who did such a terrible thing didn't see me leaving Ben's apartment. I wasn't witness to anything." She pointed to the scars on her leg. "I left Cuba with souvenirs. I don't want to drown in the East River. In two more years I have college degree."

They asked her which college and what kind of degree. She told them, "City College, degree in nursing." After they told her they'd be in touch, Cheri walked her to the door then closed the door behind her.

James got up and checked the reception area to make sure Tina wasn't eavesdropping. "What do you think?"

"Maybe he promised to marry her and changed his mind," said Cheri. "He was the marrying kind, three wives that we know of. Seriously, maybe she screwed him and he refused to pay. Or he wanted kinky sex and wouldn't let her leave until she delivered."

"I don't think so," said James. "She's a hard-working woman, earning her way through college according to her. But she could also be a liar. She might have seen somebody near the door when she was leaving."

Cheri looked at him and squinted "One way to find out if Ben was into kinky sex is to ask Ben's three wives. But how do we define kinky?"

He rolled his eyes. "I have my definition. Why don't we have a drink and compare definitions?"

"You're sneaky, you know. I don't trust you, or your definition of anything."

"Hey, I was kidding. But we should keep her as a person of interest."

"Agreed. It's possible that Tina tried to roll him if he fell asleep after sex and he caught her. Or she followed him out on the balcony, demanded more money and there was a struggle."

James nodded. "Anything's possible. Meanwhile, you investigate the Cuban bombshell while I call the Brazilian police and see what I can find out about Pepita and Luis. So far, one thing is obvious. Ben Rabinowitz was definitely not an upstanding citizen."

Cheri faced him, hands on hips. "What do you expect from an investment banker? Tina got scared because she knew she was acting under the radar screen. Ben probably called himself an honorable man in an honorable profession."

"Yeah, real honorable," said James."

"This case is getting muy interesante," she said. "And Luis is definitely looking like a person of interest since he was in New York when Ben was killed. Ask the captain if we can fly to Rio and interview Pepita and her lover."

"Que suena como una buena idea—sounds like a good idea," he said, giving her a cocky smile.

"If you're practicing your Spanish, we're out of luck," said Cheri. "They speak Brazilian Portugese in Rio, not Spanish."

"We can learn," he said winking at her. "We've tackled more difficult things together."

She pretended not to hear that. Besides, the Rabinowitz case was driving her nuts. So far, everybody involved had a motive. And it all revolved around money. Big money.

Chapter 8

The squad room sounded as if it had been hit by an earthquake. The noise level was migraine inducing. Luckily, Cheri didn't suffer from severe headaches. She was pulling off her coat when James gestured for her to follow him into a small interrogation room that was empty.

"Good news," he announced. "According to Detective Melo, Pepita's partner Luis is still in New York."

"What's he doing here?"

"I'll give you the short version," said James. "A group of theatrical producers saw a YouTube with Pepita and Luis dancing and called them. They want to produce a show with Latin dancers. Luis agreed to come to New York and talk to the producers while Pepita stayed in Brazil to run their dance studio."

"Tell me more," said Cheri.

"I don't know all the details, but Luis ended up staying here while the New York producers brought some moneyed people here from Vegas. By the way, Melo told me that most of the information he learned so far is from Pepita."

"'Because Luis is here?"

"Right, although he did speak to Luis on the phone. With Melo's accent, it was hard to follow everything he said. I kept asking him to speak slower." James pulled a piece of paper out of his pocket and placed it on the desk. Melo gave me the number of the hotel where Luis is staying. I called him little while ago. He played dumb and didn't want to talk to us. Made all kinds of excuses but finally agreed. He should be here in a couple of hours."

"Great," said Cheri. "Why didn't Melo tell us that in the beginning?"

"Seems another detective was on the case for a while, then they put Melo back on it. Who knows? The Brazilian police are known for messing up. They're also known for using force."

Cheri thought about that. "Maybe that's why Luis agreed to be questioned here. He probably heard stories about the police back home and their tactics."

"Let's use this room," said James. "I'll turn up the heat. Luis is used to heat in Brazil."

Cheri smiled.

She worked on a list of questions while James talked to Detective Melo on the phone again. Just as they cleared their desks there was a knock at the door. A policewoman stuck her head in. "Luis Morales had to cancel. Said he made a mistake when he told you he was leaving tomorrow. His flight is today."

"Thanks," said James. As soon as she closed the door he slammed his fist on the desk. "Bastard."

"We can't keep him here," said Cheri. "He's a person of interest, not a suspect,."

"Then he should have changed his flight and come to see us today."

"How about we talk to him at the airport?"

"Nah," said James. "Let him go. Detective Melo will interview him and give us the details. But we'll have to keep on Melo's ass. Everything with him is manana." He winked at her.

"Maybe we'll get to Rio after all. You never know how this will play out."

She tried not to give him a big smile but couldn't help herself. If they got the okay from the captain she was planning to buy a bikini. She'd go to an expensive store where women shop for the Caribbean during the winter and buy a bathing suit. Even that brief image of the sun warmed her.

Chapter 9

After a quick lunch at her desk, Cheri looked at James across the cubicle they shared and told him in a confidential voice, "I have an idea."

"Only one?"

"Actually two. Remember I told you about Leslie's scratches on her forearm? She said a dog at Bideawee Animal Shelter did that."

"I didn't see any marks," he said.

"She was wearing long sleeves when she came to see us, they were covered up. I saw them at her house. One idea I have is to drive over to Bideawee and check out the mysterious scratches. That okay with you?"

"Sounds good. And your other idea?"

"I want to talk to Ben's neighbors on West End Avenue."

James wrinkled his forehead. "The cops on the scene already did that."

"I know. but funny what people remember, especially when it's a woman questioning them."

"Go ahead. Leave while the weather's still good." She gave him a fake salute then grabbed her hat and coat.

She sniffed the air before stepping into the unmarked police car and recognized that smell. Snow. She wished she could snuggle under her down comforter with a CD of Native American flute music. She flashed back to stands of orange and gold trees in Montana during the fall while fly fishing with her grandfather. They both wore rubber waders for safety, but he still kept reminding her not to get swept along by the swift current.

She realized she'd been thinking about Montana a lot lately. That made her suddenly remember her little sister getting beaten up in elementary school. A gang of girls called her a squaw and her sister told them to take it back. After they started shoving her, she fought back but lost. It was three to one. When her sister got home she asked, "What's a squaw?" As their mother washed the blood off her sister's face, she told her it's a nasty word for an Indian girl or woman. "Then I did the right thing fighting them." Cheri smiled at the thought of her baby sister, now working and still fighting at her job for The Bureau of Indian Affairs.

She continued west toward the Hudson River. It was still early but with Standard Time the sun was starting to set. The red-streaked sky reminded her of the Hudson River School of paintings she had seen in museums. She wanted to buy a print of one, but she had already lined her walls with photographs she had taken of Glacier National Park, Yellowstone and close-ups of the lined faces of Native-American elders.

As Cheri coasted downhill to West End Avenue, she glanced at the stately Victorian mansions three or four stories tall intermingled with high-rise buildings built before World War 11. James once told her that those pre-war buildings had huge rooms and high ceilings. She stopped for a red light and looked out of the window. After her next promotion, she would move here. She smiled as she realized she would need at least three or four promotions. Remembering the strong winds rising off the Hudson River she had second thoughts about living this far west. If she lived on West End Avenue, she would have to climb steep hills from Broadway carrying heavy bags of groceries. If she could afford the rent, she'd do it, she decided.

It was easy locating the building she was looking for. After stepping inside, she scanned the lobby with its comfortable looking chairs and side tables She took the elevator to the fifth floor and decided to start with Ben's neighbor to his left. After flashing her badge through a crack in the door, a handsome looking woman with dark hair hesitated then opened the door all the way and led Cheri into a long narrow foyer.

"Is this is about my next door neighbor?" she said. "Didn't really know him. Sharp dresser, though, especially when he went to work. We often met in the elevator and exchanged a few words."

"About?"

"The weather mostly, but heard he was a money manager. He dressed like one so I was tempted to ask him for a stock tip."

"Did you?"

"No, would look too nervy." And stockbrokers aren't nervy? thought Cheri. Her only dealing with one taught her that lesson. Fast. A money manager was going to relieve her of her small inheritance after her father's death and invest it in penny stocks. Too risky, she told him.

"Tell me, did your neighbor live with anybody?"

"Not that I know of."

Cheri smiled warmly, hoping to loosen the woman up. It seemed to be working; the woman appeared more relaxed, willing to talk. She might be retired, thought Cheri, alone all day and glad for company. After a series of questions, the woman said there was one thing she had forgotten to tell the policeman on the scene.

"What's that?" asked Cheri.

"I occasionally saw somebody in a black, hooded coat hanging around the lobby." "Tall? Short?"

"Short, I think... I saw the same woman at Ben's door one evening. I heard a noise and looked out. The lady in the black hooded coat was standing next to the door as if she couldn't decide what to do. She spotted me and ran toward the elevator."

"Can you give me a description?" asked Cheri.

"It was hard to tell, but it was a black hooded coat. Long. Woolen. Looked expensive and the hood almost covered her face."

Cheri wanted to reach over and kiss this stranger. Instead, she asked if any other single men live on this floor other than Ben.

"At least two or three. But the mystery lady was standing in front of Ben's door. I'm sure of that."

As she glanced out of the living room window, Cheri noticed that it had gotten dark and the street lights were on. When the woman saw her peering out, she said, "I hope you head home soon, another storm expected." She smiled at Cheri in a motherly way. "Any idea what happened to the poor guy next door? Did he jump?"

"No," said Cheri. "We're calling it a homicide."

"Oh my God. Who would hate such a nice man. He had to be nice. All sharp dressers are nice."

Cheri didn't agree or disagree, just thanked the woman. "You were very helpful. This is just between us, by the way."

"Of course. Good luck with the case. And I hope the storm holds off for a while."

As soon as Cheri left she decided she to take her chance on the weather. She walked down the hallway and knocked on the door on the other side of Ben's apartment. No answer but she heard voices inside. A television? She banged harder and waited.

A woman called, "Who's there?"

"Detective Marsh." The door opened a crack and Cheri held up her badge. "I'd like to ask you a few questions. It won't take long."

A pale looking woman in her mid-thirties opened the door. A television was on across the room. The woman picked up the remote and turned the volume to mute. "Does this have anything to do with what happened next door?"

After Cheri said yes the woman told her, "I already gave a statement. Plus, I'm sick. I took the day off from work." Cheri was about to tell her, Don't worry about being sick. I won't kiss you. Just as that flashed through her mind the woman said, "I won't shake your hand, I'm getting over the flu."

"Thanks. It's going around. My partner at the NYPD had it. Just a few questions. I'll try to be brief."

Cheri went through the same series of questions she asked the other neighbor. Was Ben single? Did he live alone? Any visitors? The answers to all of Cheri's questions were the same, "I really don't know." The neighbor seemed embarrassed when she pointed to the television. I never watch it during the day. I'm too sick to do anything else."

There was an awkward silence until the woman said, "I have a keen sense of smell. I often smelled drugs coming from that apartment late at night."

"Pot?"

"Yeah." The woman laughed. "I'm not a pothead, but I know the smell from my college days. My roommate was a big user." She hesitated. "There were other smells. Once, when the door was open slightly I thought I smelled coke or hashish. I didn't tell the cops on the scene about that. I was tired after work and too distracted. Besides, I'm not an expert on drugs."

"Anything else?"

"Late at night I sometimes heard somebody knocking at his door. A drop-off, I thought, you know, drugs, then dismissed the idea but now that the poor guy is dead, I realize maybe it wasn't my imagination about possible drop-offs." She started coughing into her elbow. Cheri thanked her for her time. "I hope you feel better soon. You've been a big help, but I won't shake your hand."

Cheri darted in and out of traffic as safely as possible, anxious to get back to James. Luckily, the storm was holding off. When she reached the squad room she told him everything she had learned then added, "Sorry, I didn't get to Bideawee. It was too late. Traffic was heavy by then."

"Go home," he told her. "You had a long day." He had a coughing fit. "That damn flu. By the way, okay with you if I reserve tickets for Kati's show for first available night?"

"I'm cool with that. Will you be up to it? "

"Sure, no problem. I'll dose myself with medicine." James popped a cough drop in his mouth.

"Sounds good. She smiled and told him, "Her show is called *Suffer Queen* and it's a one-woman show."

"What if I hate it?" he asked.

"Lie... Tell her you loved the script and you loved her acting. It'll put her in a good mood. Maybe she'll let something slip."

"Why not?" said James. "You never know what people will do under stress.

"By the way, Leslie called while you were out."

"What happened? She find out the insurance policy is only half a mill?"

"Nothing to do with life insurance," he said. "She received two texts and wanted us to see them so she sent me a fax." He handed Cheri two sheets of paper. The first one read: "You knew Ben stoll my money. Your no good. Watch yor back, lady. "The text was signed JAZZ."

When she read the second one it said, "Don't be a SMARTT ASS. PAY UP or else..." Cheri shook her head. "This guy is a weirdo, can't spell either. He could also be dangerous. We have to find him before he tries to hurt her."

"Or... he tries to kill her," said James.

Chapter 10

Cheri took the call the following morning at her desk in the squad room.

"I was out for a while this morning," said Leslie over the phone. "When I got home, someone left a note for me with the doorman." She sounded as if she had been running.

Cheri covered one ear to block out the noise around her. "What did it say?"

"You have the money that Ben stole from me, Little Wifey. He invested my money and lost it. I want it back. If I was you, I'd keep my mouth shut when you talk to the cops. It was signed Jazz."

"Can you drop it off? The fingerprints might be helpful in finding Ben's murderer." Cheri was immediately sorry she had used the word murder. She should have said Ben's death. Too late. But that's what it was. A murder.

"Dropping it off today is a problem," said Leslie. "It's my morning to walk dogs at Bidawee then I have a doctor's appointment. Can't cancel either one, damn it. Tomorrow okay?"

"That'll be fine." Cheri tried to sound as casual as possible when she told Leslie, "Go about your life as usual. It could be some kook."

Cheri mouthed Leslie's name to James. He nodded.

"What should I do in the meantime? If he killed Ben he might try to kill me."

Cheri wanted to say, Stay off balconies. Instead, she made an effort to sound empathic. "After you drop off the note, we'll get on the case. Meanwhile, stay alert to your surroundings. You're a New Yorker. Use your street smarts."

"Thanks, see you tomorrow," said Leslie, sounding discouraged by the advice. "Why'd she call?" said James.

After telling him about the note she told him that Leslie plans to drop the note off tomorrow morning. She's busy today.

"Who do you think Jazz is?"

Cheri shrugged. "A client. Ben probably invested the guy's money in a stock and lost it. Now the guy wants his money back. Doesn't work that way. A broker buys and sell stocks for you until there isn't any money left. Then he moves on to the next sucker."

James laughed. "I was lucky. My sister gave me the name of a broker. Made money for me during the bull market, not a lot 'cause I didn't give him a lot. It's the bear markets that kill you and we're in one now. If my broker loses my money, think I should kill him?"

"I would if I were you," said Cheri.

A few hours later, Leslie called the police station again. This time, she sounded hysterical.

"Calm down," Cheri told her. "I can hardly understand you. What happened? Another note?"

"Worse."

"Would you rather come in and talk to me in person?"

"I will but I have to tell you something first." Cheri could hear Leslie's breathing at the other end. The poor woman sounded as if she was hyperventilating.

"It's okay," said Cheri. "Take your time."

Cheri didn't really mean it, she had work to do, but if she calmed Leslie down. it could be worth the wait.

"A man, a big man..."

"Yes?"

"He kidnapped the dog I was walking this morning."

"What?" Cheri shouted. "Tell me what happened."

"There's more," cried Leslie. "After the kidnapping, I talked to the police on the scene. They wrote up a report and I stayed at Bideawee a while so I didn't get home right away. And when I did..." She stopped abruptly to catch her breath.

"What happened there? Someone waiting for you?"

"No. It's hard to talk about."

"Come over to the police station."

"I'll be there as soon as I can. I'll cancel my doctor's appointment."

"We'll be waiting for you," said Cheri.

"I have to tell you something before I come to see you."

Cheri asked her to talk louder and Leslie practically shouted as she said. "I got home and the doorman had a package for me. I took it upstairs and...."

"What did you find in there?" asked Cheri.

"Give me a minute."

"No problem."

Leslie shrieked. "It had the dog's name on it, clear as could be."

"What had her name on it?"

"The tag on the collar. Wait," Leslie added. "there was also a note in the box."

"Take a deep breath," said Cheri. "and tell me what the note said."

She could hear Leslie breathing.

"We want the money, you rich bitch."

Cheri rubbed her forehead. "Jesus, what a nut case we're dealing with."

"I'll take a cab to the police station."

"Good," said Cheri. "And bring everything with you–the collar, tags, the note."

Leslie arrived at the precinct forty-five minutes later and apologized, said traffic was heavy. Cheri noticed she was shaking. It's not just the cold, she thought. it's exhaustion and nerves. No wonder. This guy is not just a kook. He's a psycho.

"Please find out who's doing this," Leslie whimpered. "And please find the dog." She started sobbing and Cheri passed her a box of Kleenex. "She's beautiful." Leslie added.

Detective Marsh took a break as James stepped forward. He peered in the cardboard box at the pink collar and shook his head. "Okay, tell us what happened. Start at the beginning and try not to leave anything out."

"I was walking a Cavalier King Charles Spaniel, rare to get a pure bred animal at an animal shelter. I was a few blocks from Bideawee and a man asked if he could pet the dog. I said yes and he bent down to pet her. She was a well trained dog, didn't pull, so I held the leash with only one finger through the loop." Leslie stopped and rubbed her face.

"Go ahead," said Cheri. "We need everything you can remember."

Leslie took a deep breath. "He was petting her and saying how beautiful she was. The next thing I knew he yanked the leash out of my hand and grabbed the dog."

"Anybody with him?"

"No, but somebody was waiting for him in a car parked at the curb."

"What kind of car?" asked James.

Leslie shook her head. "I'm no sure, but it had tinted windows, a four door Toyota, I think. The driver sped away while I was screaming."

"What else?"

"The kidnapper had a Russian accent. And he was wearing a blue and white ski cap with a pom-pom. I just remembered, it was a blue pom-pom."

"Actually, two men were involved," said James. "One kidnapped the dog. The other man drove the getaway car."

"You're right, I can't think straight."

"Anything else?" asked Cheri.

"No, that was it."

"Go home," James told her. "We'll get to work on this, but not much we can do right now. They're probably going to get desperate for the money so they might start calling you."

Leslie nodded and wiped the tears away from her eyes with one hand. "Meanwhile, I was told by the managers to take a break from walking dogs. And they haven't heard the latest, about the collar and the tags." She started to cry louder. "The poor dog."

Cheri watched as Leslie pulled one tissue after another out of the box. Probably a good idea she's not allowed to walk dogs at Bideawee, thought Cheri. She could cause all the dogs at the shelter to get kidnapped. She wasn't going to share that thought with anybody. Black humor. but too dark right now.

As soon as Leslie left, Cheri told James "My take? The kidnapper might be one of Ben's investors. Or could be drug related. I still want to go to Bidawee and check out Leslie's story about those scratches on her arms. The kidnapped dog doesn't change anything about Leslie being a person of interest."

"Good idea," said James. "Tomorrow morning, bright and early, we'll find out if her story sticks or if it melts like snow."

Chapter 11

Cheri arrived at the police station the next morning and called the detective on the case in Brazil. It worked out great having the one hour time difference between New York and Rio. When James arrived a little later, she told him she was expecting a return call from Detective Melo in Rio and couldn't go with him to check out the dog shelter.

"Problem is I'm still feeling punk," he said, pulling off his coat. "You check out Bideawee while I wait for the call. I feel bad about this. You've been doing all the leg work lately."

"You can make it up to me." She smiled. "Ask Melo to recommend good restaurants in Rio. And ask him about the weather this time of year."

James smiled. "We'll Google it if we go."

"You're the boss. Okay if I leave for Bideawee now?"

He nodded. She grabbed her jacket and her laptop. "I'll be back. Good luck with Brazil."

"Thanks. And don't adopt a dog. Who knows? Maybe we'll get to Rio."

As she opened the door of an unmarked Chevy Impala she looked up and recognized the familiar milky white sky. She told James that she loved snow which was the truth. She never told him that she was fearful of icy conditions on the road since she nearly got killed on one. Flashing back, she remembered a stretch of highway outside Billings, Montana where they hadn't salted the roads. At seventeen, she was a novice driver unprepared for a sheet of black ice as she drove home from a friend's house. The car swerved until she found herself staring at oncoming traffic. After she forgot what she had been taught and braked, the car shimmied all over the road. Luckily, the cars facing her were going slow and were able to stop. She quickly straightened the wheel and managed to get home safely.

She never told her parents what happened and never told James. As far as he knew, she was an experienced driver on snow and ice. She didn't want to spoil his image of her. She sometimes drove herself crazy aiming for perfection. She remembered what James once told her, "You're not perfect, but you're perfect for me." That was one of the nicest things any man ever said to her.

After driving south along Broadway, she finally reached Thirty-Eighth Street before turning east. As soon as she caught a glimpse of the East River she checked the address on her Smartphone: Bideawaee, 40 East 38th Street.

Cheri showed her badge to the woman at the desk and waited fifteen minutes before a woman walked towards her. "I'm Peggy," she said. After shaking hands, Cheri followed her down a hallway to a small windowless office. The walls were covered with photographs of dogs.

"I won't take up much of your time. You probably know by now that Leslie Rabinowitz's husband died."

"I heard that he fell from a balcony."

Cheri didn't stop to correct her. "I just have a few questions."

"Sure," said Peggy, leaning forward. "I thought you were here about that poor little spaniel that was kidnapped. Did you find the dog?"

"Not yet. We'll let you know as soon as we learn anything. Meanwhile, I'd like to go down another alley I was told that a dog at this shelter scratched Leslie's arms. Know anything about that?"

"I didn't see it happen, but I heard about it. Leslie told me that one of our dogs didn't like having a harness put on him."

On a hunch Cheri decided to lie. "I also noticed some bruises on Leslie's shoulders. Know anything about those?"

Peggy hesitated then said. "We keep it pretty warm in here. Leslie arrived wearing a short sleeve shirt under her sweater the other day. When she removed the sweater, I saw black and blue marks on her arms and shoulders."

"Did you ask her what happened?"

She hesitated. "No, actually, I didn't."

"What about the dog-napping? Think that was connected to Ben's death?"

Peggy shook her head. "Of course not. Somebody found out we had a pure-bred dog but didn't want to pay for it. That breed is very popular in New York. Perfect size for apartments and good with kids, also not a barker.'"

Cheri nodded. She remembered seeing one the other day. A nanny was walking a King Charles Spaniel while pushing an expensive looking stroller. The mother's probably a stockbroker, she thought at the time. "Do you think it's a coincidence that Leslie's husband fell off a balcony and then somebody stole the dog Leslie was walking?"

"Of course it's a coincidence. I don't see any connection other than bad luck."

"No connection you can think of?"

"No, not at all."

"Was Leslie limping the morning she incurred the scratches from the dog who didn't like the harness."

Peggy hesitated. "Limping? Why would she be limping?"

"I'm asking you."

She took a deep breath then said quietly, "I really don't remember."

"That's it for now. If you think of anything give me a call." She handed her a business card and thanked her for her time. When Peggy offered Cheri a quick tour around the kennels, she agreed. Before she left, Cheri spotted a tan and white dachshund. "I love dogs. That one would be a perfect size for my apartment."

"Want me to take him out of the kennel for you? You can walk him around."

"No thanks. I work long hours, wouldn't be fair to the pooch."

After Cheri got back, James told her that Detective Melo hadn't called back yet. He looked at his watch. "It's an hour later there, hope he didn't forget."

"He'll call," said Cheri. "It might be manana, but he'll call."

"Tell me about Bideawee."

She pulled off her scarf and threw it on her desk. "I think the manager was trying to save Leslie's ass. She never looked me in the eye, kept looking over my head or to the side as if she was lying. The only thing I learned is that Leslie had bruises on her shoulders. I just saw them on her upper arms but I tricked the manager into telling me about the other bruises."

"Interesting," said James. "Glad Bideawee wasn't a waste of time. But I'm getting disgusted with people lying to us."

"Cheer up," Cheri told him "We're going to see Kati's show *Suffer Queen*. Maybe it'll be fun." She sat opposite him and leaned forward so he could hear her over the clamor. "You know what I think?"

He shook his head.

"Kati might have killed for that part, literally. Or she killed Ben for the insurance so she wouldn't have to waitress in between jobs." Cheri smiled as she remembered her days making rounds. "It's all about who you know, but if your husband donates a lot of money to a theater like Ben did, the part is yours. She took a deep breath and exhaled loudly. "Who knows? Maybe Kati is talented. We'll find out." I'm not bitter, she thought. I had my time at the trough and enjoyed it.

Voices in the squad room suddenly erupted. Cheri heard the words "hatchet'" and "people killed." She imagined ranchers back in Montana using an ax to chop wood. Nobody used an ax or a hatchet as a weapon but this is Nueva York.

"Want to step out for a cup of coffee?" he asked. "I can't hear myself think."

"No, you go. I'll wait for Melo's call."

"Bring anything back for you?"

"Nada, gracias."

"You practicing Spanish?"

She smiled at him. "How'd you guess?"

He grabbed his jacket. "I'll be back. In the meantime, don't drive yourself crazy by asking Melo about the beaches in Rio. In other words, don't be a suffer queen."

She gave him a thumbs up and returned to her laptop. Just then, her phone rang. She grabbed it, looked at James and mouthed the words: "Not Melo."

He shrugged and told her, "Be patient."

Chapter 12

While she waited for Detective Melo's call Cheri Googled Rio de Janeiro for the third time and read reviews of Ipanema Beach and Copacabana Beach. She wasn't a strong swimmer, hated sunburns, was afraid of skin cancer but she sat there drooling over pictures of the ocean. What is the fascination? It's not a secret, she realized. It's warm in Rio, no icy sidewalks, no wind, no chapped lips, no cold feet, no huddling close to skyscrapers to avoid blowing snow.

Her reverie about Ipanema Beach was broken by the ringing of her phone.

"Hello," she said. "Como estas, Detective Melo?"

He answered in English. "We don't speak Spanish in Rio. We speak Brazilian Portugese."

"Sorry, I was hoping to get by on my college Spanish."

"That's okay," he said. "I have accent but English good."

English not so good, she thought, but answered, "Yes, it's very good. Better than my Spanish. What have you learned about Pepita and Luis?" She turned on the tape recorder.

"Is okay," he said. "You can tape our conversation."

What? How did he know? He didn't, she realized, just a lucky guess. "Did you talk to both of them?"

He coughed into the phone, apologized and said, "Yes, I talk to Pepita and Luis."

Cheri leaned forward, hoping to block out the noise around her. "Can you do me a favor?" she asked. "Speak a little louder. I'm not in a private office."

"Is not a problem," he shouted.

She wanted to tell him no need to shout but decided to keep going. "Okay, tell me."

"I'll read from my notes and add what I remember."

Cheri held her phone to one ear and stuck her finger in her other ear. Of all days, the squad room sounded like a bar during happy hour.

She decided that since everything would be on tape she could stop stressing out about hearing every word the Brazilian detective told her. Plus, his accent wasn't slight. He mispronounced words, mangled others and avoided verbs. She remained as quiet as possible and only asked Detective Melo a few times to speak up or repeat what he had just said.

They were saying goodbye when James walked into the room. He pulled off his coat and sat at the desk facing her. She smiled at him and pointed to the tape recorder.

"Detective Melo said he had an appointment, but will talk to me again soon." She stood up and stretched. "James," she said excitedly, "We have another person of interest. "I'll play the tape for you later. You'll see, Luis went over a cliff during his interview."

"Tell me."

Cheri moved closer, facing James across her desk. "Pepita looks home free unless she paid Luis to kill Ben and that's still a possibility. But the big news is Luis admitted he was in New York the day Ben was murdered."

"Interesting. Tell me more."

"Luis was one of Ben's clients."

"We learned that from our initial investigation," said James. "Learn anything else?"

"Yeah, he told me that Ben didn't just put Luis in a lousy stock. He invested Luis's money in a mine."

"What kind of mine?"

"A gold mine that was bleeding cash. A worthless investment."

"What about Ben's partner, Perry Hartman?"

"I asked Melo about that. According to Luis, Ben and Perry were partners but not friends." Cheri smiled. "I got the feeling Detective Melo played hardball to get that information out of Luis. Luis also said that that Ben and Perry blamed each other for that mine deal."

She stopped to sip from a bottle of water. "And when Melo asked Luis about Ben's will, he claimed he didn't know anything about it. Neither did Pepita. Bullshit."

"Any more info?" he asked as he popped a cough drop in his mouth.

Cberi leaned closer. "Melo is getting a list of questions together for Luis. While we were on the phone he got an important call but he's going to interview Luis again. He plans to threaten him with a lie-detector test if Luis stonewalls."

James smiled. "He did a good job for a Rio Leo. The noise in here is driving me crazy. I'm still getting over the flu and feel headache-y. Let's go around the corner to the coffee shop, I'll have hot soup for my throat, and you can finish telling me the rest."

"I have a lot more to tell you." She grabbed her jacket and scarf.

As they walked to their favorite coffee shop on the corner they huddled against the wind with their hands stuffed in their pockets. After they got settled at a table in back away from the door, James had a coughing fit and popped another cough drop in his mouth.

"This is a biggie," said Cheri, leaning close and whispering. "Luis admitted he went to Ben's apartment hoping to get the money back that he invested in that worthless gold mine. He told Melo he rang the bell. No answer, so he tried the door and found it open. He walked in quietly and stood in the hallway. That's when he saw Ben and a woman in the doorway of the bedroom. It was kind of dark, but it looked as if they were arguing according to Luis, so he hightailed it out of there. Didn't want to be part of a domestic dispute, if that's what it was."

"Did Luis go back to the apartment?" asked James.

"Claims he didn't. Doesn't sound believable but he did leave a few messages on Ben's cell. He also sent a text. No response."

"Bullshit,' said James. "First, he said he wasn't in Ben's apartment. Now, he remembers that he was there and saw Ben with a woman."

"Did Melo show Luis pictures of Kati and Leslie to see if he can identify one of them?"

"Not yet," said Cheri. "He plans to do that after I scan some pictures to him."

"If Luis is guilty, Melo is going to nail his ass..."

"To Corcovado Mountain," said Cheri, interrupting.

"Is that the huge mountain in Rio?" he asked.

"Yup. It looms over the city with a statue of Jesus on top. Big tourist site."

James rolled his eyes. She knew what he was thinking. He didn't want to talk about Jesus. He gave up on the church after attending a seminary to become a priest. Father O'Brien, that's who he wanted to be. And when he gave up the church, he gave up the idea of becoming Blessed Father O'Brien. He didn't give up on God, but he gave up everything else, including prayers. Years later, the scandal in the Catholic church didn't help. She wasn't pushing the church by mentioning Corcovado Mountain. She was hoping for a trip to Rio by saying it was a big tourist site.

James ignored the mention of the mountain and the statue of Jesus. Instead he asked, "When is Melo scheduled to call Luis back for more questioning?"

"Soon. He's going to listen to the messages on Luis' phone and check out any texts to or from Ben."

"You hungry?"

"No. I'll eat after the theatre."

He laughed. "Your usual goat cheese and cucumber sandwich?"

"You kidding? I vary my meals. Tonight is grilled elk with a side of buffalo and some grass, the edible kind."

James shook his head and smiled. The waitress took their orders and they waited for her to walk away before continuing. "Tell me something. Are Pepita and Luis from Brazil?"

Cheri shook her head. "According to Melo, she's a native of Brooklyn. Real name is Paula Walkwitz. Changed it to Pepita Alvarez."

James rolled his eyes. "And her boy toy?"

"He's from the Bronx."

Somebody at the table next to them asked to borrow the ketchup. "Keep it," said Cheri.

James emptied a second packet of sugar in his coffee, stirred it, then moved the cup aside to make room for his bowl of soup. "What did Luis do before he became a dancer?"

Cheri tried not to scowl but couldn't help herself. "He was a crack addict if that counts as a profession. Luis didn't want to admit it but Melo got that information from his computer."

James thought about that. "Luis do time in the pen?"

"No, he had a sympathetic judge who ordered rehab and community service."

"Holy shit," said James. "Maybe that's how Luis raised the money he invested with Ben. Selling drugs."

"Claims he's clean. Said he made a killing on a racehorse. Wait, there's more," she whispered. "There was an arrest for assault and battery in a bar in the Bronx. The guy who Luis punched later dropped the charges."

James looked at his partner across the table. "There's something I don't understand. Why did Luis admit he was in Ben's apartment the day of the murder? He could have lied."

She leaned closer so James wouldn't miss a word. "You'll appreciate this. Melo told Luis that the surveillance camera in Ben's lobby showed him near the elevator in Ben's building."

James rubbed his face and grinned. "This detective is sharp. Glad he's on our side."

"If Luis becomes a suspect, we'll get to Rio," she said.

"And if he's not?"

"We'll do the honorable thing and frame him." She watched the expression on his face and said quickly. "You know I'm kidding. I don't want to go to Rio that badly. But we'll have something just as good. We'll send the perp up for a long time and hope he doesn't have a sympathetic judge this time. This is not a case about a few ounces of cocaine. This was cold blooded murder."

Chapter 13

As soon as Cheri arrived at the police station the next morning, she spotted a stack of files on either side of James's desk. In the center was an iPhone. "Morning," she said. sniffing the cologne that James was wearing. It had a woodsy odor like pine trees and reminded her of hiking in the mountains of Montana.

"Remember this?" said James, holding up the phone. "It was found in the apartment where Ben was murdered. Sorry, good morning." He swiveled around to face her. "We listened to the messages."

"I remember the phone," she said. "What about it?"

"I decided to scroll through again to make sure we didn't miss any. Sure enough, we missed one. Listen to this." He put the cell on speakerphone. The voice was deep but garbled. "Hello, Ben, this is your buddy. You never returned my call, so I'm calling a second time. I invested in your goddamn gold mine. And I want my money back. I'll expect my cash returned by this evening, or else." They listened a few more times trying to trace the accent before the line went dead. Cheri stared at her partner. "That's the same damned mine that Luis invested in. Maybe Ben put all his clients in that piece of crap."

"That's what we have to find out. We're scheduled to talk to Kati after her show. Maybe she'll have some info for us."

"Any other interesting messages on that phone?" she asked.

"Two from Leslie that we already listened to which indicates she had this number. Most of his calls were on his other phone. Seems he kept this phone for special people, like the friend who threatened him and his soon-to-be ex-wife."

"Crazy dude," said Cheri. "He was married three times but never bothered to get divorced. He was technically still married to Pepita Alvarez, alias Paula Walkwitz." She crossed her arms in front of her. "Why do you think he saved a threatening message?"

James shrugged. "Maybe he wanted to report it to the police but never got around to it."

She took a deep breath and smiled at him. There was a piece of tissue paper stuck to his chin, had evidently cut himself shaving that morning, but she didn't mention it. "Maybe Ben kept the message as evidence in case somebody tried to kill him, but too late. Somebody already did."

"Jesus," he said, sounding exasperated. "Benjamin Rabinowitz had more enemies than the Godfather."

She pointed to his chin. "You cut yourself shaving?"

"Thanks for reminding me."

He removed the paper, stood up and threw it in the trash. "By the way, the phone number from the threatening call isn't traceable, probably a throw-away phone."

She shrugged. "Figures. Maybe it was Jazz."

"Why do you think that?" asked James. Cheri leaned forward, one finger on the side of her nose. "If Jazz was one of the investors and wants to get his money back from Leslie, he might have called. He also had a partner in crime with the dog-napping. Leslie said the guy had a Russian accent. This guy's accent could've been Russian."

"Too bad it wasn't clear," said James. "Speaking of the mob, there's a Russian Mafia in Brooklyn. They live in Brighton Beach. You up for a ride to the ocean?"

Cheri nodded. "Sure. I'll research the Mafia online first, maybe I'll find someone who used the alias JAZZ." There was another outburst in the squad room and Cheri heard the words "Serial killer." Then she heard someone shout, "They caught the guy. He was hiding in a dumpster."

She looked at James. He had his fingers jammed in his ears. His hearing was more sensitive than hers because he had gone to fewer rock concerts.

The outburst finally subsided. James stood up and stretched his back and shoulders. "You lucked out. We'll get to the ocean after all. The Atlantic Ocean at Brighton Beach. While we're there, we should sample some Russian delicacies."

"Anything but caviar." said Cheri. "Tried it once, didn't like it."

"I hated it," he said, "Too salty."

She considered the name of the guy who kidnapped the dog. "Maybe it's Jazz-sky or Jazzconovich and he shortened it. I'm anxious to drive out to Brighton Beach and talk to some Russians."

"Tomorrow," said James. First, let's check the criminal database for Russian sounding names. You do that while I call Detective Melo in Rio. I have a few questions for him."

"Got it," said Cheri. "Don't forget we're seeing *Suffer Queen* tonight, starring our very own Kati."

James nodded. "I'm looking forward to that. Maybe she'll tell us what she knows about that apartment."

Chapter 14

They left the police station early so they would be on time for *Suffer Queen.* James parked on Barrow Street and they walked over to the Cherry Lane Theater. A group of teenagers dressed in oversized clothing were hanging around smoking pot. Cheri recognized the smell and turned her head. She never loved weed, made her sluggish, then gave her the munchies, despite trying not to gain weight.

It was bitter cold and the sidewalks were covered with patches of ice. Cheri wanted to take James's arm, partly because she was afraid of slipping on the ice and partly because it would feel good. She kept her thoughts to herself as she pointed to a homeless man asleep in the doorway of an apartment building. He was covered with sheets of newspaper.

"Damn shame in this cold," said James. "They could find him dead in the morning." She nodded then looked away. What could she do?

They arrived at the theater early and were seated in the third row. Cheri checked out the set: a wooden coat rack, two chairs and a kitchen table. There was a calendar on a cork board with a picture that said Riley's Irish Pub. She elbowed James and pointed. His ancestors on his father's side came from County Cork. James always talked about taking a trip to

Ireland after he's finished with alimony payments. He's a good guy, thought Cheri. As far as she knew, he was never late with a payment.

She looked at the cover of the Playbill and thought about Kati. This is probably a juicy role. Good enough to kill for, especially with fractures in the marriage according to Ben's partner, Perry.

As Cheri looked around the small off-Off Broadway theater, she remembered the first show she had ever seen–a children's production of *Rapunzel.* Before the show was over, she told herself, That's what I want to do. As she watched Kati move to the edge of the stage in semi-darkness, she experienced a nudge of envy. Part of her still missed the theater. But she didn't need roommates anymore, the way she did during her acting days, and she didn't worry about paying the rent. She also had a perk at the NYPD, a handsome detective as her partner.

The stage lights came up and Kati stood center stage with a spotlight on her.

She began: "I've a story to tell you," Kati pronounced in an Irish accent. "And I don't want you to call me a Suffer Queen just because I'm Irish."

Cheri felt immediately engaged in the play and in Kati's performance as Rosie Ahearn Keene.

Kati continued:

"Tell me, why do women blame themselves when a man strays? I even wondered, Do I have a stinky vagina? That's it. I blamed it on a stinky vagina."

James cocked his head and smiled. Cheri howled at the line, along with most of the other women in the audience. This was Greenwich Village, after all. It wasn't a conservative audience. A few minutes later, she glanced at James again. He was finally laughing out loud. From the opening few lines, Cheri was drawn into the life of the character.

Kati went on in a lilting Irish accent about her plans to get revenge on her husband by meeting a mate online.

"I thought about a face-lift, but I'd have to wait too long before going on a date. My cellulite? I'm getting that under control. I've been using Brillo. I have to admit Brillo might not work, but it feels as if it's working. It should. It's painful enough. Now you know why I call myself a Suffer Queen. The Brillo scrubbed the skin off the palms of my hands. Look, see for yourselves. You can't be a full-fledged Suffer Queen unless you suffer for your body...."

Cheri whispered in James's ear, "She's good."

He nodded.

The show ran a little over seventy minutes. After it was over, Kati received a standing ovation. And as soon as she stepped out of the stage door autograph seekers were waiting for her, along with several of Kati's friends. She excused herself, walked over to the detectives and told them that a coffee shop nearby was fairly quiet at this hour. After kissing her friends good-bye the three of them set off for the restaurant two blocks away.

As soon as they walked into the coffee shop, Cheri smelled toast, coffee and scrambled eggs. She was hungry but decided to wait. Coffee would tide her over until they were back uptown. James said he could wait also. The three of them ordered coffee. Kati added an English muffin with jam on the side.

"Any chance the play will get moved uptown?" Cheri asked.

"There's talk about that," said Kati. "But one-woman plays don't make a lot of money."

James waited for the shop talk to end then leaned forward. "Where were you the day Ben died?"

Kati answered in a flat voice. "I was home learning my lines."

"Anybody with you?"

"No, it's a one-woman play."

"I noticed," he said.

"Didn't step out for food?"

Kati shook her head. The waitress brought three cups of coffee and Kati's English muffin. She spread jam on the muffin and started eating. "I never eat before a show," she told them. "I'm starving."

James nodded. "Did you go for a walk?"

"No."

"Go out for dinner?" asked Cheri.

"No." Kati was starting to sound irritated. "I was alone the entire day. There are a lot of lines to learn."

Cheri caught a glimpse of Kati's foot under the table. She was tapping it nervously. James put his coffee cup back on the saucer. "Did you expect to receive Ben's entire estate, including his life insurance?"

Kati stared back at him. "I wasn't expecting Ben to die and I wasn't hoping he would. I loved him. He wouldn't have invested in *Suffer Queen* if he didn't love me. That was a show of faith." She started fiddling with her wedding ring, trying to twist it around to the back of her finger but it was too tight.

"Do you own a black coat with a hood?" asked Cheri.

"No. I use my bike to get around town so I wear a helmet. A coat with a hood wouldn't work."

Cheri stared at Kati, busy spreading jam on the other half of her muffin. "What about bad weather when you can't use your motorcycle?"

"I wear a ski jacket but it doesn't have a hood."

There was silence at the table as all three sipped their coffee. The back door opened and a blast of cold air filled the small restaurant.

James stirred two packets of sugar in his coffee. "What about the apartment on West End Avenue?"

"What about it?" said Kati.

"Any idea why Ben kept an apartment there–so far from the financial district? What kind of business was he running there?" asked James.

"I don't know," said Kati. "He never told me about that apartment."

"You were married to him," said Cheri. "You supposedly knew the man. Ben's partner, Perry, didn't know about it. Leslie didn't know about it. You didn't know about it. Doesn't that make you curious about why he was so secretive about that place?"

"I guess so, but I don't know." She sat back, and wiped her mouth with her napkin.

"Was he involved with drugs?" asked James.

"I don't know."

Other women?" said Cheri.

She shook her head. "Definitely not. He loved me."

Cheri said pointedly, "If there was hanky-panky going on, most women might want revenge. What about you?"

"I'm not a vengeful person and he wasn't unfaithful. We had great sex."

The detectives looked across the table. Kati finally said, "I'm dead tired. I also have two shows tomorrow, a matinee and an evening performance. Instead of continuing, can I come to your office next week or the week after? This is a tough show, and it's all on my shoulders. I don't want to let the playwright or the director down."

Cheri nodded and handed her a business card. "Here's another card in case you lost the one I gave you. We'll check our schedule and give you a call with an appointment."

"Sounds good. Thanks for letting me go home." She opened her wallet to pay her share. James said, "I'll take care of it."

Katie picked up her hat and coat and walked out of the coffee shop.

"What do you think?" James asked.

"She knew about the apartment," said Cheri. "Did you see her eyes?"

"Sure did. I'm thrilled that they had great sex. But the dude wasn't faithful, not with a secret apartment and a card from an escort service on his desk. And I bet he didn't sleep home."

The back door opened again and there was another blast of cold air.

"Right now, I think all the wives look suspicious," said Cheri, "including Pepita even if she wasn't in New York. Her lover was here when Ben was murdered. And Luis had a motive. He was scammed out of thousands of dollars with that phony gold-mine."

The door opened again and Cheri said, "It's cold. Let's high-tail it out of here."

"We'll drive uptown and eat where we know the food," said James. "My treat."

He left cash on the table to cover the check and a tip. "Right now, I'm beginning to think it was Leslie who killed Cock Robin. Money is a strong motivator."

Cheri nodded. "But Kati had a strong motive, too. Revenge for Ben screwing around." She stopped and thought about the theatre. "I've acted on stage. I think Kati dug into some of her own experience for that role in *Suffer Queen* or she's a damned good actress."

James didn't comment as they walked out of the restaurant into a bitter cold night. She huddled close to him for warmth. After he slipped and nearly pulled her down, she chuckled. "I was scared of black ice, so I held your arm."

"I won't fall. Would be too embarrassing."

"Let's get back on our own turf," said Cheri. "Better food and they salt the sidewalks."

"I agree. Hang on. Do you have ice-skates, by the way?"

"No. I have cross-country skis. My mom just shipped them to me."

"I'm starved. How 'bout you?

"I could eat a goat, forgot about the cheese."

He held her elbow as they walked toward the car. "We have our work cut out for us. Now we have to figure out who hated Ben the most."

Chapter 15

Giorgio's Grill was popular for breakfast. lunch, and dinner, even brunch. Cheri and James ate there often. They walked nearly thirty blocks in good weather and drove in bad weather. But they liked the owners and the warmth of the place. Cheri also liked the exposed brick walls. They reminded her of an Off-Broadway theater where she had performed shortly after arriving in New York. Their favorite booth in back was available. Cheri smiled as she settled in. She was frustrated about the Rabinowitz case, but the smell of brewing coffee lifted her spirits.

James shook a dusting of snow off his collar then sat opposite her. A waitress poured coffee for them and took their orders.

Leaning forward, Cheri spoke softly. "I brought the file along. We could have a working dinner."

James tapped the table as he grinned. "Good idea, except I'm paranoid about talking in public."

"There's nobody here."

He looked around and nodded. The place was empty. The drinking crowd would arrive later. After he glanced at a few papers in a cursory way, he stuck everything back in the file.

"So what do you think? she asked. "What's your theory about the case?"

He shrugged. "Not sure yet."

She watched him as he shuffled his thoughts. She loved his methodical way of weighing all the facts.

"I hope Kati doesn't have another excuse not to talk to us next week," he said softly.

"We'll tell her she has to talk to us," said Cheri. "We played nice-nice letting her go home after her show because she was tired but no more."

"We have her on hold," he said. "We'll fit her in next week even if she says she has a show that night."

Cheri nodded. "She'll have to tough it out, the poor prima donna. Meanwhile, I'd love to fly to Rio and talk to Luis. Something doesn't gel. Luis told Detective Melo he wasn't in New York then changed his story and said he was here on business."

"What kind of business?" James asked.

"Something to do with a television show featuring Latin dancing."

"What about Pepita?"

"She had to stay in Brazil to meet with a group of producers about a possible nightclub act in Rio."

He held up his half empty coffee cup and gestured to the waitress. She re-filled it and said she would be right back. Cheri inhaled deeply, taking in the scent of maple syrup. Somebody at the counter was eating pancakes. She was tempted to tell the waitress she wanted a side of pancakes with her soup but too fattening, especially with butter and maple syrup.

They stopped talking when the waitress returned with their food. After reaching for ketchup, James said, "I think Pepita might have given her lover an incentive to whack Ben, especially if she was expecting big bucks from Ben's will. I bet the two of them racked up debts in Rio. They opened a dance studio, paid rent, probably bought special costumes."

Cheri said in a near whisper, "All three wives had a motive. Now, we have to work on the other angle—opportunity. So far, two of out three had the opportunity plus Luis. And Jazz." She laughed and added, "All that JAZZ."

He winked at her across the table. "Don't forget the mystery lady in the black hooded coat. She might be a link in the case," he said, wiping his mouth with a napkin. "Same with the missing tape from the lobby of the apartment building. Doubt they're both a coincidence."

They ate quietly while the waitress returned to ask if they wanted more coffee. They said no thank you, then waited until she was out of hearing range.

Cheri rubbed her temples as she thought of the possibilities. "Damn, I know it's early, but I'd hate to see this turn into a cold case. I wouldn't have liked Ben. He was a bigamist, for Christ's sake. And a liar. Still, I'd like to see the perp behind bars."

"It won't become a cold case," said James. "Not if we keep working on it."

They ate slowly, not saying much until James told her something about Ben, and Cheri asked him to speak louder.

"I said he was also a fraudulent stockbroker. Listen, I'm not comfortable here. It's starting to fill up. We should go back to the station." He hesitated. "Or we can go to my place."

Cheri smiled. "For business? Or monkey business?"

"Mostly business–of one sort or another."

She stared into his dark eyes. *Damn, I'm like Alice falling down the rabbit hole.* After she grabbed two fries from the side of his plate, she decided not to respond to his comments. Instead she said, "Good fries."

"Help yourself." He winked at her as she took one more. She rubbed the dry skin on her hands then applied Chap Stick to her lips. "This dry weather is a killer on my skin. I feel like an alligator"

"You look pretty good to me."

She nearly said, You look pretty good to me, too, but stopped herself. "Thanks," she whispered and leaned back in her chair. They were getting too close for comfort–literally and figuratively. "Let's pass on going back to the station tonight. I'll work at home."

"No problem," he said.

When she finished eating he pulled out his wallet. "Ready to go?"

"One sec." She drained the remains of her coffee then smiled at him as she pulled on her coat. The cold weather, plus working together on the Rabinowitz case, made her crave physical closeness. She figured that was probably why she was eating so much lately, especially chocolate. She was eating bars of dark chocolate, going to the gym, then eating more chocolate. At least, the chocolate was good for her heart.

As she waited near the counter for James to pay, she wondered why she had so much trouble forgiving him. He had a lousy one night stand but he apologized. She remembered their last vacation together on an island in the Caribbean. He called room service one night and ordered three dozen oysters and a bottle of wine.

She moved closer to him outside the restaurant, hoping to avoid blowing snow.

"Have a good weekend."

"You, too," he said. "I'll walk you to your car."

As soon as they reached her car they stood on the corner saying good-bye for the second time.

"By the way," she said, "I'm cooking Indian fry bread tomorrow for Caz."

"She sick?"

"No, she's worried about her losing her job. Lot of lay-offs." Cheri was tempted to tell him, I'll drop some fry bread off at your place after I see Caz but stopped herself. This was the second time tonight that she almost put her foot in her mouth.

"I can bring some fry bread to the station on Monday if you'd like. You can nuke it."

"I'd love that. See you Monday morning. Should be an interesting week."

She turned uptown and lowered her head against blowing snow. That's when she resolved to wake up especially early the next day and cook Indian fry bread for Caz. As she opened her car door she realized how lucky she was to have the use of a precinct pool car. Otherwise, she'd be riding the subway with the other suckers trying to find a little warmth. Seeking warmth made her think of James again. She shifted gears and thought about the Rabinowitz case.

When Cheri arrived home, she poured a glass of white wine for herself and sat on the couch thinking about Life with a capitol L." Too tired to practice kickboxing she went into her kitchen and dug out her grandmother's recipe for Indian fry bread in a notebook labeled "Montana." One day when she wasn't busy, she'd scan all her grandmother's recipes into her computer.

After she found the recipe for fry bread she opened her laptop and checked for messages. Nothing new from forensics and nothing from Detective Melo in Rio. She thought about Jazz and making a trip to the Russian neighborhood in Brighton Beach, Brooklyn, alone or with her partner.

Next she pulled up Google hoping to find Russian surnames starting with the letter "J" as in Jazz. She couldn't believe it. There wasn't a letter "J" in the Russian language. She stared at the list of Russian last names on Wikipedia but the phonetic alphabet in English skipped "J" and went from "I" to "K." She scrolled up and down looking for the missing letter, then decided it didn't exist. Maybe Jazz got that nickname for his love of music. He might have gone to clubs where they played jazz or he played a sax or clarinet. She was tempted to call James and tell him what she just discovered. After checking the time she decided it was too late. It could wait until Monday morning. She stared at the Cyrillic alphabet wondering how Americans learned to read the Russian language. She always wanted to become fluent in another language, preferably Italian. She could take classes at night, but she worked long hours.

She finally logged off and got ready for bed. The thought of "J" missing in the Russian language kept her awake. So did the thought of somebody kidnapping a dog.

Just as she was about to doze off, fire engines roared past. Even with the blinds closed, she could see the flashing lights. Is New York ever quiet? she wondered. It is–when your bedroom doesn't face the street and the windows of your apartment are better insulated. She wasn't rich and realized she never will be. But she loved her job. It was a challenge. And she loved working with James. He never treated her condescendingly, never called her a girl or Good Girl.

She shifted gears back to the Rabinowitz case. She had a hunch that Ben's murderer was somebody they already interviewed. Now, they had to figure out which one.

Chapter 16

After a quick breakfast of yogurt and fruit, Cheri pulled on a pair of ratty sweatpants and a tee-shirt. Then she slipped in a DVD and started kickboxing. The Martial Arts Competition is coming up, she reminded herself. With that in mind, she started kicking higher and harder. but it was difficult in her apartment's excuse for a living room. Even if she moved everything out and had an empty room, the space was still small. She had friends at the gym who did that–got rid of all non-essential furniture. When you visited them you sat on cushions or on the floor. She considered that once but ruled it out. She lived close to the gym. They had late hours so she was able to get there even after a long day at work.

Keep kicking, she told herself. Higher, higher. She kept it up until she developed a stitch in her side and stopped to rub it. She continued for another fifteen minutes. Enough, she decided, especially since she planned to hit the gym after visiting Caz.

After assembling all the ingredients for fry bread, she checked the time on her phone before calling Caz. She didn't expect her to pick up so she left a message: "Hey Sleeping Beauty, give me a call when you're ready for company. I'll bring over some fry bread."

Ten minutes later, Cheri's cell rang.

"It's me," said Caz. "I was in the shower. I'm hungry. A half hour?"

"Little more," said Cheri. "See you soon."

While she waited for the fry bread to cook she checked her phone. There was a message from Tom. "Sorry if there was a misunderstanding. I'm still planning to leave a ticket for you for opening night." The other message was from James. "My buddy can get me two tickets for any Broadway show you want to see for your birthday. Let me know your choice. I'd also like to take you to dinner. We can drive down to the Odeon or go somewhere in the theater district. Let me know so I can make a reservation."

She lifted the fry bread out of the pan, blew on a small piece and tasted it. It turned out great. She wrapped a piece for James and covered the rest to bring over to Caz.

Grabbing her keys, the fry bread and a plastic container of honey, she walked down the hallway and rang the bell. Caz opened the door dressed in jeans and a white tee shirt that said, NEW MEXICO: NOT REALLY NEW AND NOT REALLY MEXICO.

"Like the logo?" she asked.

"Love it," said Cheri. "When were you there?"

"Few years ago. You'd love Santa Fe. Great hiking." She inhaled deeply. "Smells good." Cheri remembered that Ben's partner said he'd been there recently. Popular place, she thought.

They sat on wooden stools at the kitchen counter and ate fry bread drizzled with honey When Cheri told her friend about the two messages, Caz said, "Two handsome men. I don't even have time for one."

"You will," said Cheri. "Meanwhile, you're working on an interesting assignment."

"Magazines aren't doing well in this digital age. Don't know how long they'll keep publishing. Maybe I should change careers like you did."

"What are you thinking of doing?"

Caz wiped her mouth with a napkin. "Maybe pole dancing."

Cheri laughed. "Let's open an after hours club. We'll call it Pole Cat. We can give lap dances, too, charge extra for that."

"I can just see the headline in The Daily News," said Caz. "NYPD detective discovered doing lap dances at an after hours club." Caz suddenly looked serious as she stared across the table at her friend. "Were you scared before you changed careers?"

"Yeah, didn't know if I was doing the right thing giving up the theater for the Police Academy. Why?"

"Print journalism has changed a lot."

"What about an online magazine?"

"Don't think I'd like working from home. I like being around people.

Cheri smiled. "Then pole dancing might be a good idea."

Caz poured more honey on her fry bread. "Giving up acting must have been hard."

"It was. I also worried about other people's reactions. Like if they would say, Cheri went from being an actress to being a detective. Strange..."

Caz poured coffee for both of them, then put sugar and cream on the counter. "Guess I'm not the only insecure person in New York."

Cheri laughed. "Only another eight million."

Caz took a sip of coffee. "Any regrets?"

"Nope. I'd do it again." She wiped her mouth with a paper napkin. "My turn to ask you a question. Did you ever want to have children?"

Caz nodded. "I did, still do. Maybe I'll adopt a baby in China. That's where my father's side of the family comes from–Beijing. What about you?"

Cheri shook her head. "I don't want to get on the mommy track."

They switched to discussing new restaurants in New York, figuring out which ones they could afford. They decided almost none before Cheri checked the time on her phone. "I better to get to the gym. Practice time, then I have work to do." She stood up and pulled her keys out of her pocket. "And you have to get back to work, too." She leaned over and kissed Caz's cheek. "It's always good to talk to you, de-stresses me."

"Same here," said Caz. "Before you leave, tell me about the new case you're working on."

"Can't talk about it now. But I might be driving out to Brighton Beach soon, to a neighborhood called Little Odessa, also known as Moscow on the Hudson."

"Be careful," said Caz. "I saw a program on TV recently about a Russian mob in Brighton Beach. They're known for using brass knuckles."

"That's who I'm going to investigate." Cheri put her cup of coffee close to the edge of the counter, then quickly moved it back. "It's just a preliminary trip, but thanks for being concerned."

As Cheri walked back to her apartment she smelled Polish pierogies. Jewish chicken soup, Italian lasagna. After she opened the door to her apartment, she grabbed her coat and scarf, then stopped to look in the hallway mirror. Her skin looked pale from lack of sun all winter. Worse than that, she suddenly developed a premonition about her upcoming trip to Brighton Beach, and it wasn't a good one. Her family called her a witch because of her ESP. A niece once asked her, "Why do they call you a witch, Aunt Cheri? You don't have a long nose." So far, most of her hunches were right-on. If this one turned out correct, she could end up in trouble or dead.

Brass knuckles, she thought, as she locked the door. The Russian Mafia would use them. She reached for her gun; she felt vulnerable without it. After she worked out for two hours at the gym, her premonition about Brighton Beach returned. This time it was worse than before.

Chapter 17

Standing under a hot shower on Monday morning Cheri relished her first perk of the day But when she stepped out of the tub the tile underfoot was freezing. She hopped back to her carpeted bedroom.

After pulling on a black turtleneck, a white V-neck pullover, jeans, and a pair of black knee-high leather boots, she decided she could pass for a hooker on Eighth Avenue then wondered if a hooker wears a Catholic medal of the Virgin of Copper. But dressing like this was one way not to look like a detective. She grabbed her gym bag with a pair of sneakers and a change of clothes inside and pulled a leather coat out of her closet.

When she arrived at the police station she stopped at her desk. James was already at his computer. "Hey, Cheri," he called, engrossed in what he was reading. "C'mere. You gotta see this."

"Be there in a sec." She handed him the fry bread and he thanked her, then she stood behind him and looked at the screen.

"Interesting," he said, without looking up.

She stared at his computer screen until she finally realized what he was showing her. "How did you access Ben's computer?"

"Friend of mine. I'm technologically challenged, but my buddy Ron-Joe isn't. I told him what I needed and he hacked into Ben's computer. "

"How are we going to use evidence that was accessed illegally?"

"Good question, but I'll worry about that during the trial. Meanwhile, this'll help when we question Leslie again. Besides, Ron-Joe owed me a favor."

"What kind of favor?"

"He was picked up for selling grass. Good kid, was only trying to earn enough money to go to school to learn a trade."

Cheri smiled. "So, he handed you the dope and the evidence disappeared?"

"Something like that. My buddy is looking for deleted texts and e-mails on Ben's Smartphone also."

James kept scrolling down. There were innocuous e-mails to Pepita about the weather in Rio de Janiero. Ben also wrote that he had eaten at a Brazilian restaurant in New York and asked her how to pronounce "churrasco." Petpita's return e-mail spelled it out phonetically for him: "shoe-HAS-ko."

"Gracias, senorita," Ben replied. "I bet the Brazilian food in New York isn't as good as in Rio. I'll fly down one of these days and you can take me to your favorite restaurant. How's Luis behaving, by the way?"

He pictured her smiling as she wrote, "He's a pain in the culo just like you, but I still love you."

"What do you think of that?" asked Cheri.

"I think she was teasing him. Or hoping for a belated Christmas present." He continued scrolling down. The next group of e-mails was addressed to investors. He and Cheri had trouble following discussions about puts, calls, options, ETFs. When they tired of Ben's world of high finance, they took a break.

"So tell me, who do you think took out Ben, the bigamist?"

He sat back and rubbed his face while he tapped a Magic Marker on his desk. "Not sure, but I'll lay it out for you: Pepita told the detective in Rio that the divorce was her idea. I bet she lied. Ben probably dumped her for Leslie. He also conned Pepita out of alimony. According to Detective Melo, Ben bought her a one-way ticket to Rio. She's older and smarter now, maybe figured it was time for pay-back."

"They broke up years ago," she reminded him. "Doesn't make sense to wait so long for revenge."

James scratched his chin while he considered that remark. "Yeah, but if he dumped her, she might have been carrying a torch for the guy hoping he'd come back to her. And if she struggled financially after arriving in Rio maybe Ben refused to help her."

Cheri shrugged her shoulders. "Ben also conned Luis out of money so Luis had a motive. And the opportunity. Between the two of them, they might have hatched a plan to kill Ben."

"Good point," said James. "And there's still Leslie. Let's not forget about her."

"I haven't," said Cheri. "She comes across as too nervous for someone who's innocent."

"Ben was good to Leslie initially," he said. "She even gave up her music career for him. She might be bitter about that, especially since he dumped her for Kati. Plus, we know Leslie's hurting for money. That Ponzi scheme probably took a big chunk of her money."

Cheri nodded. "I have a feeling Ben deliberately dragged out the divorce proceedings and screwed her out of temporary alimony. Maybe in the end, she figured his life insurance was worth more than alimony."

She popped a Certs in her mouth and listened as James continued. "Then we have Kati. Ben bankrolled her career and invested money in the show she's starring in before he got tired of her, too. Similar pattern with all his wives."

"And being an actor, Kati probably worried in the past about a weekly paycheck so she married a Sugar Daddy. But I bet he controlled the purse strings. Sugar Daddies do that."

He turned to look at her. "How do you know?"

"I've had a few over the years."

He raised his eyebrows but didn't respond. After he turned back to the computer she opened a tote bag and pulled out an apple. "So far, we have three feisty women and one rich womanizer who scammed everybody. All we have to figure out is who wanted Ben dead the most."

James nodded. "Put yourself in the heads of those three women and see who you come up with."

"I'll try." she said, rubbing the apple on her slacks. "But you know, you can love someone and still be able to murder that person."

She waited for James to ask, Speaking from experience? Instead, he followed up with more ideas about Leslie. "I thought she came across as a phony with her volunteer dog-walking and her bird watching in Central Park. She's also up-tight. Maybe she doesn't like police stations or doesn't like us delving into her life." He swiveled his chair around. "Don't forget, we still have to interview Ben's investors."

"We'll get there," said Cheri. She stood behind him as they stared at the computer.

"By the way," he asked, "How's your playwright boyfriend?"

"He's gone."

"Gone? Like out of town, you mean?"

"No, out of my life. I broke up with him."

James chuckled. "You didn't like his play?"

"I liked his play. I didn't like him."

He continued scrolling down through e-mails until he stopped abruptly.

"Holy shit," she cried. "Do you see what I see?"

"Sure do. Ben and Leslie were planning to leave the country together and use phony passports." James threw a candy wrapper in the trash. "Let's get her back here! I'll give her a call right now."

"Cheri listened while he called Leslie and left a message."

"Guess you heard my message, but I bet she won't call me back. She's scared to be in the same room with me. I'll keep calling and leaving messages."

"Maybe she saw your caller I.D. and didn't pick up."

"She can run," he said, "but she can't hide under a rock for too long."

"What do you think about me driving out to Brooklyn now and trying to find out what I can about Jazz?"

"I don't feel good about you going by yourself. You're talking about a dangerous Russian mob. I'd go with you, but I have to wait for my buddy, Ron-Joe. Give it a day, or two, and we'll go together."

She shook her head. "I'd like to go today. Plus, we're snow-less in Manhattan. I should take advantage of that. I won't approach anybody I think is connected to the mob. I'll just scope it out, see if Jazz even lives there, then we'll go back together in a few days."

He turned and locked eyes with her. "Take care of yourself. I need my partner."

"I will," she said and smiled at him. She didn't tell him about her premonition. The image of brass knuckles on a beefy Russian scared the hell out of her.

Chapter 18

"I still don't like it," he repeated. "I'd rather you wait. Don't forget, call the Brooklyn cops for back-up if you get in trouble."

She turned and faced him. "Don't worry, I won't tell the Mafia I'm a detective looking for a Russian psycho who kidnapped a dog and possibly killed a stockbroker." She also told James she'd been to Brooklyn before–the gentrified sections like Park Slope, Williamsburg, Brooklyn Heights, Dumbo. "Seriously," she added. I'll just scope out the scene and see what I can learn, then we can go back together."

He looked up and nodded.

While she was getting ready to leave, Ron-Joe arrived. James introduced his buddy to Cheri. They shook hands then the two men went into an interrogation room for privacy. Before James closed the door he mouthed three words to Cheri, "Watch your back."

She was tempted to tell him it was impossible to see her own back but she let it go and gave him a thumbs up.

No snow, no ice. She felt good. So what was bugging her? That sense of foreboding from Saturday afternoon after leaving Caz's apartment was still with her. She shook her head, adjusted the seat in the unmarked police car to make room for her long legs and reached for her gun. It was there. This is only a scouting expedition to try to find out about Jazz and anybody who knows him. What is my problem? she asked herself. But she never had a bad feeling like this before.

She stopped at a light and pulled out a CD. Show tunes. Just what she needed. She would get through this and reward herself with a ticket to a matinee at the theater. Tickets were expensive. But what the hell, she'd splurge for a change and see a Broadway musical.

As she merged into the right lane, traffic got heavier and some guy with a dented front fender was too close for comfort. What did he care? His car was ready for the junkyard. She tried to relax and enjoy her trip to the ocean, even if it was in Brooklyn and not Rio de Janeiro, but the guy behind her kept inching closer.

After merging onto the Belt Parkway, she got a whiff of salt air. This is going to be fun, she told herself. But she planned to do what James suggested and watch her back.

She turned onto Shore Parkway, drove six tenths of a mile and ended up on Guilder Avenue. I'm here, she told herself as she looked around and saw boarded up shops and seagulls. No people.

She locked the car and headed toward the ocean. There was that sense of foreboding again. She figured it was probably due to the abandoned look of Brighton Beach in winter. Seagulls dipped and cawed as they pecked at crumbs on the boardwalk. She turned right on Brighton Beach Avenue. More nothingness. Cold, gray sky. The only activity concerned the gulls and a few hardy joggers in light jackets wearing woolen hats pulled tight over their ears. The smell of the saltwater was making her hungry. Maybe she would find a place for seafood and have a plate of hot shrimp with spicy sauce. She also craved a cup of coffee. Later, she decided. She wanted to see what she could learn about Jazz then she'd drive back to Manhattan and get a jolt of caffeine near the police station.

As Cheri turned and looked behind her, she remembered James's words of warning, "Watch your back." I'm being paranoid, she thought. There isn't anybody following me. She fingered the muzzle of her gun and felt protected. That's when a man tapped her on the shoulder. She jumped nervously and said "Yes?"

When she turned around she saw a homeless man with his hand outstretched.

She reached in her purse, grabbed a dollar bill and handed it to him. "Good luck," she said. "Don't drink."

He shook his head and with breath that smelled of tobacco and alcohol gasped what sounded like his last words, "God bless you."

"Thanks, I need it." She headed away from the empty boardwalk toward a street with shops so she could inquire about Jazz.

The first shop she walked into sold antiques. She nearly blew her budget by buying a black Russian lacquer box with a red firebird painted on top. It represented a famous Russian folktale. She knew that from reading about Stravinsky's ballet, "The Firebird."

"You want help?" asked the shopkeeper.

"I'm just looking," said Cheri, as she turned the box upside down and glanced at the price. "I'll come back," she said. It was awkward being the only customer in the shop. She liked the box but didn't want to spend a couple of hundred dollars. The artist's signature was inscribed on the bottom, a Vladimir somebody. She loved all the Russian arts: ballet, music, theater, opera. *Crime and Punishment* was one of her favorite novels.

Next, she went into a Russian bakery. There was the earthy smell of freshly baked bread and she imagined a sign on the loaf of black bread that said, "Eat me." Will power, she told herself. She kept breathing deeply until the clerk looked up. "Da, I help you?" She nodded, then asked the clerk if he knew a man named Jazz. "Nyet," he told her. He smiled, showing a mouthful of gold teeth.

Cheri continued going into shops. In each one, she asked about someone named Jazz or Jazzky. Finally, after the fourth try, a woman with a thick Russian accent said "Jazz? Crazy guy who walks up and down boardwalk plays clarinet?"

"That might be him," said Cheri. Do you know where he lives?"

The woman walked to the front of the shop. "Jazz no live in Brooklyn, live in Manhattan, work there. He has cousin, Sergei, here."

"Where?" asked Cheri. "Where does Jazz visit Sergei?"

The woman pointed. "There. In house on corner with bars on windows. Is not a jail, why they have bars? Is safe here, safer than in Russia."

"I agree," said Cheri.

"You have been to Russia?" said the woman, excitedly.

Cheri shook her head and said, "No, not yet." Moscow and St. Petersburg were on her bucket list, but they were too far and too expensive. "Where does Jazz work?" Cheri asked.

The woman pointed again. "Somewhere in big city." Remembering the few words she learned on Google, Cheri said, "Spasibo," thank you, to the shopkeeper. The woman said, "You speak Russian?"

"Nyet, " said Cheri. "I just shot my load." The woman laughed even though she probably didn't understand what load Cheri just shot.

She walked out of the store and looked for the house on the corner. When she spotted the right one, she saw that it did indeed have bars on all the windows. Even from a distance she could see that the bars were so close together even a cat couldn't crawl through.

A little voice told her, You did a good job scouting. Go back to Manhattan and come back with James.

She ignored the little voice and headed straight for that big dark corner house.

Chapter 19

Cheri walked up the front steps of the porch and looked through the window. What little she saw between the bars was not vying for a spread in Architectural Digest. There was a ratty looking sofa with holes in it, an armchair opposite that and a standing lamp behind it with a crooked shade. She looked through another window into a dismal looking kitchen. An open bag on the counter had Kentucky Fried chicken spilling out of it. Next to that were two empty vodka bottles, an empty bottle of brandy, and three empty glasses.

As she continued peering through the window, a man grabbed her from behind and snatched her purse.

"No," she screamed. "Give that back to me."

He dumped everything on the ground and as Cheri bent to pick things up the burly stranger grabbed her ID and badge.

"What you want, Detective?" He spoke with a thick Russian accent.

"I'm looking for a friend."

"Friend?" He twisted her arm and practically threw her into the living room. Two men in grubby tee-shirts stretched over pot bellies appeared at the top of the steps.

"Who is this?" one asked.

The biggest of the three–the one who had grabbed her purse said, “A detective. “She's looking for a friend. Anybody recognize her?”

The men said in unison, “Nyet.”

“Who are you looking for?”

“A friend,” said Cheri.

“What's her name?”

She thought fast and pulled up a name from a Russian novel. “Natasha.”

“What you want with her?”

Cheri tried to sound as convincing as possible. “She sells Russian lacquer boxes. No taxes, black market. You understand black market?”

“You're lying,” said one of the men.

“Take care of her,” said another.

"Listen," said Cheri, “if Natasha doesn't live here, I'll leave right now. Sorry to bother you.”

The three men started arguing, mostly in Russian with a few English words interspersed. She understood, “meeting, conference, and the Boss.” They finally agreed to have their meeting before the Boss shows up.

Good idea, thought Cheri. She looked around the room. Even though the windows had thick iron bars nobody locked the front door. Those goons were so drunk they were barely functioning. Each one probably thought the others had locked the door. They were big and strong and Cheri suddenly felt sick to her stomach.

When they were all assembled downstairs, they decided to have their meeting in the kitchen, leaving somebody to watch her. The guard seated himself on a straight-back wooden chair, his short stubby legs outstretched. He laid a pistol with a mother of pearl handle on his lap. He stared at her for a while then closed his eyes and breathed loudly through his mouth. When he opened his eyes, Cheri said, "Spasibo, please, let me go. I'll look for Natasha somewhere else." He laughed and said something in Russian that sounded like curse words.

She realized that she still had her gun. The Russians were so out of it, they forgot to search her. As she inched closer to the end of the couch, the guard leaned back snoring loudly. She heard the name Sergei mentioned in the other room and remembered the shopkeeper told her he was Jazz's cousin. They spoke of Sergei as if they were invoking the name of God.

The man guarding her stirred a few times as if he was having a nightmare and he reeked of alcohol. Maybe he'll pass out, thought Cheri. The mobsters in the other room continued arguing in Russian. Every now and then, she understood a few words. One of the men said, "Kill her." Another said, "We wait for Sergei. He's the Boss."

A phone rang in the other room. Someone picked it up and said "Hallo," then spoke in Russian. After he hung up he told the others, "Sergei, three blocks away. Here soon." The guard opened one eye, blinked a few times and stared at Cheri as if he had forgotten who she was. He kept one eye on her then closed that one, too, and started snoring again.

As soon as he appeared to be sleeping soundly. Cheri reached for her gun. Just then the guard stirred, jumped up and tried to grab her weapon. When he couldn't reach it, he sucker-punched her in the chest. While they grappled for the gun, she kicked him in the groin. With adrenaline still flowing, she kicked him a second time. He doubled over in pain and screamed. She was almost out the front door when the two goons ran out of the kitchen. They tried to catch her, but they were too wasted to run fast. One of the guys aimed his gun at her, but was so drunk he couldn't shoot straight and missed.

Within seconds, there was chaos once they were out in the street. People screamed, ducked behind cars or behind trash cans ready for pick-up, while mothers pulled their children inside dilapidated houses.

Cheri was breathing hard and, with trembling hands, tried to unlock her car door. After a few missteps with the house key she got the door open, jumped in and locked it. "Come on, come on," she shouted. "Don't stall now. Hurry up." As soon she got the car started, she looked in the rear view mirror. None of the goons were in sight. Maybe they ran back for their cars. When she didn't spot them behind her, she figured they were too drunk to drive. She tried to catch her breath as she drove with one hand, then called the Brooklyn precinct and gave them directions to the house. "Be careful," she cried. "They're armed and dangerous."

"We know that place," said the dispatcher. "We're on it."

Cheri left her name and number and said she would be waiting for the cops so she could fill them in.

As soon as she saw her Brothers in Blue she did a U-turn, tires screeching, as she drove to the Russians' house and jumped out of the car. She quickly filled the policemen in as they headed toward the front door, guns raised. Within minutes, she heard a series of shots and hoped it was the mobsters who got hit, not the cops. She finally saw the cops walking the three perps out of the house; they were all cuffed. One of them had blood dripping from his forearm. Another had blood dripping from his forehead. There were more sirens as police cars arrived.

Cheri took a deep breath before she started driving away from the Boardwalk, away from the house, and away from the Russian mob. She zigzagged in and out of traffic, constantly checking her rear-view mirror. No need to check in back, she finally told herself, but she felt paranoid by then. She started shaking as she realized how close she came to being shot. Slow down, she told herself. After dodging more than one bullet she didn't want to get killed in a car accident.

As soon as she reached West Forty-Eighth in Manhattan, she pulled over and checked her cell. Three messages. One from a policeman in Brooklyn asking her to call him back. The other two messages were from James. "WHERE ARE YOU? CALL ME." He sounded frantic.

Chapter 20

Cheri was pulling off her jacket when she noticed James staring at her, a worried expression on his face. "Glad you grabbed a cup of coffee. You probably need it."

"Yeah, I do. We drink too much coffee but better than drugs." She seated herself at her desk opposite his.

"Okay, tell me what happened."

She took a sip of coffee and exhaled loudly. "I came face to face with a a bunch of crazy Russians. When I saw them through the window of a house, I didn't have any intention of dealing with them until one of the Russkies dragged me in. They'd been drinking vodka and brandy before I arrived, or I'd be dead." She brought him up to date about the scuffle for her gun, the chaos in the street, and the Brooklyn cops leading the perps away.

He rubbed his forehead as worry lines popped up between his eyebrows. "Sorry you had to go through that by yourself. Go on." She continued while he sat shaking his head. "You have an angel. Not bad for somebody who doesn't believe in them."

"It's not that I don't believe. I never met one." She smiled, then continued telling him what happened in Brooklyn. "Those gangsters all have good lawyers. They'll probably be out on bail before we have dinner tonight." As she rubbed the pain in her chest, she wondered if she had a collapsed lung. The pain was getting worse.

"What happened to your chest?"

"One of the goons used me as a punching bag."

"The bastard. Too bad you didn't shoot him."

Cheri grinned. "He didn't get away with it. I kicked him in the groin."

"I knew your kickboxing would come in handy one day." He leaned forward and tapped his hand on the desk. "By the way, think you should see a doctor about your chest?"

"Nah, it's just black and blue. It'll go away. Your turn," she said. "Tell me what your buddy Ron-Joe discovered about Ben's deleted texts and e-mails."

James's phone rang and he indicated to Cheri that he had to take the call. She sipped the rest of her coffee while she listened to James. He told the caller "Thanks for calling me back." He ended by saying, "Talk to you soon, buddy."

James hung up and faced Cheri. "I'm sure you know who that was. Ron-Joe did us a big favor, wanted to thank him a second time. We might need his hacking services again."

"So tell me what you learned."

"Bottom line, Ben hired a man named Sergei to kill somebody."

"Ben took out a contract on somebody?"

"You got it. Try to guess who it was for."

"One of his wives?"

"Guess again." said James.

"A mistress?"

"That's four guesses," said James. "Benjamin Rabinowitz, upstanding citizen and honorable stockbroker, wanted Sergei to knock off his partner. Looks like Perry knew too much about the gold mine scam and Ben worried about the SEC coming down on them for securities fraud if Perry squealed. Ron-Joe pieced all that together from calls, e-mails, texts."

"When was the hit supposed to happen?"

James looked at her and grinned. You won't believe it. It was scheduled for today."

."Holy shit," she muttered under her breath. "Just had a thought. Maybe Perry found out about the contract."

"That's my drift," said James. "If Perry discovered that his beloved partner wanted to whack him, he might have decided, You first, buddy. Perry could've pushed Ben off the balcony, or hired a hit man to do the job."

Cheri rubbed her face and exhaled, trying to ignore the pain in her chest. "Not far-fetched, especially when you're dealing with Wall Street and the Russia Mafia. We should pay Perry another visit. Besides, we love the Wall Street area. I can't believe that Ben, with an MBA from Harvard, was stupid enough to leave a paper trail."

"Desperate people do stupid things," said James. "Plus, his drugging didn't help."

"I can drive to Wall Street next time if you want."

"Nah, it's okay."

Cheri shrugged, leaving it up to him. "We should also interview our witness again. She might have remembered something she saw from the window."

"Fine," said James. "Meanwhile, we'll hand the Russian Mafia over to the FBI, let them deal with it. With any luck, the goons will get deported. We still have to find Jazz, or whoever the hell he is."

"I agree," said Cheri. "But I don't think Jazz killed Ben. He was hoping to get his money back so he wanted Ben to stay alive. It was after Ben died that he started harassing Leslie."

"But he's scaring the hell out of her," said James.

Cheri nodded as she put her cup of cold coffee on the desk. She was developing a headache from all the noise in the squad room, plus the room was too hot. "There's more," she said. "A woman in Brooklyn told me that Jazz lives in Manhattan, but visits his cousin Sergei in Brighton Beach. She sat back and shook her head. "Should be a cinch. Only eight million people living in New York." She was worrying about solving the case when James said, "We'll crack this case, don't worry."

"You read my mind," she said. They continued working for a few more hours until James told her, "Let's pack it in. Long day for both of us."

While they stood in front of the police station later, breathing like dragons in the cold air, James told her again, "Take care of the bruise."

"I will, thanks."

Later that evening, Cheri checked her e-mail for the second time. There were several notes related to work, including two from the Brooklyn police station, which she answered, before opening a note from Caz.

Hey, Cheri,

"I've been thinking, maybe I'll buy a food truck."

Cheri:

"You serious?"

Caz:

"Yeah, I'm burned out, need a change. I'll need some recipes from you."

Cheri smiled at Caz's idea, then sat back and thought about the Rabinowitz case and the ties between Ben and the Russian Mafia. The connection was Jazz. He was one of Ben's clients and might have introduced Sergei to his stock-broker. And Ben hired Sergei to whack his partner.

The pain in her chest had worsened. If she wasn't better tomorrow she would call her grandmother, tell her she fell and needed a home remedy, maybe an herb. She pictured her grandmother saying, Who hit you? ESP was strong on the Native-American side of her family. Now she needed ESP to help her find Ben's killer. James always stressed logic, but she believed in logic and hunches.

She moved from e-mail to news on the Net. It was late, but she never went to sleep without checking the latest news.

"Holy shit," she cried, while she stared at a photograph of a partially burned out building in Brooklyn. It was the same corner house, same bars on the windows, same scene in Brighton Beach.

She picked up her cell and called James.

"Yeah, hello, was just about to call you," he said. "Sergei, the guy they called The Boss, was identified near the front steps trying to escape. If he'd been in the house with the other guys, he would have been toast, but he was badly burned. That's why the others haven't been identified yet." He hesitated. "I'm reading the story on the Net while I talk to you."

"Saw that," she said. "The police are calling it arson. They think someone was watching that house, then moved fast. The fire must've been set right after the guys were let out on bail. Wait a minute," she cried. "I just read online that a rival gang might have torched the house for revenge."

She waited while he read. He was a slower reader than her. "The Russkeys did us a favor," said James, whistling. "Looks as if Perry Hartman might be home free now, especially if Sergei was the one Ben hired to kill Perry."

She tugged on her lower lip while she thought about all the facts they had so far. "Sergei might also have been the one driving the getaway car when Leslie's dog was kidnapped."

"That's possible," said James. "Meanwhile, we should concentrate on finding Ben's murderer, that's top priority. Right now, we have the three wives plus Luis as persons of interest."

"You forgot somebody," said Cheri. "Ben's partner, Perry Hartman. He might have played the revenge game after he discovered Ben took out a contract on him."

James hesitated. "Anything's possible in a homicide case."

Chapter 21

As soon as Cheri arrived at the police station, she pulled off her woolen watch cap, said good-morning to the policewoman at the desk and stepped into the squad room. There was pandemonium: phones ringing, loud conversations, jarring arguments. Worst of all, the thermostat must have been mistakenly set at sixty degrees. She was rubbing her hands together for warmth when she smiled at James and asked if there was anything new in the Rabinowitz case.

"Nada," he said. "No trace of anything under Ben's fingernails, probably pushed from the back as we suspected. And nothing's been stolen as far as we can tell. His laptop was impounded but thanks to my buddy, Ron-Joe we have access to what's on there. Sorry, how are you?" he asked, swiveling around in his chair.

She pulled her hair back with both hands then tucked a few loose strands behind her ears. "How am I? Frustrated about this case. So far, we have one witness who swears Ben wasn't alone on the balcony but she can't describe who she saw, not even if it was a man or woman. Just a dark figure. We have a missing tape from the security camera. And we have Luis, who told Detective Melo he saw two people on the balcony purportedly arguing, so what did he do? He fled. Wasn't even curious enough to call out."

"As soon as possible, we need to interview our witness again," said James. "She was directly across the street, might have seen something she's not telling us. We'll promise her anonymity and no leaks to the media."

"She looks to be in her early sixties," said Cheri. "Her eyesight might not be great, But I agree we should talk to her again."

"You look like you won the lottery. What's up?" he asked.

"I just figured out how to get Leslie to tell us more than she did."

"Want to share the info?"

Cheri nodded. "I'll bet a hundred bucks she never stopped loving Ben and knows more about his life, financial and otherwise, than the other two wives. He even managed to reel her back in and promised to run away with her. My take? He changed his mind at the last minute and she offed him."

"Unless somebody killed the vic before Ben had a chance to flee the country."

"I disagree," said Cheri. "Leslie lost it when he changed his mind.

Want to bet?"

"I'm not a betting man. But if I was, I'd put my money on Luis."

He looked at his appointment calendar spread across the center of his desk. "Leslie is due here this morning. Hope you didn't forget."

"No way. I couldn't sleep last night trying to figure out how to get her to open up."

James looked at her across his desk. "Do you want to interview her alone or you want me here as backup? I promise to keep my mouth shut and listen."

"I think I should be alone with her. Hang out in the other room with the one-way mirror."

He gestured with thumbs up. "It's a deal."

"This case is driving me nuts," she said, tapping her fingers on the desk. "For one thing, why does a guy become a bigamist? Try to get into his head, James, and let me know."

He shrugged. "He had his own set of rules. After he made a bundle on Wall Street he felt superior to the average man. He didn't live like an average guy, either. In addition to his monthly expenses, he rented three spaces in a midtown garage for his antique cars. Know how much those spaces cost every month in Manhattan?"

Cheri shook her head. "I haven't checked lately."

"The cost of three spaces is as much as some people pay to rent a studio apartment in the city," said James. "We're not even talking about the cost of maintenance for the cars."

She looked at him and raised an eyebrow. "He didn't deny himself anything. I also bet he was addicted to coke, especially with all his money and his crazy lifestyle."

James pulled out his phone, checked the time and said, "I'm out of here. Leslie should be arriving soon. I'll be in the other room. You know the signal if you need me. Want a cup of coffee meanwhile?"

"I'd love one."

He stepped outside, poured two cups of coffee and brought one to Cheri. Her head was buried in the Ben Rabinowitz file. Just as he was closing the door, she looked up. "When do we fly to Rio to interview Pepita and her lover boy?"

James gave her a lopsided smile. "Thought you'd never ask. I'll try to have a meeting with the captain soon. I'll do what I can to get us there. Meanwhile, good luck with Leslie. She strikes me as a liar."

"And on top of that, she had plenty of reason to be vengeful," said Cheri. "You know the line, don' t you?"

"Yeah," he said. "In this case we don't have one scorned woman. We have three."

Chapter 22

After speaking to a sergeant at the precinct Leslie was ushered into a small, windowless room. A few minutes later, Cheri walked into the interrogation room, greeted Leslie in a perfunctory manner then said, "This shouldn't take long. But first, I hope you brought me the last note you received."

She pulled the message from Jazz out of her purse and handed it to the detective. Cheri studied it briefly then slipped it in the file. A picture of a caged woman on the bottom of the note unnerved her. "Any idea who might have sent this?"

"No. Any news about the missing dog?"

Cheri shook her head.

The preliminary questions seemed to put Leslie at ease until Cheri said, "Why did Ben try to purchase phony passports for the two of you?"

Leslie's coat slipped off her lap. As she bent to pick it up, Cheri retrieved the coat and handed it to her. "Did you hear my question? Or do you want me to repeat it?"

Is she having a heart attack? Cheri wondered. The detective hopped up on the desk and watched as Leslie rubbed her mouth with one hand. The two women continued staring at one another until Leslie said, "I don't know anything about phony passports."

"We have e-mails from Ben to a man named Jake. Ben asked him to provide him with phony passports for himself. And his wife."

"That's simple," said. Leslie. "That was Kati. Ask her about it. Ben and I were in the midst or a divorce."

"Ben referred to you specifically."

Leslie appeared taken aback then quickly regained her composure. "I don't know anything about passports."

"Do you know anybody named Jake?"

"No."

"Can you tell me about Ben's plans to skip the country?"

She shook her head.

"We're going to find Jake, so you would be wise to tell to tell us who he is and why you and Ben were planning to leave the country."

Leslie shifted in her chair as if she was sitting on a tack. "I don't know anything about that. Ben was secretive, as you know, especially with an apartment on West End Avenue. Maybe he used my name accidentally, meant to use Kati's name."

"The names aren't even close," said Cheri. "And I'm sure he knew the difference between the two of you."

Leslie cleared her throat so loud, Cheri wanted to jump up and offer her a cough drop. But she didn't move. She sat still, observing Leslie's fists opening and closing on her lap.

"You want to tell me anything about the passports before we find out?"

Leslie shook her head. "Nothing to tell."

"Okay."' said Cheri. "Let's shift gears for a moment. Do you own a black winter coat with a hood?"

Leslie bit down hard on her lip and looked straight ahead. "No."

"We have a tape of a woman in the lobby of Ben's apartment building. She's wearing a black hooded winter coat. Did you ever visit Ben at his West End Avenue apartment?" Cheri crossed her arms and stared.

"No."

"Ever own a coat like that?"

Leslie shook her head.

"What if I told you that the woman in the black hooded coat is about your height and weight?"

"It wasn't me," Leslie insisted. "I was never in that lobby."

"After you refresh your memory about the coat and the lobby," said Cheri, "let me know."

"I will. But there's nothing to remember.

Cheri rubbed her chin as she glared at Leslie. "It would be smart to tell me about the coat now. I know you need money, so you don't want me to find it in a consignment shop, do you?"

Leslie's eyes darted back and forth from Cheri to the one-way window. She's watches too many TV crime shows, thought Cheri. As Leslie turned back to the detective she cried, "I never owned a coat like that."

Cheri hopped down from the desk and straightened her slacks. "I have no reason to hold you, but the mystery about the passports won't be dropped. You're not planning to leave town, are you?"

"No, I'll be in the city."

"Good. Now tell me something, where were you the day Ben was murdered?"

Leslie winced at the last word then said, "It's been a while. I'll have to look at my appointment book and get back to you."

"You do that," said Cheri as she escorted Leslie out of the office.

When she stepped back into the room. James was waiting for her. "What do you think?" she asked.

"I'm starting to agree with you. She's moving from a person of interest to a suspect. She looked scared, especially when you asked about her alibi and the black hooded coat." James sat back and continued, "It's possible that Ben changed his mind about running away with Leslie. She got pissed, went to his apartment to talk to him and..."

"Pushed him off the balcony," said Cheri, finishing his sentence. "Did you catch the expression on her face when she insisted she never went to the West End Avenue apartment? Bullshit. They were planning to leave the country but they didn't get together to talk in private?"

"My guess?" said James. "Ben changed his mind about fleeing because a business deal was about to pop. There's one thing a stockbroker loves more than women."

"Money?"

"You got it. Meanwhile, I think Leslie will find an excuse to come back here, hoping to clear things up. Let her mull this interview over. She'll come to the conclusion she needs to clarify her alibi, and maybe shift the focus to Kati."

"I have the same feeling," said Cheri. "But we'll have a few surprises for her when she returns and she probably will ask to come back. I bet she'll bring her attorney with her next time."

"This is getting interesting," said James. "Meanwhile, I have a call in to Detective Melo, in Rio. He's supposed to call me back soon. Hope that doesn't mean manana."

"I get the feeling he wants to nab Luis so he can lay his hands on Pepita. You've seen her picture?"

James nodded. "Great legs. Can see why she's a dancer. Maybe Pepita is the reason Melo is so intent on putting Luis away. I'll put his call on speaker phone later so we can both listen to him."

After several incoming calls, James gestured to Cheri. "It's Melo." He turned on the speaker phone and told him, "Detective Marsh is with me."

"No hay problema," said Melo. "I have a lot to report. Is good time?"

"Very good," said James.

"Morning," said Cheri.

"Buenos dias, Senorita Marsh. Too bad we are not on Skype. I would love to look at you while we speak. But Skype is not my choice for looking at pretty women."

James rolled his eyes. Cheri said, "Maybe O'Brien and I will fly down to Rio one of these days."

"You will be my special guests. Meanwhile, I would love to nail Luis' culo to the top of Corcovado Mountain."

"What happened?" asked James.

Detective Melo took a deep breath and cleared his throat "I will start at beginning. Will take time."

"It's okay," said James. "Take all the time you need."

Cheri pulled the tape recorder off her belt, turned it on and set it in the middle of her desk. "I'm taping this, Detective Melo."

"Is fine with me," he said before continuing. "Luis was supposed to be at police station yesterday, ten o'clock. I call Pepita to remind her. She says they will be here."

"Did they show up?" Cheri asked.

"Let me continue. No, they not show up. At twelve o'clock, I call Pepita and she said Luis ran away."

Cheri looked at James. He shook his head and shrugged while they waited for Detective Melo to continue. "So Pepita and I decide to search for him. This is interesting part," he said. Pepita told me Luis has sister living in a favella so we decide to look there. You know what is a favella?"

"I know," said Cheri. "I read guide books. Tell O'Brien."

"It is worse than slum," said Detective Melo. "It is squalor. And the favella where Luis's sister lives is in hills above Ipanema Beach, but the two worlds never meet."

"I get it," said James. "Go on."

"I pick Pepita up in police car and it is raining. You know rain?"

"Sure," the two detectives in New York answered.

"No, you don't know rain until you come to Rio," said Melo. "So, I am driving with Pepita. But I cannot see through wipers and we are climbing hills. Water doesn't drain in favellas. I am driving through lakes when suddenly Pepita screams STOP. I stop car. Pepita jumps out and grabs a baby rolling down hill about to drown."

"What?" Cheri shouted.

"Yes, happened," said Melo. "Just then baby's mother comes running downhill, says baby crawled out of house. She lifts baby from Pepita's arms and...."

"Get to the point! Did you ever find Luis?" asked James, sounding impatient."

"I'm getting to that. We find house where Luis's sister lives. As I am parking, Luis runs out of house and down street faster than giraffe. He ran even faster when he saw me get out of the car."

"What now?" asked Cheri.

"I have warrant out for Luis' arrest."

There was silence on the phone. The New York detectives were processing the news while Melo waited for more questions.

"What about Pepita?" asked James.

"She was screaming, 'Come back, Luis.' But he no come back. You know what?" Melo asked, "I am thinking all the while,

If I don't nail his culo to top of Corcovado Mountain, she will do it. Aye caramba, I have important meeting now," added Detective Melo. "Will finish story later."

After hanging up, Cheri turned off the tape recorder and looked at James, "What do you think?"

"He's either scared of the police in Rio because they have a bad rap or he's guilty. Your choice."

"I'd say good chance he's guilty," said Cheri. "Here's why: Luis was in New York at the time of Ben's murder. And he has a motive–loss of the money he invested with Ben in that screwy gold mine."

A few hours later, while James was out getting a sandwich, Cheri answered a call. A woman at the other end said, "Is this Detective Marsh?"

"Yes, who is this?"

"This is Pepita in Rio de Janeiro."

"Hola, Pepita. You have good news about Luis, I hope?"

"No, it's not good. Did you know that Detective Melo arrested Luis and threw him in jail?"

"We didn't know," said Cheri.

"Yes. Melo threw Luis in jail for non-compliance, leading a detective on a chase, and trying to punch Melo when he finally caught up with him. But Luis is innocent."

"So, why did he run away at the favella? And why did he take a punch at Detective Melo?"

"The police in Brazil make German Shepherds look meek. You haven't seen Detective Melo. He is big and fat. Luis looks like a Flamenco dancer."

"Luis might be innocent," said Cheri. "But he's missing some brain cells. You don't punch a detective."

"I know that," said Pepita. "And Luis is very sorry now."

"What do you want me to do?" asked Cheri.

"Ask Melo to let Luis out of jail. I'll make sure he keeps his next appointment."

I know what you'll do if he doesn't keep the next appointment, thought Cheri. You'll nail his ass to Corcovado Mountain before Melo gets a chance to do that.

"What should I do?" asked Pepita." She sounded more exasperated than ever.

"Here's my idea," said Cheri. "Urge Luis to take a lie detector test. I mean practically strong-arm him to agree. If he takes the test and passes, Melo will get off his ass. Comprende?"

"I understand," said Pepita. She sounded as if she was crying and kept sniffling until she said, hold on and probably pulled out a Kleenex. "I'm back," she said finally.

"You're a person of interest, too," said Cheri. "You were still in Ben's will. Did you know that?"

"How could that be? We divorced years ago."

Cheri pressed her hand to one ear to block out the noise around her. "You must be out of the loop, Pepita. He never legally married Leslie or Kati.

"What? He stayed married to me?"

"You got it. Didn't Ben's lawyer tell you the news?"

"The attorney was in a hurry plus it wasn't a good phone connection. I assumed he meant that Ben never divorced Leslie or Kati, but our divorce was legal."

Cheri shook her head and tried not to get angry at the craziness between Ben and his wives. Ben's lawyer said he told all three wives about Ben's bigamy. *Was Pepita telling the truth or pretending she didn't know?*

There was silence at the other end of the line until Pepita asked incredulously, "So, I stand to inherit all the money?"

That was a quick response, thought Cheri. "Either that or you'll be implicated if Luis becomes a suspect. Do him a favor, tell him to write out a timeline of everybody he saw that day, and where and what they talked about."

"I asked him about that," said Pepita. "He said he was alone that day in New York. All the appointments with theater producers were the day before. That's why he tried to see Ben. He had the time when Ben asked him to come over to the West End Avenue address, not his Wall Street office."

Cheri said, "If Luis was alone that day he should volunteer to take a lie detector test. Melo can administer it."

There was silence at the other end of the phone. "What if Luis refuses? He's very stubborn."

The noise in the squad room was nearly deafening. Cheri thanked whoever was in Heaven that she had perfect hearing. "Either he takes the test or Melo will keep his promise to nail Luis to the top of Corvado Mountain."

"I will try," said Pepita. "And I'll tell him what Melo said."

Cheri hesitated for a second, then moved to the other side of her desk where it was a little less noisy. She held the phone and practically screamed. "You seem to have a lot of influence over Luis," said Cheri. "Meanwhile, I have to get back to work. Call me if he changes his mind. Also, warn Luis that if he becomes a suspect, he'll be dealing with the New York Police Department. My partner, Detective O'Brien, will make Melo look like a stuffed monkey."

Chapter 23

When James returned with a cup of coffee for Cheri along with a raspberry Danish, she told him about her conversation with Pepita while he settled himself at his desk opposite hers. "We might get to Rio, after all," he said. "But I know it'll be a hassle for you."

"Yeah, you might have to go alone." She laughed before continuing. "After talking to Pepita, I came up with a theory. I think Pepita and Kati might've hooked up with Ben for his money. They were both young, wanted careers. Leslie really loved him and was crushed by his philandering. She had the strongest motive for revenge."

James looked up from his laptop. "Prove it. I bet you can since you have such a strong hunch."

Just then Cheri's phone rang. She picked it up and mouthed the name Leslie to James, then held up her index finger while she listened. She put the phone on speaker phone and both detectives scowled when Leslie said, "I just received two new texts from Jazz."

"Read them to me," said Cheri.

"The first one said, 'I don't want to tell you again, be careful what you tell the cops.'"

"And the second one?"

"It says, 'Part of your divorce settlement is mine. Ben stole from me. I want my money.'"

"How were they signed?"

"The same: JAZZ, no other name. And the spelling is atrocious, as usual."

He has to be psychotic to kidnap a dog, thought Cheri. But how far will he go to get his money? Before hanging up, she told Leslie, "Bring your cell with you when you come to see us."

The next afternoon, Cheri ushered two women into the interrogation room. Just as they had expected, Leslie arrived with her attorney.

James stepped forward. "Detective James O'Brien," he said shaking the attorney's hand. Cheri also shook hands with the attorney, Gayle Robinson. The law firm she was with sounded like, Robinson, Robinson, and Windshield Washer, reminding Cheri of a line in a Marx Brothers movie.

The lawyer had such a serious expression on her face Cheri wondered if she thought she was standing before the Supreme Court. Leslie showed the detectives the two texts she received from Jazz then slipped her Smartphone back in her purse.

"My client wants to clear up a few differences and asked me to come along," said the attorney. "I had to be uptown anyway, but I hope this won't take long."

"Shouldn't be long," said James. He pointed, and the women seated themselves at a long, rectangular table opposite the detectives. After a few minutes of small talk about another snowstorm moving east, Cheri asked Leslie if she was walking dogs again.

"Not yet," she answered. "They'll let me know."

Leslie studied Gayle's face. No reaction so far. Leslie remained guarded, especially when James brought out the file marked "Ben Rabinowitz, Homicide." He pulled a sheaf of papers out of the file and pushed three pages toward Leslie. "Recognize these?"

She looked at her attorney who nodded, indicating Leslie should answer.

"Yes. They're from Ben, addressed to me."

Cheri recited the dates of the e-mails then said, "In this one, Ben asked you to get back together with him, didn't he?" She moved the paper closer to Leslie and her attorney. The two women read them and Gayle nodded again. The e-mail read: "I made a mistake marrying Kati. You and I have a long history together. I still care for you. No. Make that love you."

Leslie took a deep breath then said, quietly, "Yes, this is from Ben."

James pushed two more e-mails in front of Leslie. Gayle put on a pair of bifocals and read them. The next note read, "Come away with me, Leslie. A new start for both of us."

Cheri pointed to the e-mail. "Did you receive this e-mail?"

Gayle asked for a break for her client, and the two women stepped to the side of the room. Cheri possessed almost bionic hearing and heard Gayle speaking even though she was practically whispering to her client. "Listen, sweetie, you have to say you received that e-mail because ... blah, blah, blah. Besides, it's always best to tell the truth.... blah, blah, blah..... Ready?"

Leslie nodded and followed Gayle back to the table.

"Did you receive this e-mail?" asked James.

Gayle turned to Leslie and nodded.

Leslie whispered, "I did."

"And what did you reply?"

"I don't remember."

"You don't remember?" Cheri said. "Pretty lame excuse, if you ask me. I asked you last time why Ben was planning to use phony passports. You said you didn't know. Any ideas you want to share with us now?"

"No. He never discussed that with me."

"Was he in some kind of trouble with the Securities and Exchange Commission, or any other Federal organization?" asked James.

"I didn't know about any trouble."

"Did you agree to leave the States with him?"

"I don't remember. It was a while ago." She stopped and turned to her attorney. Gayle looked at Leslie and nodded. She obviously wanted her client to answer that question. The two detectives watched the interaction between the two women but didn't say anything. Cheri realized they were throwing Leslie off more with their silence than with rapid-fire questions.

Leslie finally blurted out, "I loved him. We had a great relationship for years. But I don't know anything about the passports. When he told me he made a mistake marrying Kati, I was willing to get back together. In fact, I thought we were still married, never had any idea about his bigamy."

Gayle touched Leslie's arm lightly, an indication to stop talking

Leslie looked at her attorney then turned to Cheri. She bit her lip before speaking then said in a quiet voice, "Have either of you loved a man so much he was able to reel you back in?"

Cheri smiled but didn't answer.

Gayle appeared neutral. More important, she seemed anxious to put an end to the questioning. "I think my client answered all of your questions today. And she doesn't know anything about the passports. Any reason for more questions?"

"One more question," said Cheri. "You walked dogs the day Ben died. What else did you do?"

"I went birding in Central Park."

Cheri stared at her with narrowed eyes. "You never mentioned that before."

"I didn't think it was important."

James moved closer. "You were closer to Ben's apartment, that's important." He stopped then added, "Anything happen in the park that might be important?"

"Nothing that stands out. She hesitated then said, softly. "I tripped over a rock and twisted my ankle."

Cheri moved closer and stared at Leslie. "I thought you told me a dog pulled you."

Leslie swallowed hard as she addressed her lap. "That happened earlier. It got worse after I tripped in the park."

Cheri made a mental note of that then asked, "Where did you go after Central Park?"

"I was home the rest of the day icing my ankle." Cheri wondered if her response had been rehearsed, possibly in front of a mirror. Kati was the actor, she could have pulled it off. Leslie came off too stiff.

"Anybody with you in the park?"

Gayle looked at Leslie as if to say, Answer the question.

"No."

"See anybody you know?"

"Nobody."

James stepped forward, arms crossed in front of him. "Did you go to a doctor or the E.R. for that ankle?"

Cheri noticed Leslie staring straight ahead, avoiding James's eyes. "No, I went straight home. I even took a taxi instead of the bus."

"Were you home all evening?"

"Yes, my ankle hurt pretty bad."

Gayle moved forward and told Leslie. "Tell them about the taxi, sweetie."

Leslie took a deep breath. "When I came out of Central park there was a taxi parked at the curb as if the driver was waiting for somebody."

"When did you remember that about the taxi?"

"Last night."

James stepped forward. "Go on."

Leslie continued. "When I asked if I could get in, the driver said yes." She rubbed her face as she looked at the detectives. "I remembered something else this morning. The cab driver had an unusual last name on the dashboard. A long Russian name. I don't remember it and even if I could I wouldn't be able to pronounce it."

"We think he was following her," said Gayle. "This happened before the texts started."

"Remember anything else unusual about that day?" asked James.

"No, it was an ordinary day except for the cab driver."

"Leslie told you everything she can remember about that day," said Gayle. "Can we leave now?"

"You can," said James. Turning to Leslie, he added, "Don't leave town. We might need to talk to you again."

When Cheri handed the women business cards she looked specifically at Leslie. "If you think of anything else of importance, let us know. We'll be in touch if we have any more questions."

Leslie stopped near the door and checked her cell. She exclaimed loudly, "Oh, no, another one." She hurried back to the detectives and handed Cheri her phone. Cheri read the text aloud to James. "You can run. Bitch. But you can't hide."

"He's persistent," said James. "Until we find him, be sure to look around when you're outside. Then he repeated what Cheri had told her, "You're a New Yorker. Use your street smarts."

Chapter 24

A policewoman rapped softly as she opened the door. "Mrs. Rabinowitz, the Third, to see you." She winked at the reference to "The Third."

"Give us five before you send her in," said Cheri.

The policewoman stuck her head further inside the door. "This wife was in the other day, wasn't she?"

Cheri nodded. "She's back for an encore."

After the last visit, a short one because Kati pleaded with them to let her leave to attend a rehearsal, Cheri didn't insist that Kati get fingerprinted. Instead, Cheri used a pair of latex gloves and picked up Kati's coffee cup. Using a brush and fingerprint powder she dusted the cup. With the use of fingerprint tape she lifted prints from the cup. After she finished, she affixed the fingerprint tape to a special card and preserved Kati's prints in a plastic bag. She and O'Brien had a feeling they would need them. Now, they had more questions for Kati.

While they were getting ready for the interview Cheri turned to James. "Lot of gold mines in Brazil. We might need to talk to Luis in person."

James nodded. "I'd love to go, but it's up to the captain."

Within minutes, there was a knock on the door. After saying, "Come in," a policeman ushered Kati into the interrogation room. Dressed in form-fitting black leather pants and a black turtleneck, she held a black leather motorcycle jacket over one arm and a helmet in her other hand. The outfit reminded Cheri of the line in the Russian play, *The Seagull,* by Anton Chekhov. After Masha, a character in the play, is asked about being dressed in black, she wryly answers, "I'm in mourning for my life." But not you Kati, thought Cheri. You're not mourning for Ben. Or for yourself. You're going to be a rich widow.

The two detectives nodded then Cheri straddled a wooden chair opposite Kati. "We'll try not to keep you long." Without skipping a beat, she said, "We enjoyed your performance the other night."

Kati smiled broadly. "Thanks, I worked hard on that show."

"It paid off," said Cheri. At that moment, the expression on the detective's face changed as if to say, Down to business. "Tell us, did Ben normally work late into the evening?" James moved aside, quietly watching.

"Yes, he was a workaholic."

"What hours did he usually work?"

"He left home about 8 A.M."

"And what time did he arrive home in the evening?"

"That varied. He often stayed late to return phone calls. We also ate out a lot, and I sometimes met him midtown and drove home with him."

James picked up the questioning. "So he didn't have a set pattern?"

"No."

"Did you accompany him to business meetings?"

"Not usually. I often had rehearsals in the evenings. "Kati looked at her hands spread out on her lap and nodded. Despite the grilling, she appeared calm. It's her training in theater, thought Cheri. Directors always ask actors, What's your motivation in this scene? Kati would've answered in this case, To appear nonplussed.

She's doing a good job of that, thought Cheri as she asked the next question. "Did he call you to say he wouldn't be home the evening he died?"

"No, he was out of town."

James followed up by asking if Ben usually called to say he'd be late.

Kati thought for a second then said, "Sometimes."

"But he didn't check in that evening?" James's voice suddenly sounded louder and more strident. No more Mr. Nice Guy, thought Cheri.

Kati was fidgeting with her wedding ring when she said, "No, he didn't check in that night."

"Did you think that was odd?"

"No, because he told me that morning that he had a business meeting in Boston. He planned to fly home the next day and go straight to work. I didn't expect him Tuesday night, so I ate dinner alone."

The detectives exchanged glances and Cheri took over. "Did you talk to him on the phone while he was in Boston?"

"Once, I think."

"But the last time you saw him was Tuesday morning and you didn't find out until late Tuesday night that he died, correct?"

Kati nodded.

"Did Ben have a lot of friends?" asked James.

Kati turned her head from one to the other like watching a badminton game. The questions were being lobbed at her at a faster pace and she was beginning to appear anxious.

"He had a lot of business colleagues," said Kati. "I don't know if that qualifies as friends."

"What about his partner, Perry? Would you say they were friends?" asked James.

"Perry was a business associate and partner. They were also friends."

Cheri took over the questioning. "Have you ever been to Ben's bachelor apartment on West End Avenue where he was pushed from the balcony?"

"Kati twisted the wedding ring on her finger as she crossed and uncrossed her legs, then practically whispered. "No, I've never been there."

Moving closer, Cheri was now in Kati's face, making it harder for Kati to avoid eye contact. "You sure you were never at the West End Avenue apartment?"

"Very sure." Kati bit her lower lip and waited while Cheri checked the tape recorder.

"You said you never visited Ben's bachelor pad. Is that correct?" said James.

"Correct." Katie took a deep breath as she brushed her hair off her forehead.

"Is it possible you visited Ben's apartment and forgot?"

"I never visited," Kati insisted.

Cheri leaned in closer. "Not even a short visit?"

"NO," she said, raising her voice.

"Strange," said Detective Marsh. "Your fingerprints were found in Ben's West End Avenue apartment."

Kati looked from one to the other as the detectives waited for her to speak.

Chapter 25

"Okay, I'll tell you what happened." Kati took a deep breath. "Ben brought me to his apartment on West End Avenue shortly after we returned from our honeymoon."

James picked up the questioning: "Why did he suddenly decide you should get a glimpse of his bachelor pad? You lived together before you were married. Why didn't he take you before?"

Kati pulled on her bottom lip before answering. "He wanted me to see his condo before he gave it up. We were happily married by then so he wasn't planning to spend time there anymore."

"Any idea of the date?"

"No."

"Was that the only time you were there?" said Cheri.

"Yes."

James interjected. "But he was planning to give it up, correct?"

"Correct."

"Didn't he own the condo?"

"Yes. And he was going to give it up as soon as he could sell it."

"Was it in his name only?"

"I'm not sure. After we got married he told me he was going to put it in both our names. I don't know if he ever did. He was planning to sell it."

Cheri picked up a crumbled napkin and threw it in the trash. "Did you ever see the Title to the condo with your name on it?"

Kati looked sheepish. "No. But I never saw his divorce papers either." She started to say something then changed her mind. "Will this be over soon? I have to go over some notes I got from the director last night including script changes. Playwrights do that all the time, even at the last minute."

"Were you out on the balcony at any time during that visit, or any other time?"

Katie stared straight ahead and said, "No, I wasn't curious about that. Nothing special about it. It faces a noisy street."

The detectives looked at each other then at Kati. "We won't keep you much longer," said James. "Tell us what you did in Ben's condo."

"I don't remember. It was a while ago."

"But you were only there once," said Cheri, "so it was a momentous day. Ben pretty much told you he was through catting around, was even giving up his bachelor pad by selling it. And you can't remember what you did?"

Kati balled one hand into a fist underneath the table. With the other hand, she held her coffee cup while she looked at the two detectives. James was standing a few inches from her, waiting. He reminded Cheri of a seal hunter, ready for the kill.

Cheri moved closer to Kati then said, "Can you refresh your memory? Anything stand out?" Kati's manner reminded Cheri of a woman she had once met, the president of a company whose employees referred to her as The Dragon Lady.

They wore the same type of knee-high leather boots. The better to kick you my dear, especially when you're down.

Kati looked at the two detectives hovering over her and rubbed her eyes with one hand. "We didn't do anything special. Ben just wanted me to see his bachelor pad as I said, before selling it. He took me around the apartment, showed me the all the special features, like the granite counters, marble floors...." She hadn't finished when James interrupted and asked if he showed her the balcony.

"I don't remember, but he probably did. It came with the apartment, or condo, whatever you call it."

"So," said James. "What else happened that day in Ben's bachelor pad?"

"Nothing. Just what I told you."

There was another exchange of glances between the detectives as James nodded to Cheri as she moved closer and stared at Kati.

James stood to the side, arms crossed over his chest and stared through squinted eyes. He finally uncrossed his arms then spoke so softly Kati had to lean forward to hear him. "All the lab results are in. Your fingerprints were found on an antique box in Ben's desk," he said, "The box was filled with marijuana. Want to tell us about that?"

Chapter 26

Kati asked for a second cup of coffee then seemed to wait for the caffeine to kick in.

"Your answer," said James. "We're waiting."

She took a deep breath and folded her hands on her lap. "Okay... When I met Ben he was a recreational user of weed. It got worse after his business problems started."

Cheri was about to ask another question when James raised his hand indicating he wanted to interject. They worked well together, never interrupted, never contradicted each other. "We believe that Ben was pushed off the balcony," said James. "But since Ben was a heavy user is it your opinion that he might have gotten stoned and fell?"

"I don't know," said Kati, fidgeting with her ring again. "He had a lot of enemies. He was always threatened with lawsuits. But he smoked pot even before we were married." She stopped abruptly. "Now it turns out we were never legally married. I still can't believe it."

Neither can I, thought Cheri, and I wasn't even married to him. What a con artist. "Let's get back to the day you visited the apartment," she said. "Your fingerprints were also found on the bed Ben used."

Kati didn't respond immediately, but Cheri could tell from the fear in her eyes that she was starting to feel like a cornered animal. "That's not possible," she said.

"Fingerprints don't lie," said Cheri, pointedly.

Kati took a deep breath before she started speaking. "The day I visited, Ben told me he bought some great weed and wanted us to share it. I asked him to bring it home with him later. He said he wanted to get stoned and make love in his bachelor pad for the last time."

"His swan song?" asked James.

"Yeah, except he didn't call it that. He called it... " Kati looked at her lap and added, "Not his swan song. His Farewell Fuck. That's what he called it."

"That is descriptive," said Cheri.

James winked at his partner."Did you smoke the weed together?"

Kati nodded. "But then he got so stoned we never made love. He was also drinking Scotch."

"But before he passed out from so much alcohol," Kati added, "he told me something I didn't know."

"What's that?" asked James.

Kati looked at the tape recorder then looked straight ahead, avoiding eye contact with James or Cheri. "Ben was being investigated by the SEC for insider trading. Worse than that, he was being investigated by the FBI for selling shares in a gold mine that had gone bankrupt. He lost a lot of his clients' money." She quickly said, "It wasn't his fault about the mine. He lost a lot of his own money. The owner of the mine lied to Ben, even sent him phony statements. He was planning to fly down to Brazil before he died."

"Did Ben tell you who else knew about the FBI?"

Kati looked around the room, her eyes finally settling on a calendar with a photograph of skiers. She continued staring at the calendar before answering. "Ben's partner, Perry, knew about the FBI investigation. So did Leslie."

"Leslie?" Cheri looked confused. "How did that happen?"

"She invested some of her own money in the gold mine–money she had inherited from her parents. I heard him talking to her on the phone one day. He said he had a way of making the money back. Ben was Mr. Comeback, making and losing more money than most people make in a lifetime. One of his investors probably killed him." She burst out crying and pulled a Kleenex out of her pocket. She covered her eyes with both hands and sobbed.

The detectives waited for the crying jag to be over. Was she acting? Or does she really miss him? Cheri wondered.

"Did Ben's partner, Perry, have money invested in the gold mine?" asked James.

"Yes. They discussed it on the phone. And I overheard bitter arguments about the mine. Believe me, Ben was very charming. He could have sold timeshares for condos on the moon. He was also a compulsive gambler. He bet on derivatives, calls, puts. He tried to explain those terms to me, but I still don't understand what they mean. I understand gold. They use it to make jewelry and gold fillings." She stopped speaking, seemingly emotionally exhausted.

She's a good actor, thought Cheri, and wondered if Kati married Ben to further her acting career. There was something to be said for marrying well. But Ben was a pot-smoking, deceiving son-of a bitch. The man had no integrity. Cheri was glad she had never crossed paths with him while she was studying acting. Who knows what she might have done for a career in theatre? The fire in her belly was her strength. And her weakness. This wasn't the time to think about that. But she couldn't condemn Kati for marrying a sugar daddy. The theater has a strong pull.

"Can I leave now?" Kati mumbled. "I have to learn new lines by tonight."

James and Cheri looked at each other. They had a unique way of communicating: with winks, nods, upraised eyebrows. "You can go in a few minutes," said James. "No reason to hold you, but don't leave town."

"Are you kidding? I'm finally in a show that's getting attention in the theater world. I wouldn't leave New York now."

"A couple of questions," he said. "Did Ben ever do anything out of the ordinary while he was stoned?"

Kati thought for a second. "Yeah, he tried to talk me into flying down to Brazil with him to check out the gold mine."

"That's not so crazy." said Cheri.

"That part's fine, but he wanted to travel down the Amazon River. He was so stoned he promised me a gold nugget the size of my fist if I went with him. I said, no thanks."

Cheri wondered how much Kati was inventing. The Amazon jungle was a bit over the top, especially for a broker who wore custom-made suits to work. Besides, Leslie told them that Ben traveled to London to order bespoke suits which he wore with custom-made shirts and gold cufflinks.

"Ask Leslie about the gold mine." said Kati "She knows more about it than me. They were married a long time."

Cheri crossed her arms in front of her. "Let's get one thing straight. Was Ben planning to leave you?"

"Of course not!"

"We discovered that Ben ordered phony passports. He and Leslie were going to leave the country. He was going to leave you high and dry"

Kati shrieked, "What?" She looked around the room as if hoping to discover a hole to jump into. "Okay," she said. "Here's what happened. When the gold mine proved unproductive Ben became desperate. He told me more than once he was afraid for his life, said some of his clients would kill to get their money back. But I don't know anything about phony passports or offering to take Leslie with him. She lives in a fantasy world. She might have made that up."

James ignored that last comment and continued his line of questioning. "We have a list of his clients. We'll talk to them and we'll interview Ben's partner Perry again. Anything you want to add?"

"No." She glanced at her watch.

When they didn't say anything, she said, "It would be a good idea to talk to his partner, Perry."

"We'll do that," said James."

"Meanwhile, there are some loose threads," said Cheri,. "For example, what did you do in Ben's apartment after he got stoned. He did get stoned, right?"

"Yeah, I told you he drank Scotch and smoked weed."

Katie grimaced, either in disgust or she's faking it, thought Cheri. She was too good an actor not to use her talents. "What did you do while he was stoned, drunk, whatever?"

"I waited for him to wake up," said Kati. "He had books and magazines, so I read."

Cheri locked eyes with Kati. "You didn't even go out for a short walk?"

"No. Why would I leave?"

"You tell us." said Cheri.

James placed his coffee cup on the desk. "You can go now. We'll be in touch."

As soon as Kati walked out of the interrogation room, James asked, "What do you think of wife numero tres?

"She's lying," said Cheri. "After Ben passed out she didn't stay there and baby-sit."

"I agree. She took care of business and we'll find out what that was."

Chapter 27

Seated behind his desk the next afternoon James picked up the Rabinowitz file. Cheri was seated opposite him. "Here's what I think," he said, "Kati probably knew Ben was catting around. He probably wasn't spending nights at their apartment, either. So, what do you think Kati did while Ben slept off the Scotch?"

Cheri thought for a second. "She snooped around."

"I agree," said James. "But she was probably afraid he'd wake up, so what would you do in that case?"

"What would I do?" she repeated. After thinking for a second she told him, "I'd make up a duplicate key to that bachelor pad. That way I could go back one day while he was at work and nose around his finances."

"That's what I was getting at," said James.

She smiled and said. "Two detectives' heads are better than one. I have an idea, let's check out all the locksmiths in a wide radius and find out if anybody resembling Kati was in to make up a key. We'll start midtown and work our way uptown."

"Good idea," said James. "We can start today."

Cheri opened her desk drawer and held up a photograph of Kati. "I saved my Playbill from *Suffer Queen.* This should help." She turned back to her laptop and pulled up the names and addresses of all the locksmiths on the West Side. After she was finished she told James, "Ready? Let's go."

As they continued walking downtown, they stopped in front of a huge billboard announcing the season for the Public Theatre at Lincoln Center.

"You drooling yet?" he asked.

Cheri nodded.

They climbed the steps to the plaza. The Metropolitan Opera, with its huge stained glass Chagall windows, was in the center near the granite fountain. In good weather, there would be tables and chairs surrounding the fountain and people would be ordering food and drinks from a small kiosk before the show started.

A brisk wind buffeted them so they continued moving. It was too cold to stand still. James suddenly stopped at the bottom of the steps. "I'd be happy to buy tickets to the Metropolitan Opera if you'd like to go with me. I only went once, on a school trip."

She smiled at him. "Thanks, maybe another day. Meanwhile, we better start hitting those locksmiths before there's a full-blown storm. She looked up at the sky. "It's not looking good. Shopkeepers might decide to close early." As they turned the corner she told him, "I have an idea, how about buying tickets for the top tier of the Met? You mind sitting in the nose-bleed section? Won't be as expensive."

"I don't mind. I'll check online, see what's available and get back to you before I order. I might not be able to get seats for a few months. They sell out."

That's okay. You're a sweetheart, you know?"

"I always told you that."

"That makes two of us who love you," she said. "Me. And you."

Their first stop was on West Seventy-Second Street near Broadway. The tiny shop was packed with customers. After seeing how crowded the place was, Cheri realized it was a long shot that a busy locksmith would remember Kati even after showing him a photograph.

When they didn't have any luck at the first place, they walked five blocks in the freezing cold to the second shop on the list. This time, the locksmith didn't speak English fluently. He shook his head when they showed him Kati's picture. "I no see her."

Their next stop was eight blocks away. When they came up empty again, they decided to stop and eat. They had skipped lunch and were starving. It was snowing by then and the wind was picking up. A poster in the window of a travel agency advertised cruises to the Caribbean. They stopped and smiled at each other but kept walking until they reached one of their favorite Chinese restaurants on Broadway. Their shoulders kept rubbing, their hands kept touching and Cheri flashed back to the wonderful evenings they spent together, listening to music or watching a movie.

They settled in at a booth in back of the restaurant. It was nearly empty except for a few people buying take-out. The smell of shrimp was making Cheri salivate. After they ordered, James scanned the addresses of the rest of the locksmiths in the area and said, "Let's keep going unless you're too cold. In that case, we'll continue next week." She agreed and told him her feet were freezing, even through her boots, and her fingers felt numb. They looked out of the window. It was snowing harder. Even if they went back to the police station to pick up a department vehicle, driving would be a bitch, they decided.

"Here's the thing," Cheri whispered. "No leads except for one witness who says she saw two people on the balcony. And the only fingerprints we have in the apartment belong to Kati but in the bedroom, not on the balcony. And they smoked pot. Big deal. A lot of people would have loved to kill Ben. He was a con artist and a bigamist."

The waitress brought their food and James told her to dig in while the food was hot. "We'll catch a break," he said between bites. "The old lady across the street is sharp and her eyesight's pretty good. She'll get over being scared. And don't forget, Luis is still a person of interest. Too coincidental that he was in New York the day Ben was murdered. Plus, the trip to Rio is still a possibility." He winked at her. "It's a long shot don't forget, but could happen."

"Don't worry, I won't start packing." She reached for her cup of hot tea. "There's also Ben's partner, Perry. We have to interview him again. Plus that weirdo, Jazz, who keeps harassing Leslie." She rubbed her lower back and groaned. "Too much sitting in front of my laptop lately." After adding hot mustard to their food, they ate hungrily, not talking, despite their original plan to discuss the Rabinowitz case. After they finished eating, James whispered something about Ben and she had to ask him to speak louder.

"I'm not comfortable here. I don't like talking about a case in public. It's one of my fetishes."

"You develop any new fetishes?" she asked.

"Yeah, I'll show you one day."

She smiled as she rubbed her hands together. "It's cold in here."

"I agree. They're saving on the heat while I develop pneumonia. Let's go back to the station house."

"Cold there, too, and it's a long walk back."

"Any suggestions?" he asked.

"We can go to my place," she whispered.

"You serious?"

She smiled at him and nodded. She felt awkward telling him she'd been thinking about it for a long time. It came to a head, bad pun, she realized, when Caz told her, Glad you broke off with Tom. Go back to James. He made a mistake, sure, but you can learn to forgive him.

James looked at her across the table. "I don't want you to feel pressured. You comfortable about me going back with you?"

"I wouldn't have suggested it if I wasn't serious."

After they stepped out of the restaurant, they discovered that it was snowing heavily. As they headed north, they had the wind in their faces. Cheri lifted the hood on her jacket as she watched James duck his head under his coat collar.

"Wish I had ear muffs," said Cheri. "I have a pair back in Montana. I'll ask my mom to send them to me." She laughed. "They're mink. No kidding. I bought them on a whim in a fur shop after Christmas. They were on sale."

"Mink?" he repeated then laughed. "With all your cracks about Wall Street, didn't know you were a capitalist."

"Just mink earmuffs," she murmured, then ducked back under her hood.

After she opened the door to her apartment she wasn't surprised to find the radiator quiet. "Heat's off," she told him. "The landlord's saving for a trip to the Caribbean."

"That's Nueva York. If we buy a brownstone together, we'll keep the heat going day and night."

Half an hour later they were drinking their favorite red wine from California.

"Let's do it," he said, standing up and taking his glass of wine with him. "There's one place warmer than your kitchen." He took her hand and led her into the bedroom. Her bedroom resembled a stage set–all neutral colors with old sepia photographs of Central Park after a snowstorm. As soon as they were under the covers Cheri didn't even mind the cold sheets. Everything in this room comforted her: the down quilt, the throw pillows, her childhood teddy bear, and a blue-footed booby, a gift from the Sierra Club after she sent them a donation.

As they lay back on the pillow Cheri rested her head on James's chest. She wondered why he was quieter than usual until he said, "Your playwright boyfriend hasn't come back, has he?"

"Told you, he's gone."

"For good?"

"For good." She rubbed his chest. "Instead of the Metropolitan Opera, think you can still get tickets for the Broadway show starring Franco?"

"You using my body for theater tickets?"

She jumped on top of him and laughed. "No, I'm using my body to see Franco. But don't tell him."

"It's almost your birthday. I'll ask my buddy if he can get tickets for that show."

She leaned over and kissed his cheek. "I would love that, thanks. Now, don't move." She jumped up, raced across the cold tile to the kitchen and returned carrying a can in her hand. She held it up. "For later," she said and placed the container of whipped cream on the table next to the bed. "You didn't forget, did you?" He laughed as he squeezed her shoulder. "No, I didn't forget."

After they made love she fell back on the bed, arms outstretched and took several deep breaths. A few minutes later she cried, "Show time," reached over then handed him the can of whipped cream. After James spread whipped cream all over her breasts, Cheri lay back with her eyes shut and purred like a kitten while he licked it off. "This is the best dessert," he whispered. She moaned as he continued licking the cream off her body.

"My turn," she cried. They reversed positions so he was on the bottom. She spread whipped cream on his stomach, then kept sliding down until she was lying between his legs and applied whipped cream to his lower body. As she gripped his hips and thighs they were just as she remembered, solid as rocks from all his years of jogging. He kept whispering, "That's nice, that's nice" as she licked the rest of the cream off. Then he fell back on the bed like a satisfied lion. She rolled over on her side, legs straight, and lay with her back to him before she pulled herself into in a fetal position and curled herself into him.

A few minutes later, James was snoring lightly. She waited a while then tapped him on the shoulder. "I'm sorry. I don't think I can do this."

"Do what?"

"I don't think you should sleep over. I'm not ready."

He took a deep breath and mumbled, "You're telling me now? Okay, I understand. You want to take it slow."

"Yeah, it's too soon, but I'm glad we made love." She pointed to the window. "At least it isn't snowing anymore." She knew that sounded feeble, but she couldn't help herself. She was scared of getting hurt again.

He caressed her arm and whispered something about feeling used then said, "But I'll get over it." He got up and dressed as if he was sleepwalking, even left his shirt-tail hanging out of his pants and pulled his sweater on backwards. Cheri didn't say anything. She felt guilty about asking him to go out in the cold, but things were moving too fast. She shouldn't have slept with him. It was too soon. Wasn't it too soon? Yes and no, she thought.

After he left, she went over what just happened until she decided to stop beating herself up. Just as she was about to fall asleep, a line of fire engines drove past, sirens blaring. She lay on her back, satisfied from making love with James. Before she fell asleep she told herself, We'll make it. We just have to connect the dots then we'll crack the Rabinowitz case and celebrate. She kept whispering the word "dots" until she rolled onto her side and slept soundly.

When she woke up the next morning, she reached across the bed for James. "Sent him home," she whispered in a groggy voice. Dumb? No, not dumb. They were moving too fast. But now that we've moved up the ladder, she thought, there was no going back.

While she dressed for the day she remembered a documentary she had seen years ago about the police in Rio de Janeiro. She planned to tell James about it. She even remembered the name: Elite Squad "Tropa Elite." It was about the police in Rio who shoot first and ask questions later. That made her sick. But that won't happen to Luis, she told herself. If he cooperates.

She looked forward to seeing James soon, but they would have to play it cool. No touching, no secret looks, just discussions about the Rabinowitz case or the captain would send them on a trip. Not to Rio, but to the slaughterhouse.

Chapter 28

The next time Detective Melo called Marsh and O'Brien in New York, he reported that Luis was let out of jail after he promised to show up for an interview."

"Did he show up?" asked James.

"Si."

"Tell us what happened," said Cheri.

"I'm leaving for meeting in few minutes," said Melo. "I can't stay on phone long but wanted to check in, as they say in the States."

"That's okay," said Cheri, "no problem. Can you just give us a quick briefing?"

"Pepita was here with Luis. I make exception for her to stay with boyfriend. And she tell him, Tell the truth, Luis. Detective Melo can't help you if you don't tell the truth."

"What did he say?" asked James, leaning closer to the speaker phone.

"He tell Pepita, In the past I smoke weed, even sniff coke. I never commit murder."

Cheri asked, "What did Pepita say?"

Melo laughed and Cheri could picture a smirk on his face. "Senorita Detective Marsh, Pepita sat quiet, hoping Luis will talk to me. He did, but I still don't believe him. And I warn him that if he doesn't want to be suspect, he should take lie detector test. I make him promise, then I ask him again what he saw in Ben's apartment."

"What did he tell you?" said James.

"He tell me same story about two people near bedroom except this time he said, Maybe it wasn't a woman with Ben. Maybe it was a man talking to him. Cheri inhaled deeply and rapped on her desk trying to remain patient. "What did you say to him?"

"I shout at him, Maybe was kangaroo you saw."

Cheri and James exchanged glances, clearly exasperated with this method of gathering information about a person of interest thousands of miles away. "Go on," said Cheri.

"I have to leave for appointment soon but I finish story. Pepita was annoyed with me for saying maybe was kangaroo. She said, Luis, let's go."

"Not so fast, I tell them. We have to get something straight. Was it a woman you saw? Or was it a man with Ben? Luis looked at Pepita like little boy and said, 'I don't know.'" Melo cleared his throat. "I told Luis, get out of my office. When you come back, don't tell me again that you don't know. And If you don't take lie detector test, I throw your culo back in jail.

Cheri thanked Melo and asked him how the interview ended.

"We set up appointment for next time. And I warn Luis, tell me everything that happened, not just say I'm innocent. Means nothing." Melo hesitated as if he was trying to remember everything. "Here's the thing, Luis had opportunity. When I tell him that, Pepita look angry and Luis look like baby about to cry. After few minutes we all say, Hasta luego."

As soon as Melo stopped speaking Cheri told him, "We know this is hard but you're doing a great job with a difficult witness. Keep in touch."

"Si, I do that. I hope you will come to Rio, Detective Marsh so I can take you to dinner."

After the call ended Cheri looked at James and said, "What do you think?"

"I think Luis is going south as a person of interest. He's fast becoming a suspect. I'll have another talk with the captain about a possible trip to Rio."

"We really need to talk to him in person."

James nodded. "I'll do the best I can."

When Cheri checked her e-mail at home that night she found e-mails from forensics and a note from an investigative reporter at The Daily News asking for an update about the death of Benjamin Rabinowitz.

She wrote back, "No comment." Then Cheri thought about Leslie. She had called earlier that day to say she was going to visit an elderly aunt in Queens and would come into the precinct as soon as she got back in a day, or two.

Hope she makes it there without a mobster trying to kill her. thought Cheri, *And if she arrives safely, hope she makes it back in one piece.*

Chapter 29

Two days later, Leslie called the police station to report that she just returned from Queens. "I also received a package while I was away, just picked it up from the doorman."

"What was it?" Cheri asked.

Leslie hesitated, then said softly, "A doll. But not an ordinary doll." She stopped to catch her breath. "It was missing a leg."

"Oh, no," said Cheri. "Any idea who left it?"

"No, but I had a phone call a little while ago."

"What did he say?"

Leslie composed herself before she finally answered. "Next time it won't be a doll."

As Cheri listened, she mouthed the name "Leslie" to James. She gave him a thumbs down and told Leslie to hold on. She covered the mouthpiece with her hand and told him, "Not good. I'll tell you later." She went back to the call and told Leslie, "After the guy dropped the doll off, he probably won't hang around waiting for you to leave. Here's what I want you to do. Go out right now, buy a wig and a cane. Also, get some old lady clothes, maybe second-hand. Wear them home from the store and wear that disguise every time you go out. Got it?"

"Yes, no problem."

"Could you identify the guy who kidnapped the dog if we send a few pictures to your computer?"

"Doubt it," said Leslie. "I'm sorry."

"You sure? Or you're scared?"

Leslie didn't answer and Cheri continued "What did the guy on the phone sound like?"

"He had a thick Russian accent. I think there were two people involved. I heard someone in the background yelling at the speaker, telling him what to say."

"Both sounded Russian?"

"Yes."

"Get that disguise ASAP. Be careful going in and out of your building and come see us as soon as you can. You received James's messages I assume."

"Yes, sorry I didn't respond. Hope it's okay."

"It's not okay," said Cheri, pointedly. "We wanted to talk to you. We still do. Get here as soon as you can." She leaned over her desk and told James about the phone call Leslie received with somebody in the background prompting the caller.

"This guy who's calling Leslie. He's probably using a cell that can't be traced."

"We'll keep searching for him," she said.

James propped his feet up on his desk and leaned back. "Jazz could be an innocuous goon who just wants his money back. His cousin Sergei from Brighton Beach might have been the aggressor–he was the Boss. I have a feeling that after Sergei died as a result of the fire, Jazz didn't know what to do so he hooked up with another member of the Mafia for back-up. That's who Leslie probably heard in the background."

Cheri thought for a second. "Damn, we know that somebody connected with the Russian mob left the doll. I hope whoever he is isn't watching Leslie. She needs that disguise ASAP. I hope she doesn't get killed before she buys it.

That evening, James approached Cheri outside the station. "My place is warmer than yours. Want to stay overnight?" She grinned. "I was hoping you'd ask."

Their first stop was her apartment where she packed an overnight bag. Next, they ducked into their favorite Thai restaurant for hot soup and Pad Thai. After they arrived at his place, they each checked their e-mail then went to bed early. They were both exhausted.

Propped up in bed the next morning, Cheri watched as snow kept piling up outside. People were trying to duck the wind using their coat collars, hoods, scarves. Too windy for an umbrella, she decided. They'd turn inside out. She closed her eyes and pictured a giant octopus as she wrapped her feet around James's calves. "Calamari," she murmured.

"Yeah, we're octopi," he whispered in a sleepy voice. She smiled, glad he heard her.

After showering together, they downed a quick breakfast of energy bars, orange juice, and coffee. "I hope your place isn't bugged," she said. "The captain won't appreciate two of his detectives getting out of bed together."

"No problem. Besides, it was a working dinner." He pointed to their laptops on the kitchen counter.

"Good point. I was starting to feel guilty." She pulled her hair into a pony tail as she looked out of the window. The sun was starting to peek through the clouds and she became hopeful that the sunshine would make it easier to get around. "We should get going and visit the next locksmith on our list," she said as they stepped out of his apartment building. He nodded as they stepped over a snowbank pushed to the curb by a plow. They headed north, faces lowered, bucking the wind on their way to the locksmith's shop on Columbus Circle. Before James opened the door he asked if Cheri had the copy of Kati's photograph.

"It's in here," she said, tapping her briefcase.

After they showed the man behind the counter their IDs, he told them he was the owner. Cheri showed him Kati's picture. He nodded immediately and said he recognized the woman in the photograph.

"Did you make up a key for her?" asked James.

"I didn't make up one key," he said. "I made up two. Here's why I remember. She asked if she could tape a flyer to my window advertising a show she was in. It was an interesting name for a play."

"What was it?"

"Something with the word *Suffer* in it, a name I wouldn't forget."

Suffer Queen? asked James.

"Yeah, that was it," said the shopkeeper.

"You have a good memory," said Cheri. "Anything else unusual happen?"

"That's unusual enough. She was smart. She waited until after she paid for the keys then took out a stack of flyers. I told her she could put up one." The tiny shop was filling up with people who wanted keys made up. The detectives waited until the shopkeeper finished waiting on customers then inquired if Kati ever came back.

"Nope, never saw her again. Made up two keys and she seemed happy. She was even happier after she taped a poster to my window."

Cheri looked at the bare window.

"I took it down a few days after she was here. Figured a few day of free advertising was enough. I don't want people thinking they can use my window for their notices." They thanked him and stepped outside. "Two keys," said Cheri. "Why do you think she made up two?"

That's the next question on our list for Kati," said James.

Chapter 30

During her next meeting with Detectives Marsh and O'Brien, Kati stared at the wall over their heads, not looking at them at all.

James leaned forward and said pointedly, "We found out that you made up a key to Ben's apartment. Want to talk about that or you're tired again?"

Katie's eyes darted back and forth until she finally looked at James. "I'm not okay. I'm exhausted from performing in a one-woman play, plus it's hot in here." She looked from one to the other again, obviously hoping one of the detectives would say, You're right. I'll lower the heat. Nobody moved even when Kati started wiping her face with a Kleenex.

"Nothing we can do about that," said James. Cheri knew Kati was sitting under a vent with hot air blowing on her. She hoped that being uncomfortable might prompt her to talk so she could get out of there.

"You going to talk to us?" Cheri asked, finally.

"It's been a long day for us, too," said James. "We all want to go home."

Kati pushed up the sleeves of her cardigan and looked around. "Okay, the two keys," she said, taking a deep breath. The detectives waited, didn't say a word. "Before Ben got stoned, he asked me to go out and make up an extra key for him. He told me he needed it for the cleaning lady. After we smoked some weed, he remembered he needed the key that day." Kati looked down, as if studying a cracked tile. "Ben also snorted coke that day. As long as I knew him, I begged him to stop using drugs, but he just blew me off."

"Go on," said James. "Don't stop now."

Kati pulled a Kleenex out of her pants pocket and wiped her forehead. After taking several deep breaths she continued. "He told me if he fell asleep, I should get the key made up, said he'd be up when I got back."

"Go on," said James, sounding impatient. "It took you long enough to open up. What happened next?"

Katie did her Kleenex routine again, seemingly desperate to get out of there. She's not exaggerating about the heat, thought Cheri, staring at beads of perspiration on Kati's upper lip.

"While he slept I took the key and headed downtown. I knew he'd be out for a while, knew how coke affected him. I also grabbed my briefcase stuffed with flyers. After I had the key made up I asked the locksmith if I could put up a poster for my show. The locksmith said yes and I...."

"Just a minute," said James interrupting. "We found out you made up two keys. Why?"

She twisted a strand of hair around her finger and whispered, "A personal reason."

"There are no personal reasons in a homicide case," James replied sharply. "Either you tell us your reason, or you're not leaving until you do. Your choice. Okay, one key for the cleaning lady. Who was the other one for?"

Katie picked up her coffee cup and stared inside as if there was a message for her. "The other key was for me," she said finally. "I wanted to go back to the apartment while Ben was traveling. I suspected he was playing around and wanted to find out if I was right."

"What else did you suspect?"

She wiped her neck with the Kleenex this time. "I suspected Ben was seeing his ex-wife Leslie. He'd been talking about her a lot lately. I was hoping to find evidence of that."

"Why Leslie?" Cheri asked.

"Be specific," said James. "We're not mind-readers."

"Here's why," said Katie. "There was something in Ben's voice whenever he said Leslie's name that made me suspicious. When I asked him if he was dating her, he screamed, You're paranoid." She took a deep breath. "That's why I made up the second key."

Cheri leaned closer. "After you had those keys made up, did you use one?"

Kati swallowed hard. "I used one twice. I swear to you, only twice."

"What did you find?"

"The first time I found condoms, dope, and threatening letters from an investor named Jazz. The letters were in Ben's desk. I never heard of him."

"And the second time?" asked James. "Same items?"

"Yes, except the letters from Jazz were missing. I thought maybe Ben took them to the police. I couldn't ask. He'd know I was snooping. Everything else was the same but neater. Guess the cleaning lady had been there. No, she didn't know the cleaning lady's name. Kati looked around the windowless interrogation room. She turned pale as if she was getting sick.

After being asked, Kati tried to remember the dates she went to the apartment. It was recently, but she insisted it was not the day Ben died. She was home studying her lines. Cheri had the feeling Kati was lying about that day, but she didn't press it. Neither did James. Instead, they asked about the letters from Jazz. "Any return address or zip code?"

Kati shook her head. "Neither."

"What did the letters look like?" James asked.

"Plain white printer paper. Both letters said the same thing: 'You cheated me. I want my money back. Or else. The dude couldn't spell, by the way."

"Never mind that," said Cheri. "Was Ben especially distracted around that time?"

Kati nodded, said she tried to draw him out about his business problems but he kept saying he was about to close on a merger. Everything would be fine after that. He also said he had to travel to Rio de Janeiro to talk to somebody about a gold mine. She looked sheepish as she added, Now that I'm telling you everything, I was always jealous of Leslie. And Pepita." Kati immediately looked as if she regretted telling them that but didn't take it back, even added, "especially Pepita. "Did you ever see her?" She didn't wait for an answer, instead blurted out, "That caused me to snoop but I never hurt Ben. I loved him. We were happy. He changed when he started to have business problems."

"In what way?" said Cheri, moving closer to Kati.

"He became brusque with me. He invested in my show, then he didn't want to listen to my problems with the director. He kept telling me, I have problems of my own. Talk to a girlfriend."

"Did he ever hit you?"

"No. Of course not, but I had the feeling he wanted to run away from his problems. He was planning that trip to Rio. When I finally asked him if he was going to see Pepita, he told me I was insecure." It was hard for me, women were always throwing themselves at Ben. He exuded power."

"You have your own power," said Cheri. You're in a hit show."

"It's Off-Broadway, not on Broadway. And actors are a dime a dozen."

Cheri frowned, tired of Kati's dissembling. "Are you willing to take a polygraph test?"

There was a slight hesitation. "I'll have to think about it."

After she finished her cup of coffee, Cheri asked about Ben's partner, Perry. "You told us he was an investor in the gold mine. You keep adding and subtracting things. Is that still a fact?"

"I believe he was an investor," Kate replied. "Ben cornered everybody expecting to sell shares in that mine. I'm not sure the mine was even a money maker. I got that idea from Ben as he kept getting more and more depressed about business."

The heat in the room was starting to get to Cheri, but she didn't offer to turn it down. "Did you buy shares in the mine with your personal money?"

Kati took her time answering. "I inherited some money from an aunt and gave it to Ben. He promised me I'd double my money, maybe even triple it."

"Did you?"

"You kidding? I lost everything."

"The deal might have been a Ponzi scheme," said Cheri, "especially if Ben knew the mine was unproductive."

After another hour they told Kati she could leave, said they'd be in touch.

"Interesting about the cleaning lady," said Cheri as soon as they were alone again. "We need to find out what she knows about that apartment. "I'll start calling every cleaning service in New York tomorrow morning and try to find her. Think it's possible in a city of eight million people?"

"I have faith in you."

Chapter 31

The next time Cheri stayed overnight at James's apartment, he told her in the morning, "Give me a fifteen minute head start, then leave." She locked the door behind him and lingered over a cup of coffee while she read a theater review in *The New York Times.* Fifteen minutes later she locked the door to his apartment. The cold weather was making her hungry again so she stopped for a warmed-up blueberry muffin then headed to work.

James didn't look up when she entered the squad room. They didn't arrive at the same time or leave at the same time except on business. And they didn't t eat together in the evening anywhere near the police station.

Cheri set up her laptop and Googled Cleaning Services in the vicinity of Ben's apartment. Finding the person Ben hired was like searching for a button on a New York City street.

While James was on the phone she heard him mention Rio de Janeiro. They would need plane tickets, he said, and two hotel rooms. Cheri heard that part clearly. Also meals and a rental car. James mentioned Detective Melo in Rio. Yes, they've been in touch with him.

Cheri was on the phone when he hung up. He coughed, gestured to his throat and mouthed the words "I'll be right back."

After he returned he dropped a bag of cough drops on his desk. He gave her a look of what's up. She held up her index finger indicating he should wait until she got off the phone. "No luck so far," she said. "I'll keep trying."

While Cheri continued working on the cleaning lady angle, James searched police records for anybody nicknamed Jazz who had been arrested.

"Whew," said Cheri, finally hanging up. "Think I got a lead. I finally reached the superintendent of the building Ben lived in. Told him I have an elderly mother living nearby and I need to hire a cleaning lady for her. Said I heard the woman Ben Rabinowitz hired was excellent."

"Smart thinking," said James. "What did he say?"

"He didn't want to give out any names at first. I had to beg, plead, and cajole until he gave me the name."

James laughed. "Your theater background comes in handy."

She nodded. "He finally said he has a woman he recommends to people living in the building, a friend of his."

"Did you get her name and number?"

"Yup. We should talk to her right away. If she's not home we can ask neighbors about her, tell them we need references before we hire her to clean for us."

James grabbed his laptop and his coat. Cheri did the same. They were at the door when he ran back and grabbed a handful of cough drops. "Drive or walk?"

"Let's drive," she said. "You still have a cold."

"Nah, just a frog in my throat."

They headed uptown, talking all the while, trying to figure out what to expect from the cleaning lady. "Maybe Ben died before she got to clean," said James.

"I don't think so," said Cheri. "Remember Kati said the apartment was neater the second time she went there? I doubt

Benjamin Rabinowitz straightened up, doesn't strike me as the domestic type."

Definitely not domestic. And definitely not a monogamist. But Cheri kept her thoughts to herself. *Not a good idea to bring up monogamy.*

"Tell me something," he said, as he stopped for a red light. "What's your sense of Ben Rabinowitz now that we know a little more about him?"

Cheri shrugged. "Not sure. He sniffed coke yet he managed to be successful. He cheated on his wives yet attracted three attractive, intelligent women."

"What else?"

"He was charming, bright, well-dressed, well educated, attended Harvard Business School." The light turned green and James stepped on the gas. Cheri hesitated for a second then said, "He also had more than his share of enemies, including Jazz, whoever he is. Ben was unscrupulous. That mine deal probably wasn't his only breach of ethics. But success doesn't necessarily connect with integrity."

"No kidding."

"What about our trip to Rio? Any news?"

"Not looking good," said James. "The captain agrees that it would be good for us to go there but too expensive. I was going to tell him to save on a second hotel room."

She looked at him as if he'd suggested they attach Velcro to their shoulders and fly to Rio. She smiled. "That would have gone over big."

As soon as they reached the building James parked in front and used the police decal, then they climbed three flights of worn steps and rang the bell for apartment 4D, Rita Alvarez.

A teenager wearing a tattered chenille robe answered. She kept the door partly closed with the latch on while she asked what they wanted. Cold air seeped in through the crack in the door.

They flashed their IDs and the girl jumped back. "We didn't call you," she said nervously.

"Who is it?" a woman shouted from the other room.

"Mami, you better come here."

A Latina woman about forty-five years old appeared. She was dressed in jeans and a heavy sweater. She was wearing sturdy walking shoes used for cleaning expensive apartments and condos, like Ben's.

"Si? Can I help you?"

"We're looking for Rita Alvarez. A superintendent on West End Avenue told us she does cleaning jobs in that building."

"That's me. What's the problem?"

"No problem. Just want to know if you ever worked for Benjamin Rabinowitz."

She hesitated before answering. "I cleaned for him a few times. Nice man. Gave me a bonus for Christmas plus a box of chocolates por la familia. What's wrong? Sick?"

"Not sick," said James. "Dead. Guess you don't read the paper or watch the news."

"Dead? Mon Dio, I'm sorry to hear that. He told me he was flying to Brazil on business and would call me when he got back."

"When was that?"

She stopped to think then said hesitantly. "About two weeks ago, I think. I haven't seen him since."

She opened the door wide and led them into her tiny, but immaculate living room. The television was on, and she gestured for her daughter to turn it off. "I'm home because I'm getting over the flu, but now my daughter has it. Tomorrow I go back to work. I need mucho dineros. I'm sure you understand."

"Sure," said Cheri. "Did you ever meet anybody in Benjamin's apartment? A friend? Relative?"

"Nobody."

"Ever?" Cheri stared into Rita's eyes.

"Never." Rita hesitated for a moment. "I saw a woman there once."

"Remember her name?"

"Of course. She was Mrs. Rabinowitz."

"What was her first name?"

"I don't remember."

"They showed her a picture of Pepita,

"No, that wasn't her." They showed her pictures of Leslie and Kati. Rita shook her head. "His wife wasn't any of those women. He just said, 'Meet my wife.' Didn't say her name. But he said she's from Italy. He also said she doesn't speak English. Maybe he didn't want me to ask her any question. But I mind my own business."

"Did his wife look unusual in any way?" Cheri asked. "Like a puta?"

"A hooker? No," said Rita. "She looked too high-class. Pardon me for saying, maybe a high class hooker." She covered her mouth and laughed. Her daughter, who was standing next to her, rolled her eyes.

"Can you describe her?"

"No, I only saw her once. After I arrive, his wife come out of the bedroom and say he would pay me. I ask him, don't you want I should clean apartment?"

"What did he say?" asked Cheri.

"He said 'Next time.' I figure something there he don't want me to see." She giggled. "Maybe sex toys. But not my business."

After a few more questions that didn't go anywhere, they thanked her for the information and left their business cards. "Buenas dias," said Cheri.

"Buenas dias,"' she replied, bowing her head as if the detectives were royalty. "I'm sorry to hear Ben died. I'll call if I have more information." When Cheri reached the door, Rita added, "Ben was rich man. And handsome. Did he have more than one wife?"

"He had three wives that we know of," said James.

"Busy man," said Rita. "No wonder he didn't have time to clean." She chuckled. "His wife didn't clean, either."

No, thought Cheri, none of them cleaned.

As soon as they were outside the apartment building Cheri turned to James. "Are you thinking the same thing I am?"

"I think so. The so-called Mrs. Rabinowitz that Rita met was the woman from the escort service."

He touched Cheri's arm. "We need to talk to our witness, Tina, also known as a masseuse, also known as Mrs. Rabinowitz to the cleaning lady."

After a quick stop for coffee, they paid a visit to Tina. She had to be prompted a few times, but finally said she saw a cleaning lady in Ben's apartment. She was only there a short time when the woman showed up for work. Ben told me he forgot she was coming. I was surprised when he introduced me as his wife."

"What else did he say?"

"He told her I was from Italy, didn't speak good English. I played along. I get paid for stranger things."

"Anything else you want to tell us?" said James.

"Nada. That's all I remember. I left soon after that and he paid me extra, said he was sorry he forgot about the cleaning lady. So, turned out to be a quick massage."

James squinted at Tina. "You told us you went to Ben's apartment only once."

"I make mistake. I was in his apartment twice."

"You sure?"

"That's all. Twice, I swear."

"You remember anything else?"

"Nada," said Tina. "It was quick visit. In and out."

Thanks," said Cheri, apprehensive about this so-called masseuse who had business cards that read "Escort Service" on one side and "Masseuse" on the other.

"If you think of anything else, give us a call," said James. "You still have our cards, I hope."

"I have them, no problem."

After they returned to the police station, Cheri and James decided to interview Ben's partner Perry the next day then they'd work on finding Jazz. They were sure he had an accomplice. Another psycho who replaced Sergei. Cheri still had a hunch Leslie killed Ben. All the more reason, she thought, for her and James to keep Leslie safe from the Russians. She figured Jazz wanted to keep Leslie alive, too, despite his threats. She was worth more to him alive than dead. It was her money he wanted, not her dead body.

Chapter 32

The next day with no phone calls expected, Cheri told James, "Let's drive down to Wall Street and have another talk with Ben's partner, Perry. Lunch first?"

He nodded. "Good idea. I'm starving."

After stopping at a nearby coffee shop James ordered a burger. Cheri ordered a tofu salad. "I'm a Suffer Queen," she said.

He laughed at the reference to Kati's play. "Speaking of which, what do you think about Kati's excuse for making up the key?"

"I have a feeling there's more to it than she told us. We need to question her again."

He thanked the waitress and waited. As soon as the waitress was out of earshot they went over what they had so far. They also discussed the mystery woman in the black hooded coat. "Maybe it was one of the wives hanging around the lobby undecided if she should make an unexpected visit to Ben," said James.

Cheri nodded as she reached for her cup of coffee. "Could be. Whoever it was didn't want to be seen on the camera. Damn it, so many loose ends." She was feeling discouraged again until James reminded her that they might still fly to Rio to interview Luis. "It's a long shot," he added, "so don't get your hopes up."

"Then don't bring it up. I'll drool all over you if you mention Rio one more time."

"You can do whatever you want all over me. We should live together," he whispered.

Cheri did a double-take. "Not sure the boss would approve of that, either. Besides, we came close to that once, remember? It didn't work out."

"Yeah, but we're older and smarter now."

When she didn't answer, he asked her to at least think about it. She promised she would. Their food arrived and they ate in a hurry, anxious to get to Wall Street.

After James paid, they walked to the car and headed downtown. Traffic was heavy, as usual, and Cheri listened while James told her, "When I grew up in New York, a lot of people took subways. Now, everybody drives, damn it, plus there's Uber and Lyft."

She nodded, although she was secretly thrilled to have the use of an unmarked car. When they finally reached Perry's office building they had to go through the same routine as the time before. Security was so tight, Cheri wondered if investment bankers were hated that much. There was a lot of news in the papers lately about Wall Street regarding hard drugs and billionaire divorces. Maybe Ben's behavior was typical of the Wall Street culture, she thought. She wondered what her relatives in Montana would say about the lifestyle of stockbrokers.

As they waited for somebody from Perry's office to come downstairs for them Cheri whispered, "They have more security here than any place in New York, including Kennedy airport. But like you said, this is where the power is, and everybody loves power."

A thin woman in her thirties stepped off the escalator, waved to them and escorted them upstairs. Perry was on a long-distance call, but would be with them shortly. Fifteen minutes later, they were ushered into the luxurious office Perry shared with his expensive art collection, metal sculptures, and a fake parrot perched in an antique Victorian cage. "This is new," he said, pointing to the bird. "A gift from my wife for my birthday."

They complimented his wife on her imagination then sat across from him at a desk wider than the Grand Canyon.

"What can I do for you?"

"Know anything about a gold mine that Ben sold shares in?"

There was silence as Perry appeared to be mulling over his answer. "Not much. We stayed out of each other's business. Here's the thing," said Perry. "Too much money to be made in stocks and bonds. I didn't need shares in a gold mine. High risk."

Cheri leaned forward, one hand around the arm of a wooden chair. She fell in love with this piece of furniture the first time she saw it. She especially loved the rattan seat. She was a sucker for rattan or wicker. "You said you pretty much stayed out of that investment," she offered. "That's like being a little pregnant. You either invested or you didn't. Which is it?"

Perry pulled a gold toothpick out of his breast pocket and poked at a back tooth. "I'll explain," he said, sucking on the toothpick before putting it away, "Ben was a huge risk taker. Making big money requires taking big risks but Ben was what we in this business refer to as a cowboy. He went for broke. The gold mine was that kind of investment so I only dipped my big toe in. It wasn't money I couldn't afford to lose so when I lost a little I wasn't devastated. It was petty cash for me. Can't say the same for Ben. I kept telling him the mine was going south, He refused to listen. First rule of Wall Street, don't fall in love with a stock. Or a gold mine."

"Interesting," said James.

He's bull-shitting, thought Cheri. Watching his eyes and body language were a dead give-away, especially the index finger placed on the side of his nose. He invested heavily in that mine and had a motive to kill his partner. Now she and James had to prove it. That might be tough. A lot of Ben's papers were missing. They were working with an incomplete list of investors and incomplete statements for the mine. They had to bluff their way through.

"Did you ever travel to Brazil with Ben?" asked Cheri.

"Brazil? Not me. I'm not a lover of the Amazon. I'm not even enamored of South America for that matter, except for Rio during Carnival. That's different." He stood up and reached for a hardcover book on his book shelf. He opened it and pointed to a photograph. James and Cheri waited for an explanation. "This is an indigenous tribe discovered a few years ago in the Amazon jungle in Brazil." He pointed to the picture with his index finger. "If you'll notice, they're carrying bows and arrows. I doubt those are just for hunting. I didn't relish becoming meat stew."

"Are they really cannibals?" she asked, "or just a throwback to an earlier time?" She resented the inference to indigenous people as cannibals. Being one-quarter Assiniboine, she was sympathetic to Natives especially in America and never forgot the poverty on her family's reservation in Montana.

Perry continued his monologue about the primitive nature of Indians until Cheri said, "I'm one quarter Native American."

"You don't look it."

"That's not the point," she replied. "Native Americans were screwed out of land, gold. and, most of all their culture. Did you ever read about the boarding schools they were sent to? They were punished if they spoke their native language."

"I read about that," he said with a shrug." He doesn't care, she thought. Insensitive bastard. Anxious to get back on track she asked him, "Where were you the day Ben died?"

"Had just gotten back from Santa Fe, was in meetings all day, even late into the evening. You can check. We're in the midst of taking a company public so it's been hectic the last few months. This is a hedge fund," he told Cheri. "Do you understand what we do?"

"I know about hedge funds," she said pointedly. She hated his condescending manner and was tempted to say, I know what you do. You invest other people's money until they don't have any left. She didn't smile this time, wasn't concerned about appeasing him. "We'd like a list of your employees," she added, "so we can interview them. It's to your advantage that you're cleared as a suspect."

Perry appeared taken aback by the word "suspect" but didn't respond.

"Did you leave the meeting for any length of time?" asked James.

"I don't recall."

"Get us a list of everybody at the meeting. Was Ben supposed to be there, too?"

"Most likely, although he was scheduled to fly to Brazil that week. I don't remember the date. You can check with Ben's wife. I still don't believe the newspapers. They said Ben was a bigamist. That's crazy. Anyway, check with Kati."

"Thanks for the tip," said James. He leaned forward. "You and Ben were partners for a long time. Did he ever confide in you about personal matters?"

"Not often."

"Was he seeing Leslie around the time of his death, do you know?"

"Not sure, but they remained friendly. They were married a long time."

James winked at Cheri, a signal for her to make her move. She faced Perry with both elbows planted on the desk and said pointedly, "If I told you we know you were a big investor in that gold mine, what would you say?"

"Baloney. Who told you that?"

"We have a list of people who invested in the mine. Your name is on it." She moved closer, her eyes riveted on him. "Did you push Ben off the balcony after the gold mine deal soured and you lost over a million dollars?"

"And don't tell us you didn't lose that much," said James. We have printed statements."

Perry stood up. "This interview is over as far as I'm concerned." He appeared to be sweating. "That's hearsay. And even if I lost that much I have millions left. There wasn't any reason for me to commit murder, not even for money." Without shaking hands, Perry walked to his office door and opened it. "I have a meeting in a few minutes. Call me if you have any more questions."

"We'll be back," she said. "Not to discuss the indigenous people of Brazil, either."

They were outside the building before Cheri blurted out, "That bastard, flaunting his millions. Now, I'm feeling lousy about this case again."

"Don't," James told her. "Let's wait to hear what Pepita and her lover have to say at the next meeting with Melo. Luis was one of the last people to see Ben alive. And he's on the list of investors who lost money."

"True," she said, starting to feel a bit more upbeat. "We should also find out if Perry ever traveled to Brazil."

"Let's take a walk before heading back to the car," said James. "You'll feel better in the cool air."

They wended their way through the narrow streets in the Wall Street area. When they reached the bronze bull, symbol of wealth in America, Cheri asked him to take a picture of her standing next to the sculpture. "I'm not a hypocrite, I hate what this stands for, but since we need to catch a break I'll rub the bull's head for good luck."

Chapter 33

Shortly after they returned to the police station, Cheri received a call from Leslie. She sounded hysterical and spoke so fast Cheri had to tell her to slow down. "Big news," said Leslie. "I have big news."

"Okay, start again from the beginning, said Cheri.

"I just got a call from a Russian and I taped it, like you asked me to."

James, who was seated at the desk opposite Cheri, looked curious to know who the caller was. Cheri mouthed the name, "Leslie." He said "Good luck" then turned back to his computer.

Cheri spoke to the caller again. "Who called you?"

Leslie took a deep breath. "Jazz. "He said his name was Jazz then blurted out a Russian-sounding name by accident. It's on the tape, but it's not clear. He kept slurring his words."

Probably was drunk thought Cheri, especially if he was part of that vodka swilling mob in Brighton Beach. "Bring us the tape ASAP."

"I'll try," said Leslie. "You know how traffic is at this hour. I'll leave right now."

When Leslie finally arrived at the police station an hour later, she was clearly out of breath, more from nervousness than from walking from the bus stop.

As soon as the detectives started listening to the tape, they heard a man's voice. As expected, he had a thick Russian accent. When Leslie asked "Who is this," he mumbled in response, and she asked, "Who is this?"

"You know who this is. Don't play games. I no like."

"I'm not playing games."

"Phone is not good," he told her. "Talk in person is better."

"Is Jazz your real name?" asked Leslie.

"I am blah-blah-blah," he said proudly. "Jazz is nickname."

Cheri rewound the tape and they listened again. "I can't understand what he said," said Leslie.

"Me neither," said James. "I'm not good at accents or foreign names."

"I'm pretty good," said Cheri, moving closer. She shook her head and rewound the tape again. "It's hard to understand." After five tries she finally understood his name. "*Dimitri... Balabanov*," she announced, raising two fingers in a "V" for victory sign. "Okay, let's continue."

"If you would meet me," he said.

"I can't," said Leslie. She hesitated and then asked "What do you want?"

"You have the money your husband stole from me. We make a deal."

"You're wrong. I lost money in that gold mine like you. And I'm broke." There was silence at the other end of the phone. "Are you still there, whoever you are?"

"My name is Jazz. Call me Jazz. And don't make me tell you again or I'll..."

Leslie replied, "I heard you, but listen I can help you. A lawyer called me yesterday about a class action suit to help Ben's investors get some of their money back. You could get in on it."

"Why you no tell me before today?"

"I just found out. And I didn't have any way to contact you."

There was silence until Jazz said, "Give me name of lawyer and his phone number. I think about it."

"Listen," said Leslie. "You can't get any money from Ben. He's dead, and I don't have any. You have a piece of paper and a pen?"

"I have. Talk." She gave him the lawyer's name, address and phone number. "Call the lawyer soon," she said. While they continued listening, Cheri gave James a thumbs up. He smiled at her and nodded. "You won't get any money right away," Leslie warned. "It will take time, but there's a good chance you could get some of your money back. Ben left a huge estate. Know what I mean by estate?"

"I understand," said Jazz. "Getting some of my money back is better than nothing." He suddenly sounded sober. Leslie told him that the news about the class action suit was in all the newspapers recently. "Don't you read the paper?"

"I read Russian newspapers." He hesitated then said in a softer voice. "This talk about lawyers is just between us. No need for cops."

"No cops," said Leslie.

The call ended when Dimitri, a/k/a Jazz, said he would call the lawyer soon. "I no call today, busy at work."

The recording ended and Leslie let out a whoosh of air, as if relieved. "You did a good job taping, but be careful," said Cheri. "Did you buy what I suggested?"

"Leslie nodded as she pulled a blonde wig out of her tote bag.

It looks like a fright wig, thought Cheri, but she complimented Leslie on her choice and told her to wear the wig going home in case anybody was following her. "Go straight home. Call us when you get there and don't let anybody in your apartment. That means nobody, not even the super, a neighbor, a friend.

James leaned forward and stared at Leslie. "We have to see if Jazz calls the attorney. If not, we'll try to find him and bring him in, that is, if he gave us his real name. But you'll have to agree to testify as a witness if he was the one who kidnapped the dog."

"NO," Leslie shouted. "You asked me once if I'm scared. I am. I'm also not sure what the kidnapper looked like. It happened so fast."

"We'll wait and see," said James. "If he signs up with the lawyer, he'll probably stop harassing you."

"At the worst," said Cheri, "he'll bug the attorney for the money."

Leslie nodded as she adjusted the wig. It's crooked, thought Cheri, but that was okay. Leslie looked more like a bag lady than a woman who lived on the Upper East Side. They thanked her and told her to keep in touch, especially if she hears from Jazz.

As soon as they were alone Cheri told James, "The Brooklyn police can deal with the Russian Mafia. I love the name Dimitri Balabanov, by the way, straight out of a James Bond movie. "In the meantime, what do you think Jazz will do?"

"Not sure he'll call the lawyer," said James. "He wants the money, but he doesn't want to wait. And he probably doesn't believe Leslie's broke. He saw the fancy building she lives in, the street, the doorman. I wouldn't believe her either."

"Yeah," said Cheri. "But the problem is Leslie won't agree to be a witness and we can't book him without her cooperation. I don't blame her for being scared."

James shook his head. "I'm pissed. Everything hinges on her."

"But if she killed Ben," said Cheri. "We can prove it and nab her. We won't need Dimitri, alias Jazz."

"True, but I still don't trust him," said James.

Chapter 34

The following day, O'Brien and Marsh walked over to the corner diner for an early lunch. A television hanging on a wall over the counter was blaring, but they couldn't change tables. The place was full. After the waitress took their order the anchor on CNN made an announcement:

"STOCKBROKER PUSHED FROM BALCONY IMPLICATED IN INSIDER TRADING."

There was a photograph of Benjamin Rabinowitz in a suit and tie walking out of a building in the Wall Street area.

The TV reporter continued:

"The Securities and Exchange Commission issued a statement saying that the dead man was a fraudster who carried out a Ponzi scheme causing hundreds of investors to lose millions of dollars and was allegedly involved in insider trading."

Cheri and James strained to hear the next part of the announcement. "Reactions to the news ranged from colleagues who said it was a set-up and others who said that Benjamin Rabinowitz was a crook and ended up getting what he deserved."

The anchor interviewed a man in an expensive looking suit who said, "There aren't any victims in an insider trading case. If a company makes a lot of money, why not a few brokers and their clients? What's good for the broker is good for the client."

"Wait just a minute," said the anchor. "Are you saying insider trading is okay?"

"I'm not saying that. I'm saying that there are worse crimes than trying to make money for clients."

"What do you think of that?" Cheri asked James.

He shook his head and said, "Remember *Alice In Wonderland?* This case is getting curiouser and curiouser. But we would hate it if life got boring. We're action junkies."

"Us?" She laughed. "We'd sign up for a one-way trip to Mars if our jobs became boring." They asked for more coffee and decided to share dessert. They ordered cherry pie topped with ice cream. "I hate myself now," said Cheri., "but I needed it."

"We both needed it," said James. "This case is stressful."

As soon as they returned to the police station, they went into an interrogation room and closed the door. Cheri stood next to an easel with a large pad propped up on it, picked up a wooden ruler and pointed. On the left side, she had printed the word NAME. In the middle was the word MOTIVE, and on the right side was ALIBI.

James pulled a pair of reading glasses out of his jacket pocket and scanned the list. "Is that in any special order?" he asked.

"No, I just listed everybody who's a person of interest: Kati, Leslie, Luis, Pepita, and Ben's partner Perry. Woman in Black Hooded Coat is on the bottom."

"I noticed that," he said, rubbing his chin, thoughtfully.

"Regarding that coat, I'm determined to visit consignment shops and try to find that coat," said Cheri.

"Why do you think you'll find it in a consignment shop?"

She put the ruler down and faced him. "It was probably expensive and Leslie needs money. For rich women, clothes are commodities, like gold or silver. Plus, Leslie lost a lot of money in that Ponzi scheme."

He looked skeptical.

"Trust me," she said. "Plus, I was watching Leslie when I mentioned the words consignment shops. She looked scared."

"It's worth a shot," said James.

Cheri faced the chart again and pointed to the name Jazz. Under his name, she had written, "Investors in Brazilian gold mine."

Under MOTIVE she wrote the same for everybody: "Money And/Or Revenge." The ALIBI column was empty. "We could fill in the alibi for Perry, tentatively at least," said James. "He told us he was in meetings all day after getting back from Santa Fe. What else have we got?"

Cheri shook her head. "The two wives claim they were alone. Kati was home studying her lines for *Suffer Queen*, and Leslie was home nursing her ankle. Pepita looks home free. She was in Rio. Even with a private jet she couldn't have flown to New York, pushed Benjamin off the balcony and been back in Brazil the same day."

"Yeah, but Luis was here," said James. "He lost money with Ben, plus he can't account for his time that day."

"Exactly. When are we going to Rio?"

"Have to wait to hear from the Captain, but that trip is too expensive for this police department, or any department."

"I know but I can dream." She turned back to the chart. "Did I leave anybody out?"

"Tina, the hot Cuban masseuse. What are you putting down for her motive?""A question mark. We'll work on it, but for now I'll put Robbery. And bad sex. Okay?"

"He laughed. "Sure. We also have to interview Ben's clients, everybody who invested in that worthless gold mine. We ought to do that soon."

"That's next." She stood in front of the chart. "I also want to visit emergency rooms. Leslie's story about her sprained ankle doesn't sound kosher. She told us she didn't go anywhere for the pain even though it was killing her. If she visited an E.R. it won't prove she injured the ankle on Ben's balcony. But it'll prove she lied. And her lies are starting to pile up."

She went back to the column headed MOTIVE jotting notes on the side in washable purple ink. Then they pored over the list of clients who invested in the Brazilian gold mine. Cheri pointed to the name Hogwood Jones of Sagaponack, Long Island. Didn't you say you called him?"

"Yeah, there's a caretaker on the premises," said James. "The master of the house was out, never called me back. There's more. I went into the database for Hogwood. A string of arrests including domestic abuse, assault and battery."

She stopped, spun around and faced him. "Any jail time?"

"You kidding? said James "The guy probably has big bucks and a hot-shot attorney on retainer."

"What else did you find out?" she asked.

"Something very interesting. Benjamin Rabinowitz took out a restraining order against Hogwood Jones. Stalking."

"Whoa..." she cried. Want to take a drive out there today?"

"Yeah, let's do it."

"Meanwhile, I have an idea," said Cheri. "Give me a minute here. I want to check the name of one of the investors who might be Russian."

James walked over and stood behind her.

"See that name?" she asked.

"Yeah, Balaban," he said. "But Balaban is not a Russian sounding name."

"Just wait," said Cheri, sounding excited.

She pulled up Russian last names on Wikipedia and clicked on the letter "B."

"Here it is," she shouted. "Balabanov. Somebody from Russia shortened the name, probably to Americanize it."

"Holy shit," said James. "Anything on a Balaban in the computer about arrests? Jail time?"

She Googled the database. "Nada," she said. "I'll keep checking. Meanwhile, let's drive out to Long Island and check out a stalker named Hogwood Jones."

Chapter 35

The Long Island Expressway was stop and go all the way. As they approached the village of Sagaponack, Cheri anticipated seeing million dollar mansions and rolling lawns. She did not expect Hogwood Jones's home to look like an ad for a handyman's special. As soon as they laid eyes on it they agreed that it resembled a Charles Adams cartoon in *The New Yorker Magazine.*

As soon as James pulled into the circular driveway he looked around then mumbled, "Hang on. This can't be the house." The driveway looked like a junkyard with rusting auto parts, an old refrigerator, flat tires, and a dented washing machine. Cheri checked the address again to make sure it was the right place. Shrugging her shoulders she said, "This is it."

"What a mess," James mumbled. "Let's get the story on this place and on some weirdo named Hogwood Jones."

"I Googled Sagaponack," said Cheri. "Mansions sell for millions here. A lot of homes sit on what were once potato fields. But something is weird about this place. The owner of this spread was a big investor with Ben, but I don't smell money."

"Me neither. Even if the guy lost big bucks, the house would still look okay and this mess didn't happen overnight."

They rang the bell. No answer and nobody peered out of a dormer window on the top floor. "No mad woman in the attic staring down at us," said James. Looking through a side window they saw a mess of cobwebs on the furniture, walls, even ceilings as if the place had never been dusted. The place reminded Cheri of Miss Haversham's house in Dickens' *Great Expectations*. There were dusty looking lamps with torn lampshades, but none of the lamps were turned on. Lastly, they noticed a huge elm tree around the back of the house ready to land on the roof during the next hurricane. And Long Island gets bad hurricanes, thought Cheri.

She rang the bell again and heard it ring inside the house. She also smelled a wood-burning fireplace. Somebody was likely home. As they stood looking up at the brick and stone house Cheri told James, "I was in a one-act play years ago titled *This Property Is Condemned* by Tennessee Williams. I'm having a sense of déjà vu."

"Doesn't look condemned yet." said James. "It's damn run down, though. I'm surprised the town hasn't gotten on this guy's ass. Zoning boards in the Hamptons are strict. Maybe that's why the owner isn't home. He's hiding."

Following a path around to the back of the house they spotted an old wooden cabin about twenty-five yards away. There was a growling dog nearby, but before they had a chance to backtrack, a pit-bull bounded up to them, teeth bared. They stopped in their tracks while the dog gnashed its teeth and snarled at them. "Stay back," said Cheri. "Let me handle this. I know dogs."

She approached the dog and whispered, "Down, boy."

"Be careful," said James. "Don't get too close." The dog bounded toward Cheri and before she knew it, the animal was chomping on the hem of her coat.

"Leave it!" Cheri shouted. She took a deep breath, determined not to show fear. When the dog finally let go, she whispered, "Good boy," hoping to calm the animal down. But she wasn't planning to pat it on the head the way she had trained dogs back home.

"We better head back to the car," called James.

"Not yet. We need to look around first. Here's what to do," she shouted, "come toward me slowly. When you get close, stand still. You have to show a dog who's in charge. And I'm trying to show this beast that I'm the alpha dog."

James looked worried but did as she suggested. She knew he had been bitten on the lip when he was ten years old and received stitches. An aggressive dog still scared the hell out of him.

The dog didn't move until Cheri started walking away. Suddenly, the animal jumped up, nearly knocking her over. When she tried to grab the dog's collar, the animal bit the top of her hand.

"Damn," she cried, rubbing the wound.

James rushed to her side. "Lucky he didn't bite through the skin. Let's get out of here. We'll come back another time." They turned and walked toward their car with the dog still snarling. After they walked about ten feet someone shouted, "What the hell are you doing here?"

They spotted a tall, skinny man behind a row of pine trees. He stood hunched over, feet apart, a shotgun pointed at their heads. "Move and I'll shoot both of youse."

The man, who Cheri figured to be the caretaker, was wearing tan baggy pants and a dirty flannel shirt. He had a gray beard and a gray ponytail. As he moved closer, she could smell body odor. He smirked at them, showing rotting teeth among those missing. His accent sounded Texan.

Cheri called out. "We're detectives. Put your gun down or I'll shoot." She held out her hand. "Look what your dog did to me. Did this animal get shots for rabies?"

"Yeah, what's it to you?"

You're lucky he did or we'd take this animal back with us and you'd never see him again."

"Like hell you would. This dog is guarding my property. What do you want?"

"We're looking for Mr. Jones."

"Hogwood's his name."

"Is he around?" asked James, stepping forward.

"Who are you?

"We're NYPD detectives," he said, as they flashed their badges.

"Mess with Hogwood and I'll blow your brains out." He moved a step closer and grumbled. "Those are phony badges; I know a real one when I see one. You're a repo man from the bank, but you're not foreclosing on this property. Joneses have lived here going back to the late eighteen hundreds when Hogwood's ancestors had a potato field on this spot."

Cheri tried to calm him down out by saying, "Impressive place you have here."

"You lying piece of shit. It's run down 'cause people from the bank are harassing us and we don't have time to fix it up."

"We're not from the bank," James shouted. "We have a few questions for Hogwood. Is he here?"

"No. And this is my property. Hogwood gave me this cabin and I'm not letting you in. Besides, I don't think you want to go in that house. You might find a stinking dead body." As he came closer, James pointed his service revolver at the caretaker.

"You don't have a search warrant. I don't have to let you in my house or in the big house. If you're not from the bank, then you're from the zoning board. Either way, you're both lying vermin. And I just might blow your brains out. I have cancer and was given only six month to live so I don't give a shit about getting killed."

"Drop the gun," said James, "or we'll haul you down to the police station."

Cheri moved fast, did a high kick and knocked the gun out of his hand.

He looked at the ground and said, "You a kick-boxer? I don't do that fancy shit, but I can wrastle you to the ground."

James kept his gun aimed at the caretaker as Cheri picked up the gun.

"I'll tell you why I'm suspicious. Somebody came here recently and tried to talk Hogwood into selling this property to build condos." He spit a wad of chewing tobacco on the ground. "I blew his head off. That got rid of him." He started cackling then continued. "He deserved to die. So will you two if you if you keep snooping around here."

"We'll return–with a search warrant," said Cheri. "Tell Hogwood we want to question him about the death of Benjamin Rabinowitz."

The caretaker stared at them through slitted eyes. "You mean that guy who went head first over a balcony? Hogwood and I know who pushed him."

"Who?" asked James.

Silence as the caretaker grinned a nearly toothless smile but didn't answer.

"We'll be back," said Cheri. "And you'll tell us what the hell you know."

"Get your damn search warrant." He spat on the ground again then turned and walked back to what had once been an ivy-covered guest cottage on a wealthy estate. Now, it resembled a dilapidated shack. The dog remained where it had been, snarling at the detectives.

They drove to a drugstore where Cheri bought a tube of Neosporin. They also talked to shopkeepers and learned that the town has been trying to evict Hogwood for years but he has a fancy lawyer in East Hampton.

Driving back to Manhattan, traffic was stop and go again. By then, it had also started snowing.

"Do you think he could be dangerous or he's just nuts?" Cheri asked after they parked in front of her apartment building.

"We'll find out more when we go back. But I'll shoot that damn dog if he tries to bite you again." He hesitated then said. "Sorry I wasn't much help." He massaged her hand and asked if it hurt.

She shook her head. "Damn that low-life and his ugly mutt. We need to catch a break in this case."

"Don't get discouraged," he said. "We still have the rest of the suckers who invested in Ben's gold mine. And we have Leslie scheduled for Friday. She's cagey, so I'll give you a lot of space with her."

Chapter 36

"I'd love to find the hooded coat our mystery woman wore," said Cheri, after she walked into the squad room the next morning. "I'd like to check out consignment shops today. That okay with you?"

He nodded then suggested she call around first before driving all over town.

"Small shopkeepers are busy, better to check out the shops in person. I'll start near Leslie's condo and work my way along the Upper East Side."

Armed with a list of names and addresses, she grabbed her hat and coat and gave James a military salute. "See you later, probably not until after lunch."

"Good luck. And check in."

"Will do."

She picked out a department vehicle, drove east on 86th Street, then south on Fifth Avenue to 22nd Street, close to Gramercy Park where Leslie lives. She parked in front of the first shop and placed a Police Department placard on the dashboard. After stepping inside, she inquired about a black woolen winter coat with a hood.

"Sorry," said the saleswoman. "We're showing clothes for spring now, but I can take your name and number in case we get one in." Cheri doubted she'd ever hear from the woman but she left contact information

As she got back inside the car and buckled up, she was glad James had given her the okay. But after the next two shops turned into a dead bounce, she decided to try consignment shops farther from Leslie's apartment. Cheri drove north to Madison Avenue and 76th Street, more than fifty blocks from Leslie's Gramercy Park condo, but where prices were higher on everything. She had two shops in that area to visit.

The first shop was closed. The second one was L.A. Boutique Resale on Madison Avenue. She rang the bell and waited for the woman inside to open the door. After browsing for a few minutes, the owner introduced herself and asked if she was looking for anything specific.

"I've been looking all over for a black winter coat with a hood."

"I have one in the back. I was saving it for myself but I can part with it if that's what you're looking for." She walked in the back room and came back carrying a black hooded coat.

Cheri smiled at the saleswoman and told her, "Just what I want." After flashing her badge and I.D., she asked for the name and address of the woman who brought it in.

The owner appeared startled. "I can't give you that information. You need a warrant, don't you?"

"It's not necessary. This is standard police procedure, I assure you."

The shop owner didn't respond at first then whispered, "I'm going to call the local police station and check, if you don't mind."

"It isn't necessary," said Cheri, holding up her badge. "This speaks for itself."

"If you say so." The owner clasped her fingers together and continued looking at Cheri. "I won't get in trouble, will I?"

"Not at all. It's not a big case. Nothing like murder."

"Murder? I hope not."

"Petty theft," said Cheri. "That's all."

After being reassured that she wouldn't get in trouble, the owner walked over to her computer and checked the database. "Here's all the information. The woman who brought the coat in was..." The phone rang and the owner held up her index finger.

Cheri felt her heart thump as she waited for the call to end.

The owner listened to the person at the other end then said, "Uh-huh, hold on a sec." She looked for a particular dress on a rack before going back to the phone. After saying she'd hold the dress, the call ended and the owner returned to her computer. "Now, I can't find the name."

She stopped and pointed. "Here it is. A Mrs. Leslie Rabinowitz brought this coat in last week."

Cheri exhaled deeply, then asked the price.

"A hundred ninety-five dollars. It's a good coat, check the label."

"No need. It's a deal. After she paid with a check and thanked the owner, she left with the coat on her arm and a shit-ass grin on her face. She was so anxious to show James the coat she didn't call him. Instead, she drove as fast as she could through crowded Manhattan traffic.

"Look what I found," she cried, as she ran through the squad room straight to James's desk. "Leslie's coat," she exclaimed, then told him the story.

"You done good," he said, giving her a thumbs up. "Leslie's coming in tomorrow. Let's see how she tries to talk her way out of this."

Before they left for the day, Detective Melo called from Rio. He sounded disappointed as he told Cheri, "Luis still hasn't called to take a lie detector test."

He's secretly happy, thought Cheri. Now he can hit on Pepita, Melo recovered for the moment and added, "Maybe some day I travel to New York. In the meantime, if you want vacation from snow in New York you can visit me in Rio. I will take you to dinner and make sure you stay at nicest hotel in Rio. Dinner will be my treat, Detective Marsh."

"I'll keep that in mind," she told the Brazilian detective. She couldn't wait to tell Caz about the invitation and imagined her friend saying, "I'll go in place of you. He never met you. He won't know I'm impersonating Senorita Marsh." Cheri pictured the two of them laughing about that. Meanwhile, Luis was still a suspect.

Chapter 37

"Play it cool when Leslie arrives," said James. "Leave questions about the coat for last."

"That's what I was planning to do."

After a soft knock at the door, Leslie was ushered into the room. It was the first time Cheri noticed Leslie wearing foundation, blush, and mascara. She's a good looking woman. Too bad she wasted her time with that philandering husband.

Cheri offered to hang Leslie's coat up, but she chose to keep it on her lap. Suit yourself, she thought. You're not going to leave any sooner holding onto it.

James nodded to Cheri. She pulled over a chair and faced Leslie.

"First of all," said Leslie. "I checked with the lawyer handling the class action suit. Jazz, I mean Dimitri Balabanov did call and he's going over to the lawyer's office to sign papers. He told the lawyer on the phone that his cousin, Sergei, a gang leader in Brighton Beach, put him up to kidnapping the dog. The lawyer said Jazz cried and told him he was sorry about the dog. He also told the lawyer he gave the dog to his niece in Brooklyn. The dog was fine, wasn't hurt in any way."

"That's good news for you," said Cheri. "Let's wait and see if he keeps his word. If not, agree to meet him and we'll give you an empty briefcase for him and nab him when he takes it from you."

"I'm not crazy about that idea," said Leslie. "Scares me. I hope he keeps his word and I never hear from him again. He also has more to gain by working with the lawyer."

"We'll see about that," said Cheri. "Meanwhile, I'd like to go over something again. Around the time Ben was murdered you sprained your ankle so badly you thought it was broken. Yet you didn't go the E.R. or to a doctor. Why not?"

Leslie began fidgeting with her ring, a small green and blue opal set in gold. "I've sprained it so many times in the past I knew what to do. I went home and iced it." She sounded irritated then added. "We went over this before."

"That's okay," said Cheri. "We'll go over it again. Did you go out later that afternoon or evening?"

Leslie shook her head. "No. My ankle was still swollen and painful. It stayed like that for days."

"It was painful, but you didn't have it checked out?" said James. "Did you think it was sprained or broken?"

"I thought it was at first."

"Sprained or broken, which was it?"

"I thought it was broken. She stopped and coughed. "No, I mean I thought it was sprained."

"You sounded confused for a moment," said Cheri. "You need to refresh your memory." James moved closer, towering over Leslie. "Did you injure that ankle on Ben's balcony?"

"No," she shouted. "I was never on Ben's balcony."

"The results should be back from the lab soon. We'll find out if your fingerprints were on that balcony," said James. He winked at Cheri and she picked up the questioning. "According to Ben's cell records, you spoke to him on the phone the day he was murdered. Did he call you?"

"Yes."

"Did he want to see you?"

"No. He called to ask me the name of an art gallery. He wanted to sell a painting." She hesitated. "That's all, very short conversation."

The detectives waited, giving Leslie time to offer more information. When James asked if there was anything she wanted to add, she shook her head. There was silence until she blurted out, "There is something you should know. It doesn't have to do with me, but it's important."

"What is it?" asked James.

"Kati was stealing from Ben." Leslie loosened a scarf around her neck. "Ben lost a lot of money in the bear market. He was trying to make a come-back and Kati knew that. But she kept treating her friends to expensive restaurants."

"Who paid the bills," asked James.

"Ben paid them. He paid all her credit card bills. She didn't pay for anything."

"Go on," said Cheri, in an intimate tone. She noticed that James hung back, giving the women plenty of space as if they were two ladies having a friendly lunch.

"Here's the thing," said Leslie, playing with the shoulder strap on her purse, "Ben wasn't happy with Kati from the beginning of their marriage. They led separate lives and kept separate checking accounts."

"Go on," said Cheri.

"Ben transferred money into Kati's account instead of giving her cash, easier that way, he said. But after a while he noticed that money was missing from his account."

"How do you know?" asked Cheri.

"He asked my advice about how to handle that."

James cleared his throat as if reminding Leslie that he was still in the room. "And what advice did you give him?" Barely looking at him Leslie said, "I suggested he stop transferring money into her account, cancel Kati's credit cards, and discontinue her access to his account."

"Did he?"

"I don't know. He died a few days later." Cheri hopped up on the desk and crossed her legs. "Let me get the story straight. Are you suggesting that after Ben cut off Kati's money's supply, she pushed him off the balcony?"

Leslie glared at Cheri then told her, "I wasn't saying that." She pulled a Kleenex out of her purse and wiped her forehead. It was seventy-five degrees in the room, but she was sweating. "I was saying she was totally dependent on Ben's money. He told me she hated that. But you know the famous saying about the theater: You can make a killing, but you can't make a living. Most actors barely make it in New York financially."

Cheri nodded as she edged closer to the end of the desk. "What else did Ben tell you?"

The detectives watched Leslie as she took a deep breath then exhaled slowly. "Kati forged Ben's signature on blank checks. She denied it when he confronted her."

James faced Leslie and said, "Let me interrupt here. Ben paid all the bills for the condo they lived in, so Katie wasn't destitute, was she?"

"No, but when Ben cut off her credit cards, she didn't have access to any cash. The credit cards were her ATM."

Cheri frowned, still mulling over the story about the poor little rich girl who lost her shopping and restaurant privileges. She stood up and walked around the desk, stopping a few feet from Leslie. "Were you jealous when Kati moved into Ben's condo?"

"No," she answered, emphatically. "Ben and I were separated by then."

"Are you happy now that he can't be with Kati?"

"Of course not!"

James moved forward and asked, "Did the bank cash the forged checks?"

"I don't know. You'll have to check with them."

"We will. Meanwhile, let's get back to the passports. We have evidence that they were for you and Ben. Anything you want to tell us about that?"

Leslie nodded. "Ben had a financial setback recently. He didn't tell me what it was. But he told me he still loved me, would get in trouble if he stayed in New York and begged me to leave the country with him." She looked exhausted as if reliving that moment had drained her emotionally. "I thought we were going to use our own passports. I wouldn't have done anything illegal."

Cheri made a clicking sound with her tongue as if they were two girlfriends confiding secrets. "It must have hurt deeply when he changed his mind."

Leslie nearly jumped out of her seat. "He didn't change his mind. He postponed our trip."

"For how long?"

"Indefinitely. He said he had business to take care of first. Then he died." She wiped her eyes with a tissue then stuffed it back in her purse.

"Bad timing," said Cheri.

Leslie nodded. "A few days before Ben died, he told me he and Kati had a huge fight about money. He told her to get a real job for a change. Kati stormed out of the apartment and was gone overnight. He thought she had a lover."

"Interesting," Cheri mumbled. "He obviously still had feelings for you."

Leslie gave her a wan smile and Cheri suddenly felt sorry for her: the older woman replaced by a flashier model. She lost her husband and now it was probably too late to resume her career as a concert pianist. She was away too long.

"I'm coming down with a cold or maybe the flu," said Leslie, sniffling. "I don't want you to catch it. Can I leave now?"

The detectives exchanged glances and James said, "Not yet. I have a few more questions. "You told us you don't own a black hooded coat, correct?"

"That's right." She looked from James to Cheri then back again like a frightened child.

"A woman in a black hooded coat was seen on camera in the lobby of Ben's apartment," said James." More than once."

Leslie looked down at her hands, clasped on her lap, and said in a muffled tone, "A lot of people in a building that size–could have been anybody."

"But you swear it wasn't you, correct? said James.

Leslie glanced around the room and settled on Cheri's face. Facing her, she said, softly, "Correct."

James nodded to Cheri then gestured toward the door. She knew immediately what he wanted her to do. She turned to Leslie and said, "There's something I'd like you to do for me. I'll be right back." There was silence in the interrogation room while they waited. When Cheri returned she had the black winter coat draped over her arm. Looking at the coat, Leslie's face turned pale, as if she might faint.

"Can you try it on for us?" asked James.

"It's not mine"

"Try it on!" he repeated.

Leslie placed her coat on the chair and pulled on the black hooded winter coat. "Odd," said James. "It's a perfect fit. Now you want to tell us the truth?"

Leslie collapsed in the chair, not even bothering to move the coat she had worn when she arrived. She covered her eyes with one hand and took a deep breath.

"Speak to us."

"I don't have anything to say. You trapped me."

The detectives stood next to each other, waiting. Leslie was stonewalling and that's probably making James pissed, thought Cheri. Leslie didn't utter a sound. Even her coughing subsided. It was silent in the room as she sat as rigid as a mannequin.

James moved closer to Leslie. "We don't have all day."

She accepted a Certs from Cheri then said, "Okay... After Ben postponed our trip I wanted to talk to him about it, but he refused to see me. I knew he was staying overnight for weeks at the West End Avenue apartment because of friction with Kati. And I knew his work hours so I waited in the lobby a few times hoping to talk to him. I had a feeling he was drinking heavily or using drugs, and I was afraid he'd get angry at me, so each time I was in the lobby I chickened out and never called him to say I was downstairs."

"That's it?" said James.

Leslie dropped her hands on her lap. "There is something else. I wanted to see if he was bringing a woman home with him. I couldn't help myself, especially with his history. I wore the coat with the hood because it covered part of my face.

"You were stalking him," said Cheri.

"I wouldn't call it that," Leslie whispered.

"So, why didn't you make a date to meet him?"

"He didn't want to see me, said I was nagging him."

"Why did you lie about the coat?" asked James.

"I was afraid you would think I killed Ben."

"Did you?"

"NO."

After Leslie handed the hooded coat back, Cheri folded it over her arm. "If you had told the truth from the beginning you could have saved me a lot of trouble."

"I'm sorry," she mumbled, her face buried in her hands.

"You can leave. We don't have any more questions," said James. "We'll be in touch. By the way, any more texts?"

"Just the one I told you about on the phone. The one that said, "Pay up, bitch, or you'll end up like Ben."

"Yeah, you told us about that one," said Cheri. "Let me know if you get any more."

"The texts might stop now that he went to see the lawyer about the lawsuit." She stood up and pulled on her down coat. As she turned the doorknob, she turned and mouthed the words, "I'm sorry," then left the interrogation room.

Cheri made sure nobody was listening outside then asked James "What do you think?"

"She obviously stalked him. Who knows what else she did?"

"Cheri nodded. "And revenge was a strong motive, especially after he changed his mind about running away with her. She said he postponed the trip. We'll never know."

James leaned back in his chair and rubbed his jaw. "She's a sick pup when it comes to love, kept coming back for more punishment. She also could have made up that stuff about Kati. We'll check it out." He leaned across the desk and whispered, "Your hunch about the coat was right."

She looked at him and smiled.

"In my opinion," said James, "Leslie just moved up a notch. She and Luis are tied for first place."

Chapter 38

Armed with a search warrant the detectives returned to the town of Sagaponack to interview Hogwood Jones, the Third. As soon as James parked, they stood next to the police car and using a megaphone called for the caretaker whose name they had since learned was Edwin.

"Edwin," James shouted. "We have a search warrant. Step outside and bring the dog with you. Put a leash on it then tie the leash to a tree. Hear me?" He repeated the message before Edwin stepped out of the cabin without the dog.

"Get the dog," James shouted. "Now."

Edwin walked towards them and mumbled something about Hogwood.

"Louder," he called. "We can't hear you."

"Hogwood ain't back yet."

"We don't care. We have a search warrant for your cabin and the main house. We'll talk to Hogwood another time. Get the animal now and tie it to a tree. I don't want my partner getting bit again. If the dog gets loose, I'll kill it, hear me?"

"I hear you, you bastard." He took his time inside while James and Cheri waited, service revolvers aimed at the cabin door. "If he comes out with his shotgun raised or with the dog off the leash, aim for the ground," said James.

"Gotcha," she said.

"Edwin, where the hell are you?" James shouted.

They waited with guns raised as the door creaked open but nobody stepped outside. "What the hell's he doing?" Cheri asked.

"The bastard is playing with us," said James, pointing his gun in front of him ready to shoot, if necessary.

Edwin stepped outside and started walking towards them, one hand in his pocket.

"Put your hands on your head," James called, "or I'll shoot." As Edwin continued walking toward them, hands at his sides, Cheri took a flying leap and wrestled Edwin to the ground while James cuffed him.

"You could have done this the easy way," she told him as he lay on the ground.

Edwin was shouting curses at the detectives as a man came running out of the main house.

"Who are you?"

"Police. Who are you?"

"Hogwood Jones, the Third. I live here. I own this house and all the land as far as you can see."

While the detectives flashed their shields and IDs, Edwin shouted, "Don't believe them. They have phony badges."

"Shut up," said Cheri, showing Hogwood the search warrant. As he walked closer she got a better look at him. He was nearly bald with an unkempt ponytail and a child's barrette on either side of his head. From his ruddy complexion and red nose, he appeared to be a barely functioning alcoholic. He smelled like a wino, too.

When Cheri researched Hogwood's background before their second trip she learned that he had attended Princeton for one year before dropping out. Evidently, the Joneses had enough money to buy their son's entry into an Ivy League school but no way of keeping him there. James ordered Hogwood to get the dog and tie the animal to a tree so they could search inside. When Hogwood insisted the dog wouldn't bite, Cheri pointed her gun at him and said, "Do what the detective told you."

After the dog was finally tied to a tree, they all went into the cabin where the detectives searched for anything related to Ben Rabinowitz.

Hogwood refused to answer any questions about investing in a gold mine. "None of your damn business who I deal with. You're talking to a Jones." After they finished with the cabin, they walked over to the main building. The house was a two-story saltbox built circa early nineteenth century, Cheri figured, with additional rooms added to the original structure.

Edwin continued screaming obscenities at the detectives while Hogwood shouted, "Shut up, you're making my hangover worse." As soon as the detectives inched their way forward, the dog pulled loose and began growling. Cheri guessed the dog's weight at approximately ninety-five pounds and she didn't feel like dealing with it again. The dog was also dirty from lying on the ground.

"Edwin, tell your dog to come!" ordered Cheri.

"If he tries to bite me or my partner, I'll shoot him," James hollered.

Edwin still didn't give the command.

"Hang on." Cheri reached in her pocket, pulled out dog treats and threw them on the ground.

"Good thinking," whispered James. "But he's going to want more."

She smiled and pulled out another handful. She threw the treats on the ground until the dog stopped growling.

Hogwood finally called, "Brutus, COME," and the animal obeyed.

Later, while searching the main house Cheri pulled a manila folder out of a desk drawer filled with yellowing papers. Scrawled on top of the folder was the name: "Benjamin Rabinowitz." Underneath that, it said, "Gold mine in Brazil."

Cheri turned and faced Hogwood. "Want to tell us about this?"

"It's bullshit, wasn't me who killed Ben. "

When pressed for an alibi the day Ben died, Hogwood cackled like a cartoon character. "Ben deserved to die, but I'll check with my private secretary. She keeps track of all my appointments. Today's her day off."

"You do that," said James," and get back to us. If not, we'll nail your ass to the front of this house." He pointed to the empty bottles strewn on the floor. "You drink too much."

"Liquor won't kill me. I'll probably rot in jail first."

Cheri exchanged glances with James but decided to let it go.

James stood over Edwin who was sprawled on the couch. "Where were you on January twelfth?"

"I was in town talking to my accountant about my trust fund."

"Smart ass," said James.

"Then take these damn handcuffs off."

"I'll take them off before we leave. Cheri continued looking at both men. "You both better have valid alibis. Until then, you're both suspects, hear me?"

"I hears you," said Hogwood.

A back wall filled with floor to ceiling bookcases was crammed with moldy smelling books. Cheri knew that James was allergic to mold. When she glanced at him, he looked as if he was going to gag. He pushed everything they needed into his briefcase, un-cuffed Edwin and suggested the two men spend the day cleaning up the mess. "This place is a pig sty."

Hogwood chuckled. "You ain't seen nothin' We cleaned up for your visit. You're the pigs, not us, you stinking coppers."

"Shut up," Cheri shouted.

As soon as they were in their car, James opened his window for fresh air. "If their alibis don't check out we'll have to come back. I'll wear a painter's mask next time." After taking a another gulp of fresh air, he continued, "Did you ever read about the Collier Brothers? The two crazies hoarded stuff for half a century. They even had a Model T Ford in their living-room."

"I read about them," she said. "They were sick-o."

"Which reminds me," James whispered. "I have to pull over."

He waited for a safe spot before he pulled over. He jumped out, his hand clamped over his mouth.

When he got back in the car she asked, "Feel better?"

He nodded. "Let's get out of here."

Traffic was heavy and he said very little while he concentrated. Meanwhile, Cheri thought about the house, the two weirdos, and the possibility that one or both of them killed Benjamin. They struck her as demented creatures. Possibly evil, too.

Chapter 39

They were working on their Motive and Alibi chart Wednesday afternoon when Cheri said, "Let's take a break. Leslie said her daughter's back from vacation. I'm going to drive out to Park Slope in Brooklyn and interview her. I called yesterday and told her I might come out today. She works at home and gave me directions."

"Good idea," said James. "I'll keep calling the suckers, I mean the investors in the gold mine."

She told him she'd check in from Brooklyn and left just as he picked up the phone to start making calls.

The drive to Park Slope turned out to be shorter than she had expected. As she drove along the along the clean tree-lined streets, she considered Park Slope an attractive place to live. Prospect Park was nearby. So was the Brooklyn Museum, the Botanical Gardens, and the main branch of the public library. All that, and she'd still be pretty close to work. Nah, she decided, she'd be too far from James. And he would never leave Manhattan. He told her that he was born in the area once called Hell's Kitchen like his mother and grandmother before him, and he would die there. Besides, his apartment was rent-stabilized.

After reaching the brownstone on Third Street, near Prospect Park West, Cheri rang the doorbell. An attractive woman in her twenties answered the door. As Susan ushered Cheri down a long foyer past the kitchen and into the living room, Cheri was greeted by the lingering smell of tomato soup and toast. One wall held a gas fireplace. On the opposite wall stood an ebony baby grand piano. There was also a collection of modern art. As soon as they were seated Cheri placed her tape recorder on the coffee table and turned it on after asking permission first.

Susan resembled her mother, Leslie, in appearance and poise. When Cheri asked if she worked at home full-time Susan nodded and said she was a computer graphics designer.

"Interesting," said Cheri. "How was the Caribbean?"

"Great, just got back."

"Good timing. We've had a little snow," said Cheri, facetiously. She planned on keeping the interview short. She wanted to get back in time to help James with calls to the investors. She leaned forward and peered at Susan. "Ben had three wives but only one daughter. You. Did you consider him your father?"

"He was my step-father but I called him dad. And he always introduced me as his daughter."

Susan smiled and Cheri noticed tiny lines forming around her eyes. Probably a sun worshipper or a skier. Maybe both.

"He was the greatest dad," Susan continued. "We went skiing every Christmas and again during spring break."

My ESP was right, thought Cheri. She figured he was a lousy husband but a good father. "You were lucky," she said.

"You know something funny?" said Susan. "Ben was a serious guy when he was dressed in a suit and tie. When he changed into jeans or a ski outfit, he loosened up." She thought for a second. "I'll sum Ben up for you. I once had a college interview during a winter from hell, like this year. I told my parents I'd cancel the appointment. Ben saw how disappointed I was. He told me, Get ready, snow never stopped me before." He drove me up to Poughkeepsie and I got accepted at Vassar."

Cheri smiled. "Nice story. Anything else you want to tell me about him?"

Susan thought for a second. "He was generous, not just with money. Money was a means to an end for him like taking my mother and me on ski trips. Even after he and my mom separated, he gave me advice about my career."

"What was your natural father like?"

A dark cloud seemed to pass over Susan's face. "Genes. That's all he gave me."

"A few more questions, then I'll let you get back to work. How did your mother and Ben get along?"

Susan laughed loud this time. "It was interesting. My mom is a die-hard Democrat and Ben was a staunch Republican."

Cheri crossed her legs and watched Susan's face closely during this exchange. "Did arguments ever become physical between them?"

"No, never. Other than politics, they had a lot in common–travel, music, skiing."

"How did your mother react when Ben left her for a younger woman?"

"My mom took it hard, especially at first. But she adjusted." Cheri wondered what Susan meant by "at first." Until she stalked him and figured out a way to get revenge? She sat and waited for Susan to continue. "She gave piano lessons and walked dogs at Bideawee. She kept busy."

They went over a few more questions about Leslie and Ben's relationship until Cheri changed course and asked Susan what she thought of her step-mother.

"Kati? She's very competitive. She hated sharing Ben with anybody, even me. I think she considered me a rival. I was his daughter." She shrugged. "She also has a bad temper."

"As far as you know, did she come from money?"

"You kidding? She lived with three roommates before she married my dad. Her parents couldn't help her financially either." Cheri leaned forward and checked the tape recorder. It was working fine. "Did you see your mother shortly after Ben died?"

"She came here the day after he died. She was distraught."

"Was your mother limping at that time?" Susan shifted nervously in her chair and said, "I don't remember."

Cheri felt encouraged by Susan's answers and continued. "Did she tell you she sprained her ankle?"

"She mentioned it in passing after I noticed her wearing an Ace bandage."

Interesting, thought Cheri, then proceeded to ask the question she'd been wanting to ask since she arrived. She leaned forward and looked at Susan as if they were old friends. "Did you try to convince her to get it x-rayed?"

There was a visible change in Susan's expression from warm to stone faced. Was she protecting her mother? Cheri wondered. And why?

"I tried to talk her into having it x-rayed," said Susan, "but you don't know my mother. She's stubborn."

Next question, thought Cheri. The most important one. "Is it possible your mother stopped at an E.R. nearby before she visited and forgot to mention it?"

"That's possible. She said it hurt pretty bad. That's why I told her to have it checked out."

Cheri felt excited about where this was going then asked, "Where's the closest E.R?"

"Methodist Hospital on Seventh Avenue."

I'm making progress, thought Cheri, I'm not stopping now. "Did your mother have any visible bruises when she visited?" Susan winced, obviously connecting the dots between a sprained ankle and bruises. "No, unless you consider her sprained ankle."

"Tell me about it," said Cheri."

"After she showed me her ankle, I told my mom it looked like it might be broken. It was huge and the color of an eggplant." Susan looked as if she wanted to retract those words then added quickly, "It's not a big deal to sprain an ankle." She stopped abruptly and said she had to make a phone call.

They took a break while Susan went in the other room to make the call. Cheri walked around the room and checked out the artwork. When Susan returned, Cheri asked if she bought all the paintings.

"My father bought me two of them." She pointed to a seascape and a large yellow and orange abstract watercolor. My dad had a good eye," said Susan. "He studied art history in college then got an MBA at Harvard." She laughed. "Then he became a stockbroker."

"Interesting change," said Cheri

They shook hands at the front door and Cheri made a mental note to visit Methodist Hospital. She needed to get back to the police station so she decided to drive instead of walk. After waiting nearly half an hour she finally spoke to somebody in the emergency room but it turned out to be a waste of time.

As soon as Cheri left the hospital she pulled out her phone and called James. "How're you doing with calls to the investors," she asked.

"Slow going. I'll need your help."

"No problem."

"What about you? Good visit with Leslie's daughter?"

"Yeah, interesting." She told him a little about it then James said, "Go home after you get back from Brooklyn. By the way," he whispered. "Got two tickets to the show you want to see for the night of your birthday."

"Thanks, I can't wait."

After saying goodbye, Cheri called a rehab facility on the Upper West Side and asked to speak to her grandmother.

"Nana," she said. "It's Cheri. I'm going to visit you on Sunday. I don't know what time. I'll call in the morning before I leave." Before saying good-bye, she added. "I love you, too."

While she was driving back to Manhattan, Cheri thought about Leslie's sprained ankle. If Leslie's daughter thought it might have been broken, it was probably more than a bad sprain. She conjured up a picture of Ben's gruesome death. *Leslie twisted that ankle on Ben's balcony.* It was only a hunch but one worth checking out.

Chapter 40

The next morning, Cheri showed up in the squad room before eight a.m. James looked up from his laptop and said, "Good morning," then leaned way back raising the two front legs of his chair off the floor. "Why are some men good fathers but lousy husbands? Your talk with Leslie's daughter got me thinking about that."

Cheri shrugged. Even with all her reading of psychology in college, some behavior wasn't easily explained. Her own father was a great dad but drank too much to be a great husband.

"Time to divvy up the rest of the investors," she said. "I'll start with the next guy on the list."

"Good, maybe you'll have better luck than me." The first man she called told Cheri that after Ben learned about the gold mine, he talked Perry into investing." Luckily, I trusted my instinct and didn't invest much money, had a feeling it was a scam."

She looked at the list of questions on her desk and started at the top. "Did Perry ever travel to Brazil?" she asked.

"Sure. He and Ben went there together at least once." She gestured to James that she hit pay dirt.

The man answered a few more questions then told her he had to leave for an appointment but promised to call back later.

Cheri continued calling investors, speaking to as many people as she could before James suggested it was time to take a break. As they shared information over coffee and Danish pastries at their desks, Cheri wondered aloud if it was a good day to visit emergency rooms and asked James what he thought of the idea.

He shook his head. "It's supposed to keep snowing. Why don't you call the hospitals? No need to drive around for nothing."

"I'm better off going there in person. I might get lousy information on the phone or be left holding on indefinitely. I'll wait until the weather clears. Meanwhile, I'll call a few more investors."

"Good idea," said James as he glanced at the list on his desk. He exhaled loudly as he shook his head. "Damn, Ben must have been a persuasive son of a bitch. Hundreds of suckers invested in a gold mine that wasn't producing anything. Don't people check to see where their money's going?"

Cheri shrugged. "Haven't you heard? The stock market runs on fear and greed. Same with gold mines." When she called an investor in Bal Harbour, Florida, she pictured an old man sitting by the pool with a trophy wife beside him. Instead, a young woman answered. Her father was in hospice. She didn't know much about her father's investments, but she took Cheri's number and promised to call back.

James looked at the list then told Cheri that the majority did live in Florida, probably in retirement communities. "Ben must have gotten one lead, then other investors followed like lemmings or he paid them commissions for more names. Places like Bal Harbour and Palm Beach are wealthy places, but retired people can't afford to lose money; no way to make it back." In addition to Florida, there were investors in New Jersey, Connecticut, Massachusetts, even Brooklyn."

Cheri opened the file and stared at a photo of Ben. A middle aged man with graying temples smiled up at her. Who wanted you dead? she wondered. She set the photo aside and looked at her list of investors again. Several people she had spoken to told her they were angry at Ben. A few were hopeful they would get their money back from the class action suit. Most had filled out forms for the SEC, the FBI, and an army of attorneys. One elderly man told Cheri, "I hope I live long enough to see some of my money returned. Meanwhile, I moved in with my son." Surprisingly, a few investors were forgiving and told her, "How could Ben have known the mine would go belly up? He lost some of his own money, too."

James leaned back, rubbed the back of his neck then glanced at the clock on the wall. "Still early," he said. "We can make a few more calls. You know something? I know the stock market runs on fear and greed, but it's getting even worse 'cause it's rigged against the little guy."

Cheri knew he wasn't bitter about the big money in New York. He told her more than once that he had pounded the streets as a policeman before getting promoted to Detective, Homicide Squad. But unlike the crooks on Wall Street he would never be able to afford a condo in Manhattan, even a one-bedroom. He still teared up when he talked about his elderly mother climbing four flights of steps to a crummy rent-controlled apartment. She also knew that he helped his mother with medical bills.

After popping a Tic Tac in her mouth Cheri continued scratching people off the list–too old, too sick, too hard of hearing.

"I called a lot of people on the list," said James, "including one guy who lives nearby, but he's not a person of interest. He suffers from Parkinson's. If the last guy I spoke to on the phone was right, Perry left the research to Ben believing the gold mine would make a ton of money, then invested a fortune."

They worked the phones for two more hours until James said, "Most of those calls were frustrating. Let's call it a day."

As soon as they walked out into the cold night they discovered that it had stopped snowing.

"Want to stop for a beer?" asked James.

"I'd love one, but I can't stay long. I promised Caz I'd drop by. She's worried about her mother."

"Sorry to hear that," said James. "Give Caz my love. How's your mom?"

"Good, busy making pottery. Selling it, too. People love Native American pottery."

"Cool. And your Nana?"

"Hanging tough. I'm going to visit her at the nursing home on Sunday.

"Would you like me go with you?"

Cheri smiled. "She would love to see you, but let's wait until she's stronger."

"No problem."

They continued walking, sidestepping piles of yellow snow until they reached a corner bar on Amsterdam Avenue. They weren't planning to eat so they hopped up on stools. James ordered a Guinness draft. Cheri asked for Brooklyn Pale Ale.

They spoke in whispers about the case until they heard, "Top investment banker was indicted today on insider trading involving a phony gold mine." They stopped talking as a picture flashed across the screen. It took Cheri a second to recognize Ben's partner, Perry Hartman, leaving the courthouse with his lawyer.

The detectives leaned forward and heard: "There continues to be an SEC investigation into the firm owned by two partners, one of whom either fell or was pushed off a balcony recently. Investors are claiming the partners ran a Ponzi scheme. For now, seventy million dollars is allegedly missing." After that brief bit, the program faded to a commercial.

"Damn," Cheri cried. "Seventy million bucks? How do you hide that kind of money?"

"You don't," said James. "You spend it on drugs, expensive booze, women. I think we might have been betting on the wrong people. Maybe Perry is our guy."

She nodded then glanced back at the television screen. The meteorologist was warning about an upcoming blizzard in the Northeast. "Just what we need," she said. "I want to drive to emergency rooms."

He rubbed her upper arm. "Cheer up. We'll close this case even if we have to work 24/7."

When Cheri got home she received a text from Caz inviting her to dinner.

"You're on," she wrote back. "I'll skip seaweed and algae for one night."

As soon as she stepped into Caz's apartment Cheri smelled sweet and sour shrimp. "Your house smells divine."

Caz laughed. "Divine? I don't hear that word often. Ready for dinner?" She set the table with a tablecloth and linen napkins.

While they ate and drank they talked about Caz being a role model for her nieces and nephews. "They all want to come to the States now and go to American colleges," said Caz. "A few want to take their skills back to China. The others want to stay here like I did after finishing college. I'm the progenitor," said Caz. "Like that word?"

"Love it," said Cheri. She helped herself to more rice and another glass of wine. After they finished eating, Cheri helped Caz clear the table.

"How's James?" asked Caz, pouring cups of green tea. "Still hot in bed?"

"Hotter."

Caz smiled as she passed a plate of fortune cookies.

Cheri broke one open and pretended to read. "Detective Marsh, you will soon solve important murder case." She laughed. "Wish it really said that. By the way, how are your plans for the food truck coming along?"

"Let me show you," said Caz. She pulled up pictures of several trucks on her iPhone. Told you, I looked at them with my brother. When the time comes, I'm going to buy one."

"You serious?"

Caz nodded. "Getting serious. Lucky I saved money all these years. Frugality pays."

They both ended up tired after a heavy meal so they took their cups of green tea into the living room and watched the news on CNN. When Cheri started to doze off she said she had to go home and get ready for bed. "Long day," she told Caz.

"Me too. See you soon. Maybe we'll go out for drinks."

"Good idea."

She walked down the hallway, opened her door and called James. He answered on the first ring.

"Any news from Melo?" she asked.

"No. But Luis is still high on our list."

"I agree. But I'm still betting on Leslie."

It was more of the same the next day. James continued calling investors and they told him that Ben guaranteed them huge profits from the mine. Later, while James was still working the phones Cheri called the next emergency room on her list. After holding on for more than thirty minutes, she hung up in disgust. She told James about her latest plan to drive to the remaining emergency rooms on her list.

"Be careful driving," he told her. "I saw a lot of fender benders earlier from remaining snow and ice."

She pulled on her jacket and grabbed an apple for the road. As soon as she stepped outside she chose a department vehicle, a newer model this time. Inasmuch as she came up with *bupkis* at all the emergency rooms near Leslie's home in Gramercy Park the last time, her latest plan was to visit Emergency Rooms in midtown Manhattan.

While idling for ten minutes at a construction site she started wishing for a hot bowl of venison stew. All the men in her family hunted back in Montana. They froze the meat until winter and cooked stew. Cheri licked her lips and could taste and smell the fragrant meat.

When she reached the first hospital on her list she parked as close as possible, but even with her police department sticker it was a trek to the entrance. Flashing her shield and picture I.D gave here easy access to the emergency room, but she still had to wait to talk to somebody. A nurse on duty at the first hospital told her the name sounded familiar. After checking her computer she said, "A Mrs. Markowitz visited the E.R. on January 15."

"Wrong name," said Cheri. *Maybe Leslie used an alias.* But she still asked why the woman showed up at the ER.

"Bad reaction to drugs," said the nurse.

Cheri crossed that hospital off her list and drove to the next one. Maybe this was a mistake. It was turning out be a pain driving around in heavy traffic.

After the third E.R. also turned out to be a disappointment she decided to head back to the police station. While walking to her car she realized how short the days still were. Lack of light depressed her and the constant smell of exhaust fumes sickened her. The drive back to the station was slow and frustrating. Opening the door, she found James at his laptop. He mumbled something unintelligible then looked up and asked, "How'd you make out?"

"I'm ready to scream," she said. "But I still have a few more emergency rooms on my list."

He closed his laptop and said, "Come on, I'll buy you a beer. That usually cheers you up."

"I'd love one," she said, "thanks."

They walked to the restaurant on the corner going over details of the case until they stepped inside. The bar smelled of beer and greasy hamburgers.

"Don't give up," he told her after they seated themselves on bar stools. "You have a strong hunch. Follow it." The bar was nearly empty by then due to the cold weather, but Cheri and James still whispered to each other.

"Don't worry," she said, digging into a bowl of nuts "I'm not giving up." She was hungry, as usual, and probably gaining weight. Cold weather caused her to eat more, plus she missed the gym a few times lately. The damn Rabinowitz case was driving her crazy.

"Would you like to stay for dinner?" James asked. "We can move to a table."

"I can't. I have a kickboxing class.

"When is the Martial Arts Competition?"

"Friday, seven o'clock at the gym."

"I'll be there," he said.

She drank quickly then wiped her mouth. "I'm going to check every hospital and E.R. in the vicinity of Ben's apartment next time. I'm also going to check the Upper East Side. I have a strong hunch Leslie had that ankle looked at."

He smiled as Cheri passed him the bowl of nuts and he dug in, popping a handful in his mouth. "It might not be necessary to visit every hospital," he said, licking salt off his lips. You could call a few."

Cheri moved closer to James. "Any news from Detective Melo about Luis?"

"No, I would've told you." He grabbed another handful of peanuts. "Did you ever see the film *City of God?*" he asked, before popping the nuts in his mouth.

"Sure did," she said. "According to the people who made that film, Rio has some of the worst slums in the world. They discovered oil there recently, but that's not going to help the poor. Speaking of Brazil," said Cheri. "On the slight chance we travel there, I bought a phrase book from Amazon. Just happen to have it with me." She pulled a paperback out of her purse. "Hello, *ola,* goodbye, *tchau*–pronounced like ciao in Italian, see you later, *ate mais,* and thanks, *obrigado.*"

"Obrigado," he said sincerely. "I'm impressed. You have a good ear for languages. I'm tone deaf."

She continued. "I made a list of places to visit to Rio but don't worry. You'll get to see the hotties on Ipanema Beach."

"I'll probably have eye strain from staring at your bikini." He signaled the waiter, indicating he wanted another beer. Cheri said no to another one, but dug into the bowl of salty peanuts. Problem was, they were making her thirsty for another beer.

"It isn't just the trip I want," said Cheri. "I'm anxious to interview Luis.

He raised his glass. "Here's to closing this case."

She clinked glasses with him and said, "Cheers." They finished their beers and James paid the bill.

"If Luis didn't push Ben off the balcony," said Cheri, "it could be one of the other investors. Somebody who knew Ben's schedule and surprised him at the apartment. Whoever the perp is, he's keeping a low profile."

They parted in front of the restaurant and Cheri pulled up the collar on her coat. The wind was howling, making her wish she was spending the night at his apartment. But things were moving too fast. She also had to get a good night's sleep. There were more emergency rooms to tackle in the morning.

Chapter 41

The next morning dawned cold and cloudy. Cheri arrived at the station at 8:30 a.m., pulled off her hat and coat and spied James hunched over his laptop. He gave her a wan smile. "Bad news," he mumbled.

Cheri stopped in her tracks. "Another stockbroker pushed over a balcony?"

He shook his head. "No, not that bad; the captain vetoed our trip to Rio."

"Figures," said Cheri.

She rarely saw him looking so down except when he was hung-over after a long weekend. But she doubted he still drank a lot when he was home alone. He was trying to cut back.

"It's hot in Rio," she told him, "and who wants to leave the city when it's all white and pretty?" She laughed. "I better get ready. Emergency rooms are waiting for me."

He gave her a thumbs up. "Meanwhile, I'll finish calling investors. I also want to set up appointments with a few people here in the city, especially one guy who might be a person of interest. So far he doesn't have an alibi. Told me he went to the movies alone, didn't talk to anybody then stayed for a second show."

"He's either a movie critic or a liar," said Cheri. "Good luck."

She booted up her laptop and retrieved her list of hospitals As she checked her e-mail, her thoughts turned to Rio. She swiveled her chair around and faced James. "Who wants to fly to Brazil anyway and deal with jet lag?"

Just as she was getting ready to leave, she took a call from Detective Melo. He told her that Luis agreed to another interview. "I set up camera and videotaped interrogation with him. I'm sending to you now," he said.

Cheri and James watched the videotape on his computer. There was a shot of a long hallway that was a little grainy with voices in the background. Cheri looked at James. "What's happening?"

James shrugged. "This isn't Hollywood, be patient."

They saw Luis and Pepita being ushered into Detective Melo's office. Melo looked at the camera and smiled, flashing two gold teeth on the side of his mouth. The first thing the detective told Luis and Pepita was that the New York cops might not be able to make it. That's the reason for the videotape. Detective Melo appeared pleased by the change in plans as if he was looking forward to grilling Luis alone.

The room was furnished with a metal desk, two file cabinets, and three rickety, wooden chairs. Displayed above the desk was a calendar with a photograph of nearly naked girls on Ipanema Beach. Melo turned on a tape recorder and pointed to a chair indicating Luis should sit.

When Detective Melo escorted Pepita to the door, she asked when she should pick Luis up. "We'll call you," he said, flashing a toothy smile. He was dressed like a pimp: a white linen suit, red handkerchief in his breast pocket and black huaraches. Cheri wondered why he was so vain. His face had traces of acne, and his large teeth gave him the appearance of a barracuda.

Pepita turned around in the doorway and blew Luis a kiss. He nodded and gave her a tentative smile. As soon as the door was closed, the detective straddled a chair as if he was starring in a Western movie.

"So tell me, were you one of Ben's clients?"

Luis nodded.

"Did you know the gold mine wasn't productive before your trip to the States?"

"I had some idea."

"How much money you lose in that mine?"

Luis hesitated then said, "A lot of money, don't know the total."

Detective Melo dragged his chair closer to Luis and asked, in a staccato voice, "Who else was in Ben's apartment the day he died?"

"I don't know."

The detective pulled a handkerchief out of his breast pocket and wiped his brow. "Who did you see on the balcony?" While he waited for the answer, he spread his legs out in front of him as if he had been riding a horse and needed to stretch. "Come on, talk me to me," he shouted.

"I told you, I don't know," said Luis, also raising his voice. "I only saw the outline of two people on the balcony."

Melo tucked his legs back under the chair and sat upright. "If you couldn't see clearly, how do you know it was two people?"

"It appeared that way."

Melo smirked. "Appeared? I guess you believe in UFOs also. Maybe it was one person and his shadow. Did you ever see a shadow before? Maybe it was your own shadow. You afraid of shadows?"

The clock on the wall kept ticking loudly. Luis turned to look at it then asked, "Can I please have a cup of coffee?"

"When we finish," said the detective.

Cheri and James sat side by side, elbows touching as the interrogation unfolded in Rio de Janeiro. Neither wanted to leave the room so they shared a cup of coffee which had turned cold by then.

Just then, Melo got up and adjusted the thermostat in the room. "I bet you're making it hotter in here," said Luis. "It's already hot." Melo grinned as he removed his jacket and hung it up. Luis wiped his brow with the palm of his hand. "Can you turn up the air conditioning?"

The detective narrowed his eyes and stared at Luis. "You're in the hot seat, that's why you're sweating. Or you have a guilty conscience." He took a deep breath before continuing. "You wear glasses for distance. Is that correct?"

Luis nodded, beginning to sweat more profusely.

"Were you wearing your glasses that day in Ben's apartment?"

"I don't remember."

Melo narrowed his eyes for emphasis. "The eye doctor I talked to told me you dropped off a pair of prescription eyeglasses to be repaired. On the phone the other day, Pepita told me that you have one pair of glasses for indoors and they were in the shop. She also told me you have a pair of prescription sunglasses and you took those to New York. Were you wearing sunglasses in the Ben's apartment when you saw two people on the dark balcony?"

"Luis shook his head and shouted "NO. My sunglasses were in my pocket."

Dtective Melo stood up and jabbed his forefinger in Luis's chest. "Pepita told me about the glasses because she knew I would find out. According to the eye doctor, you're very near-sighted." He gave one last jab. "But you don't need glasses to push somebody off a balcony, right?"

Luis rubbed his chest where Melo had bruised him and shifted as if he wanted to jump out of the chair "I did not push anybody off a balcony."

The detective shoved him further back in his chair. "Stay seated. I'm not finished with you. What were the people on the balcony doing?"

"I don't know. From their body language, they seemed to be arguing."

"Did you wait for them to stop arguing so you could talk to Ben?"

"No, I didn't think it was a good idea. I didn't want to embarrass him. I went over to his desk, wrote a short note and left.

"Aha," said the detective grinning. "You never mentioned the note before."

Luis's face was covered with perspiration. Sweat was dripping into his eyes but he didn't move. "I just remembered the note today."

The detective stood up and circled his chair, stopping next to Luis. "Did you take the elevator when you left?"

"No," Luis said emphatically. "The elevator was slow, so I ran down the steps. I had bad vibes about what was happening in that apartment."

The detective cupped his ear. "Let me make sure I heard right. You ran down five flights of stairs?"

For the first time during the interview Luis smiled. "Sure, I'm in good shape. I'm a dancer." The detective circled the room slowly, then came back, straddled the chair again and continued the questioning, his face only a few inches from Luis. "Are you aware that you were the last person to see Ben alive?"

"I wasn't the last person. Somebody on the balcony pushed him."

"That somebody might have been you. That's what the New York cops think."

It was finally lunch time and the detective said they would take a break. Melo brought a ham and cheese sandwich with a cup of coffee for himself into the interrogation room. Luis asked for a cup of fresh coffee. The detective said there wasn't any fresh coffee left. Luis asked for a glass of ice cold water, but the detective said, "Later."

"Turn on the air conditioner," Luis begged.

"Later," said Melo swallowing a bite of his sandwich. "After you answer all my questions."

From the clock on the wall, O'Brien and Marsh could see that fifteen minutes had elapsed before Melo brought a glass of water into the room and handed it to Luis. The detective remained standing, towering over Luis, then started questioning again. "Let's start at the beginning. You were in the apartment and saw two people on the balcony, correct?"

Luis wiped his brow with a handkerchief then nodded and said that was correct. He clutched the corner of the desk as if he felt woozy. Detective Melo seemed to notice but didn't stop. "What did they look like, the two people?"

"I couldn't tell."

The detective jabbed Luis's chest. "You can't tell male from female? What kind of idiot are you?"

"It was dark outside," said Luis. "Or nearly dark. It gets dark early in New York in January."

Melo shook his head. "What time was it?"

Luis rubbed his forehead with the back of his hand. "I don't remember. I wasn't wearing a watch."

Sweat was pouring down the detective's face, but he seemed determined to prove he was macho and quickly moved on to another subject. "How long have you been a recovering addict?"

Luis did a double take then said, "Ten years."

"Did you do drugs with Ben the day he was pushed off the balcony?"

"No," Luis said, pointedly. "I never used drugs with him."

"That day? Or ever?"

"Ever."

Melo held out a pack of cigarettes. Luis shook his head. As Detective Melo lit a cigarette, Luis turned his head away as if the odor sickened him. He didn't turn back until he was asked the next question. "If you don't tell me what happened," continued the detective, "I'm going to ask the New York detectives to pick you up. You won't like their interrogation methods. Now answer me," he shouted, blowing smoke rings in Luis's face. "Did you push Ben off the balcony?"

Luis reeled back from the detective and the smell of the cigarette. I never touched him, I swear to you, I was never out on the balcony." He was practically hyper-ventilating by then.

The detective glared at him. "We have your fingerprints on the desk in the apartment. You followed him out to the balcony, demanded your money back and when he refused, you pushed him. Is that what happened?"

Luis cracked his knuckles. "NO."

Detective Melo stood up and circled Luis's chair, stopping in front of him. "Right now is not looking good. The New York cops don't like your fingerprints on the desk. They fly here; they whip your ass. One thing you can do. Take lie detector test."

"I don't know." He looked scared at the mention of a polygraph test. "I'll think about it."

"If you're innocent, nothing to worry about." The detective got up and pushed his chair behind the desk. "Be here at ten o'clock tomorrow morning with your answer so I can call

New York." He turned on the air conditioner then turned to Luis. "You can call Pepita and ask her to pick you up. But wait in here, I'll send her in. Hear me?"

Luis nodded.

"Pepita is mucho loyal," said the detective. "I'm sure she'll visit you in jail." The detective chuckled. "I'll be back. And by the way, don't think of leaving town. That would make you look guilty."

Luis sat back and picked up the glass of water. It was empty by then.

"I'll be back when Pepita arrives, then you can leave with her."

Chapter 42

Detective Melo told O'Brien and Marsh over the phone that when he left the room he deliberately left the tape recorder running. "Luis and Pepita were so nervous they didn't notice. "I'll play tape for you," he said.

"Great," said Cheri, turning up their speaker phone.

The first voice they heard was that of Pepita telling Luis, "When Melo comes back tell him you'll take the test. What are you afraid of?" Cheri missed the next few words but she was getting the gist of the conversation and she figured James was, too.

"There could be a mistake and they'll throw me in jail," Luis replied.

"Nobody can pin it on you if you pass the test. If you refuse, you'll look guilty And stop walking around the room like a caged animal. Listen honey, I'll stay with you while you take the test. Melo might let me do that or I'll wait right outside the door and we'll go home together."

"I'm scared, Pepita. The cops are looking for a way out. And my track record doesn't look good."

"Please, Luis. Do it for me."

"I can't. Don't you understand? There are sometimes mistakes with lie detector tests. I don't want to be one of those mistakes."

There was a long pause then Pepita's voice, loud and clear. "Luis, you're not only making Melo think you're guilty. You're making me think you're guilty. If I'm coming to that conclusion, what will the detectives in New York think?"

Cheri said something to James and he whispered, "Sh, maybe he'll agree. Let's listen."

Pepita continued begging Luis, until she finally said, "Bullshit, I'm leaving. Don't come home until you take the test. Go live with your sister in the favella."

Luis tried to tell her something but she interrupted. "No, no more explanations. You were in New York when Ben died. You invested with Ben and lost a ton of money. What am I supposed to think?"

"Pepita," he cried, "you're not being fair."

"Fair? There was a possible murder. You're a suspect and you ask me to be fair. Get with it, Luis. I know your temper. I know you got into fights in New York. You told me that yourself."

"That was a long time ago when I was doing drugs. I don't do drugs anymore and no more fights. Don't bring up the past."

"Then take the freaking test."

"NO. Why should I? That's an admission of guilt."

"Shit," Pepita screamed. "Look, the tape recorder's been running all this time. I'm out of here, Luis. You dragged me through the mud in the favella. Now, you're risking our careers. Don't come back till you take the test. Hear me?"

"The tape recorder is running," he cried. "Stop talking."

There was the sound of high heels on the floor and the slam of a door.

When Detective Melo returned, he asked Luis, "Will you agree to take test."

"I'll call you with my decision. And you left the tape recorder running."

"Did I?" said Melo. "Was mistake. But you are innocent so you have nothing to be afraid of, right?"

"Right," said Luis, "but, you still should have turned off the tape recorder."

"Who says? You?" He laughed. "You are a stupid man. You drag this out when it could be over if you take test. Meanwhile, get your culo out of here. You make me sick."

"I'll get back to you," said Luis. He uttered something under his breath and left the interrogation room.

Melo told the detectives in New York that he'll be in touch about Luis's decision. "Great," said James. "We'll wait to hear from you."

"Hasta luego," said Cheri. "Hope to meet you one day."

"Would be my pleasure," he said, sounding excited. "Meanwhile, hasta luego Senorita Marsh."

Chapter 43

Cheri and James decided to go out for a late lunch to discuss Melo's video. As soon as they stepped outside Cheri took a deep breath. "We're having a January thaw. How 'bout that?"

"About time. How about a picnic in Central Park? I'll bring a blanket and some take-out food."

She laughed. "Would love it, but it's not that warm. Let's wait till spring."

They continued walking down Broadway with their coats over their arms, and their long sleeves rolled up to their elbows.

"I feel positively giddy about that tape recording," said Cheri. "Let's not stop at the first coffee shop, we could use some fresh air." As they waited for the light to change, Cheri ran to a corner newsstand and glanced at the tabloid. There wasn't anything about Ben on the front page.

They chose a coffee shop and took a booth in back. After they were seated, they noticed TV sets in front of them, in back, and to the side. There was also a television set hanging on the wall facing the counter. They hated the noise but didn't want to leave. After the waitress took their order Cheri said, "Hope the service is fast, I'm starving."

"Me, too," said James. "Can't go over the case until I get some food in my gut."

She laughed. "Same here. "We're like bears. By the way, just thought of something. We should call Kati back for another interview, she's not off the hook yet." James nodded as the waitress poured coffee. As soon as their food arrived they dug in, hardly talking.

Cheri noticed that all the television sets in the restaurant were tuned to MSNBC with the stock market prices running across the bottom of the screens. She was a news junkie and often watched that channel, but she wasn't interested in the stock market. They continued eating, making a few comments from time to time. until three words blasted from the TV screens: "BRIGHTON BEACH, BROOKLYN."

James's dropped his fork and stared at the screen facing them. Cheri spun around and faced the television. She craned her head to hear better, especially with all the noise in the restaurant. The picture on the screen showed Brighton Beach. Cheri recognized it immediately. A TV anchor on the scene announced that several people were shot and a stabbing had taken place. "In broad daylight," she added. Cheri took a deep breath and exhaled loudly.

"Here's what we know so far," said the anchor. "There was a gangland incident in Brighton Beach. Several members of the Russian Mafia were shot and a bystander on the boardwalk was stabbed. There aren't any witnesses so far. The alleged shooters, Russian mobsters, have been apprehended. According to the Brooklyn police the injured man was not linked to the Russian Mafia here in Brooklyn. The police are hoping witnesses will come forward with information about the stabbing." The anchor pulled out a notebook. "The man who was stabbed has been identified as..." She stumbled over the name then finally said, Dimitri Balabanov. "From what we've learned, he's expected to make a full recovery."

"Whoa, what do you think of that?" asked James.

Cheri kept shaking her head. "We couldn't have ordered a better finale for a few Russian mobsters." They stopped talking when the waitress came back to refill their coffee cups and James asked for the check.

She put the check on the table and asked if everything was okay.

"Fine," said James. "We have to get back to work. An emergency."

After they raced back to the police station, James called his buddies at the police station in Brighton Beach and asked for details. After he hung up, he told Cheri that the anchor got it right. But there was one piece of information missing. "My buddy thinks the perp was aiming for somebody else and Dimitri was nearby."

Cheri grinned. "The Russians are helping the Brooklyn cops by knocking each other off."

"Know what I think?" said James. "Jazz wasn't a member of the Russian mob. He asked his cousin Sergei for a favor and got caught in the net. The guy has lousy luck. First, he lost a lot of money with Ben then he almost lost his life today." He rubbed his chin while he kept shaking his head. "I wonder if Leslie heard the news yet."

"If not, she'll hear it soon. It's been a good day so far. First the news from Rio and now the Russian mob's getting wiped out."

"Let's celebrate," said James. "Where would you like to go?"

"Can't celebrate tonight. My big day tomorrow. The Martial Arts Competition."

"Sorry, I forgot. But I cleared the time in my diary. I'll be there."

"I'm getting nervous."

"Don't be. You're good."

Chapter 44

Friday night, Cheri was putting her laptop to sleep when her cell rang.

"Hey," cried Caz. "Just got your message. Congrats on finishing first in the Martial Arts Competition."

"Thanks. Actually, I finished first in my age group. Third overall. But I'm happy."

"You should be. Want to come over for a glass of wine?"

"Would love to. I'll be right there." Just as she was leaving, she received a text from James: Congrats, hope you got my message. Got stuck at the E.R. with my mom. She has a bad case of the flu. Still at the hospital, waiting. Talk to you later.

Cheri texted back. No problem about not being there. Will tell you all about it. Hope your mom gets better soon. xoxo.

As soon as they were settled on wooden stools in Caz's tiny kitchen, she turned to Cheri and asked, "What are you planning to do for a celebration?"

"I'm going to ride..."

"A mechanical bull?"

Cheri laughed. "No, I'm going to ride escalators."

"What?"

"I never told you this, but my biggest fear is going down an escalator so I'm going to Macy's and ride the escalators from top to bottom. I'm determined not to chicken out this time."

Caz poured more wine for them. "I can't believe it. You deal with the possibility of getting shot in the line of duty, not to mention stabbed, kidnapped, held hostage, and you're afraid of going down an escalator?"

"Yup. I'm sometimes afraid of the things you mentioned, too, but escalators are more prominent in my life. I fear they'll start building airports with only escalators, no stairs, no elevators, same with office buildings and condos in New York. I'll have to stay on the roof until they'll air-lift me down."

"They have to have elevators for the disabled."

Cheri sipped her wine then put the glass down. "But I'm not disabled, so I may not qualify to use them. You'll need a special app in the future for the truly disabled."

"No way will that happen. Your imagination is going haywire. You're reading too many sci-fi novels." Caz took another sip of wine. "When did this fear start?

"When I was a kid. Nothing happened, never got sucked up by an escalator. I was just standing at the top of an escalator one day and freaked out."

Caz shook her head in disbelief. "And you haven't ridden one since?

"I have, in an emergency. But I hold on so tight James has to pry my hand loose when I get to the bottom. Cheri laughed. "Poor James. What a partner they gave him." She thought for a second. "The nicest thing James ever said to me was 'You're not perfect, but you're perfect for me.' And I always thought I was perfect."

They laughed so hard Caz almost dribbled her wine.

Cheri leaned forward, facing her friend. "What are you afraid of?"

"Bungee jumping."

Cheri shook her head. "That's not a necessity."

"It was for me," said Caz." I had a boyfriend who used to go bungee jumping. I didn't want to lose him so I went once. That was it."

"What happened to him?"

"He died."

"Seriously?"

"Yeah." He moved to Nepal to climb mountains and fell off a cliff." She picked up the bottle of wine. "Want some more?"

"No thanks," said Cheri. "I have to get back to my laptop, also see if there's e-mail from James. But if he calls instead, I don't want to sound drunk."

"You're not at work," said Caz. "That reminds me, I saved work for tonight, too."

They clinked glasses and finished the rest.

When Caz walked Cheri to the door, she leaned against the wall, her face flushed from the alcohol. "Want me to go with you on your escalator run? I can hold your hand."

Cheri said "Good idea but no thanks."

"Good luck."

"Instead, tell me what they say in the theater: Break a leg"

"On an escalator?"

"I agree, not good," said Cheri.

They hugged goodbye, then Cheri went home to decide if she really wanted to confront her fear. Maybe I'll just live with it, she told herself as she splashed cold water on her face.

When she checked her cell, there was a message on voice mail from James. "Just brought my mom home. Before I forget, how about going to Giorgo's to celebrate your win in the competition?"

She looked at her Smartphone and decided it wasn't too late to call him back. He didn't pick up so she left a message. "Giorgio's would be great. We can have a double celebration after we close the Rabinowitz case."

Mentioning the case reminded her about Luis and the fact that he was looking more and more like the killer. James was right, she thought. Leslie and Luis are tied for first place, but her money was on Leslie by a nose.

Chapter 45

When Detective Melo called again he told Detectives Marsh that Luis showed up for the lie detector test. "He passed test," Melo said, sounding disgusted. Cheri figured that her hunch was correct. He was hoping to get Luis out of the picture so he could put the make on Pepita. The damn polygraph test spoiled his plans.

"Guess he can be eliminated now," she said. "Thanks for your help." After saying goodbye to Melo she passed the news along to James.

After they crossed Luis off their list of suspects Cheri grabbed her hat and coat and announced, "I have a few more hospitals on my list. I'm going to keep going until midnight if I have to. That okay with you? If I can catch Leslie in a lie about visiting an E.R., I might be able to coax the Big One out of her."

He nodded and said, "That's possible."

She hesitated at the door. "Forgot to ask, what are your plans for today?"

James held up a legal size pad. I'm not finished calling the suckers, I mean the investors in Ben's gold mine scam. I'm also hoping to interview the mystery investor who spends his days in movie theaters."

"Good luck," Cheri called, closing the door. "We both need it."

Resembling the Energizer bunny in a white down coat and white ski hat, she drove to the first hospital on her list: St. Luke's-Roosevelt on West Fifty-Ninth Street. After flashing her shield and picture I.D., she asked the nurse if a Mrs. Rabinowitz was seen in the emergency room on January 15th. "She might have come in for a sprained ankle and possible abrasions on her arms and hands."

The nurse checked her computer and shook her head. "Sorry, nobody with that name on that date."

Cheri thanked her and continued uptown where she repeated the same routine at Weill-Cornell Medical Associates. After waiting more than fifteen minutes, it turned out to be another dead-end.

Onward and upward, she told herself. Time to visit the chi-chi Upper East Side. She pulled the car keys out of her pocket and drove cross-town through Central Park. As she crawled through heavy traffic, Cheri looked out of the window. The elm trees were bare and the ground was frozen but there were nannies pushing strollers and joggers dressed in shorts as if it were spring.

As soon as Cheri reached New York Hospital she discovered that the hospital was huge. She had to search for the entrance to the emergency room. After she finally found somebody willing to help her. the computer came up empty. No Mrs. Rabinowitz on or about that date.

Determined not to give up or stop for a cup of coffee, she continued down her list to New York Presbyterian, on East Eighty-Sixth Street. She had a good feeling about this hospital and begged the nurse to check the computer a second time. "I don't have time," she said with an Irish brogue. "If I didn't find the name the first time, I won't find it a second time." She dismissed Cheri with a nod of her head.

"I understand. I know you're busy." She thanked the nurse on duty and left. Her hunt was going nowhere. But somebody pushed Ben off that balcony. And her gut feeling said it was Leslie, a woman so obsessed with her husband that she would kill the man she loved man rather than share him.

Next on her list was Mt. Sinai Hospital on East Ninety Sixth Street. She was running out of hospitals to visit. Cheri couldn't understand why Leslie who thought she might have broken her ankle didn't have it looked at. Afraid of leaving a paper trail?

Tired and hungry by then, Cheri considered buying a sugar-filled donut, then decided to keep going. She only had two more hospitals on her list. Her feet were ice-cold and her hands felt frozen even through leather gloves. She had hoped to hit it big in one of the earlier hospitals and head back to the police station.

As soon as she reached the door of the next emergency room she became aware of total bedlam. There had just been a serious accident. Orderlies were carrying in the bleeding and wounded on stretchers. It looked like a war zone. A bus carrying school children had been side-swiped by a truck. Bad timing to speak to a nurse on duty, she realized. She decided to walk over to Lexington Avenue, have something to eat and return later when there would be less chaos.

Stopping at a coffee shop she ordered a pastrami sandwich and a cup of coffee. She was cold and tired and her boots were torture. She pulled off her left boot and discovered a huge blister on her heel. So much for expensive, fur lined boots. She vowed to wear old hiking boots for walking from now on. After calling James, she left a message bringing him up to date. The noise in the coffee shop was deafening. Hoping to kill a little more time, she ordered a second cup of coffee and nursed it as if it was a margarita. That made her think of Rio again as she looked out the window of the coffee shop. The sun was hidden behind clouds and it looked as if it was going to snow again. This was turning into the winter from hell.

When she returned to the hospital, the corridors in the E.R. were clear and a different nurse was on duty, one who hadn't been there during the turmoil and her disposition was almost cheerful when she asked Cheri if she could help her.

"Yes," Cheri answered, showing the woman her I.D. She told her what she needed then waited. Just then, the phone rang and the nurse took care of the caller before the phone rang a second time. Before the phone rang a third time, Cheri quickly inquired about a Mrs. Rabinowitz visiting the E.R.

"Sorry, wish I could help you, but there is doctor-patient confidentiality and HIPAA laws. I believe you need to come back with a warrant for me give you that information."

"Not in this case." said Cheri, pointedly. "This is a homicide case. And I need the information ASAP."

The nurse locked eyes with Cheri, stayed like that for a second then turned back to her computer and scrolled down. "I hope I'm doing the right thing," she said. "I'm new here and I don't want to get in trouble."

"You won't," said Cheri. "You're helping to solve a murder case."

The nurse turned back to the computer and said,. "Looks as if a Mrs. Rabinowitz was here on January 18th."

Cheri forgot about the heat in the hospital, the blister on her foot, and her tight fur-lined boots and asked, "What was she here for?"

"Let me see." She continued scrolling down. "Her chart says she had a rash on her upper arms."

"A rash?" Cheri repeated. "Not a sprained ankle?"

"No mention of it. But here's something else. The doctor on duty, Doctor. Ramirez, noted on the chart that Mrs. Rabinowitz said she was under stress, something traumatic happened. She wouldn't tell the doctor what happened, just said, an accident. The patient also asked the doctor for a refill of a prescription for Raynaud's disease."

"What is Raynaud's disease?" asked Cheri.

"It's a rare disease. The blood vessels in a person's hands and feet react to severe cold temperatures or to stress. The fingers tingle and turn white."

The phone rang again. The nurse transferred the call and returned to the computer.

"Did the doctor give her a prescription?"

"The chart says yes. Raynaud's can cause infections."

"And what caused the rash?"

She scrolled down while Cheri held her breath.

"Let me see... Dr. Ramirez wrote that the rash was due to an allergic reaction."

"To what?" asked Cheri. "A medication? Please keep checking."

"I'm looking." She was starting to sound exasperated. She kept reading until she finally said, "It says here..."'

"Yes? Tell me."

"According to the chart, the patient told Dr. Ramirez that she has a wool allergy and the rash was due to her husband's woolen jacket."

"Interesting," said Cheri, wondering where Ben had been sleeping. Leslie said he was staying at his pad on West End Avenue. She asked the nurse to make a copy of the chart. "Please hurry," she added. "I have to get back to the police station ASAP."

The nurse said she could do that and started making a copy of the record.

"We need to confirm Mrs. Rabinowitz's first name," said Cheri.

"It was Leslie, right?"

"No. The name in the computer isn't Leslie. It's Kati."

Chapter 46

As soon as Kati opened the door she apologized, said she was in the bathroom. Detective Marsh noticed a suitcase and a backpack in a corner of the living-room. James's eyes indicated that he had spotted those items, too.

"We have a few questions for you," said Cheri, closing the door behind her. They stepped into the living room. Cheri turned on the tape recorder and ordered Kati to sit.

"What's this all about?" cried Kati

Cheri held up a copy of the chart from New York Hospital. "You tell us."

"First of all, where were you planning to go?" James walked over to the unzipped backpack and upended it. A passport fell on the floor. "Planning to leave the country?"

"The last performance of *Suffer Queen* was yesterday. I made a last minute decision to take a vacation. I'm entitled, aren't I?"

"Why didn't you return our calls? We kept leaving messages that we wanted to talk to you."

"I was busy."

"Is that so?" said Cheri. "We found out your play closed last night, that's why we're here this morning. Figured you'd stayed up celebrating and slept late today."

Cheri hovered over Kati who was seated on the couch like a teenager about to be grounded. "I visited New York Hospital and learned about your rash, diagnosed as a severe allergic reaction to wool." She had deliberately added the word "severe" for dramatic effect. "We have enough evidence to send you to prison for a long time."

"You're lying. You're making that up to scare me."

"We also interviewed Dick, the director of your show," added James. "We discovered that you went out the afternoon Ben died. You might have been studying your lines earlier in the day, but Dick said he called you about five-thirty to invite you to dinner. During the conversation, he overheard traffic in the background. You were either walking or riding a bus, according to him. You were also not in this neighborhood. The signal from your cell indicates you were not far from Ben's apartment."

Kati tried to stand up but Cheri ordered her to remain seated. "You're not going anywhere until you tell us what happened."

"You're wrong. About everything."

"We have enough evidence to make you our prime suspect. We have the nurse from the E.R. on tape and we have Dick's testimony."

James moved forward and stared at Kati. "Thanks to Dick, your alibi is shot," he said, turning to Cheri who picked up the interrogation.

"As Ben's third and last wife, you expected to collect everything," said Cheri.

"But there was one detail you hadn't counted on. Ben was a bigamist."

Katie was hunched over her lap, hands covering her eyes. "You're wrong," she cried. "You're both dead wrong."

James looked at her, his lips pursed in anger. Cheri knew how much he hated money-grubbing women, how tempted he was to tell Kati what he thought of her but he'd probably hold off and vent later. "You'd be wise to tell us about that evening." he said.

"Nothing happened."

"Nothing?" Cheri asked.

"I did forget to tell you one thing," said Kati "I left my apartment to buy Chinese take-out."

"You weren't hungry. That's what you told Dick."

"I changed my mind."

Cheri moved closer, arms crossed in front of her chest. "So, you took a cross-town bus to West End Avenue? No Chinese restaurants near you? This is New York."

Kati stared straight ahead, fists clenched.

"But instead of Chinese take-out, or dinner with Dick, you went to Ben's apartment. Why did you go there?"

Cheri surmised that Kati went to Ben's apartment after discovering Ben hadn't gone to Boston on business. When she asked her if that was true, Kati reluctantly said yes. She had called Ben and he said he was still in New York. That's when she told him she needed to talk to him. He said, Come over to my place on West End Avenue. I work better where it's quiet. Kati stopped abruptly and wiped her eyes with both hands.

"Go on," said James.

"I took the bus there, but when I arrived at Ben's apartment it was obvious he was high on coke and booze."

"What was he drinking?" asked Cheri.

"Scotch and soda."

"Did he offer you a drink?"

"No. He was already high so I guess he forgot his manners."

"Continue," said James.

"We started talking. About money. He wasn't giving me any. For the house for food, for anything. And he cancelled all my credit cards."

Cheri rested one arm on a round mahogany table covered with photographs and stared out of the window at the city spread out before her. *F. Scott Fitzgerald had a point. The rich are different.* Turning around, she watched James's face as he continued questioning the suspect.

"How did you end up on the balcony?"

Katie was crying harder by this time. "Ben always had a habit of shutting me out especially if we were arguing. I should have realized he was high and it was useless to discuss anything." James handed her a handkerchief, told her to keep it.

"You were about to tell us how you ended up on the balcony," said Cheri, moving away from the table.

"Okay," Kati whispered. "Ben walked out on the balcony so he wouldn't have to listen to me, but I told him he couldn't shut me out anymore. The door to the balcony didn't have a lock on it so I followed him and…"

She broke down at this point and James asked, "Was he tipsy enough to lose his balance and fall?"

"Yes," said Kati, looking hopeful. "It must have happened just after I left."

Cheri could see James's clenched jaw, a sign of his anger. "During that entire time, did you ever touch him?" she asked.

"No, why would I?"

"He didn't fall," James said pointedly. "He was pushed. I'm curious about something. Did you know you're allergic to wool?"

"Of course, but I didn't touch Ben's jacket. He wouldn't let me near him on the balcony. I was hoping to get back together, so I asked him to hold me while we were inside and he did.

But he refused to get near me when we were outside. He kept saying, 'Get your coat and leave.'"

"Where was your coat?"

"In the apartment."

Cheri moved closer, one hand pressed against her jaw. "Did you push him over the balcony?"

"NO. Of course not."

"We have evidence you did," said James.

"Ben had a lot of enemies," cried Kati. "He cheated his investors out of a lot of money. One of them probably killed him. He was fine when I left. He either fell or someone who hated him visited his apartment." She hesitated. "He even mentioned an appointment. That's why he was all dressed up."

"No, sweetheart, it was you he feared. You were the only one who had a spare key." James moved closer to Katie as he continued the questioning. "Plus, we found a note in his daily calendar reminding him to change the lock on his apartment door. He evidently didn't get to it."

"This is a hanging. You'll be proven wrong."

"We also spoke to your doctor."

"How could you find out the name of my doctor?"

"We have ways," said Cheri, picking up the questioning. "Your doctor confirmed what the record in the E.R. showed. You have Raynaud's disease. You arrived at the apartment wearing leather gloves and never took them off. Clever, no fingerprints."

Katie's coat was on top of her laptop. When she began staring at the front door the detectives nodded to each other and quickly blocked the access to the outside door.

"You had a motive," said James. "And you had an alibi until the director of your show called while you were on West End Avenue. The global positioning system on your cell isn't false."

"You're lying," said Katie.

"The GPS didn't lie," said James. "It's over, sweetheart, the show is closing."

Cheri checked the tape recorder on the table as she moved closer. "I've been an actor," she said quietly. "I understand what you went through to establish an acting career."

Kati looked up at Detective Marsh. "You told me you acted for a while so I bet you do understand. Acting is more competitive than most careers."

"I know," said Cheri. "Tell me everything."

James moved aside and let the two women talk.

Kati wiped her eyes. "Ben threatened to leave me said he was going to put the condo up for sale. It was in his name. I can't afford the rent in New York. It's gotten worse. Even with roommates, I can't afford New York anymore." Kati's shoulders slumped like a rag doll. "I would have had to go back to waitressing." She began sobbing louder than before and sniffling in between words. "No time to make rounds. No time to network. No time to take classes. No more acting gigs." She looked at Cheri. "You acted. You know."

"I sure do," said Cheri, pretending to sound sympathetic. "You constantly have to make rounds to get anywhere. And you have to go to open auditions."

"You can't spend time waitressing," said Kati.

"I had to waitress, too. I know what that's like," said Cheri, "You have a call-back and you don't know how you'll get there." She caught James's eye. He winked at her

"Ben promised he would always help me," said Kati. "He promised. He told me, You will never have to go back to a crummy job again. I'll take care of you. Forever." She stopped to catch her breath. "He didn't even come to a rehearsal of *Suffer Queen.* Claimed he was too busy."

"What a crummy excuse," said Cheri. "I would've been pissed, too. But let's get back to that night in his apartment."

"When I asked him for money," he said, "Tough. I take my words back. Go, get a real job. You're not talented anyway. He screamed, I've had enough." Then he turned and walked away from me and went out on the balcony."

"So you followed him, right?" said Cheri.

"I just wanted to keep talking, but he shut me out."

"Your arms were bare and you were cold so you asked him to hold you. He was your husband. He was supposed to be there for you."

"Yes," said Kati but he screamed, I told you, I've had enough. Get your coat and leave."

"Go on," said Cheri. "Don't stop now."

"It was like hearing my father's voice when he was drunk and he'd yell, You're not talented enough for New York, Katie. He said that to me all the time." She lowered her head in her hands.

I'm listening," said Cheri. "And I don't agree with him. I think you're very talented."

Kati looked up, tears streaking her cheeks. "You do?"

"Yes, I do. Tell me what happened out on the balcony."

"He wouldn't let me touch him. Made fun of my wearing gloves indoors. He knew I have a disease."

Cheri didn't say anything, just nodded at James.

Kati continued sobbing. "I was about to leave when he screamed. Get out, you whore. That's when he turned his back on me. He always shut me out. So I reached out and..."

"And what happened?" asked Cheri.

"It was easy."

"What was easy? Tell me."

""Pushing him. He had his back to me, but he'd been drinking and smoking weed. He wasn't steady on his feet. He went over fast."

"Over what?" asked Cheri.

"He went over the balcony."

"When?"

"After I pushed him." Kati broke down and cried hysterically. She looked at James just as he pulled a pair of handcuffs out of his back pocket. While he handcuffed her he told her, "You're under arrest for the murder of Benjamin Rabinowitz," then advised her of her Miranda rights: "You have the right to remain silent. Anything you say can and will be held against you in a court of law. You have the right to speak to an attorney If you can't afford an attorney, one will be appointed for you. Do you understand those rights?"

Kati lowered her head. "Yes," she whispered. She was breathing heavily as she cried, "But you tricked me."

"You're wrong," said Cheri as they led her away. "Confessing was the best thing you could have done for yourself."

When Cheri got home that evening, there was e-mail from James.

"We need to build our case against Kati. Will tell you my idea tomorrow morning."

Chapter 47

James suggested they interview Dick Alter, the director of Kati's show *Suffer Queen.* When James called Dick he readily agreed to be interviewed.

Two days later, a policewoman escorted him into the interrogation room where the detectives were going over their prepared questions. Too bad I'm not networking in the theater anymore, thought Cheri. She had been impressed with Dick's work on *Suffer Queen;* he didn't strike her as arrogant or conceited. She remembered reading his resume in the Playbill. It struck her as impressive. A lot of professional work Off-Broadway and an M.F.A from the Yale School of Drama.

Dick remained standing until James said, "Have a seat." He sat, one leg crossed as if he was getting ready to perform the lotus position in yoga.

James asked a few simple questions to break the ice then zeroed in. "Do you remember the night of Ben's murder?"

"I sure do," said Dick. "I hadn't been alone with Kati for several days except for rehearsals so I called and asked her to dinner that night. She said she couldn't make it. I asked her what was going on."

"What did she say?"

"She told me she had to go cross-town to visit a sick friend and might not be back on time."

"Go on," said Cheri.

"That struck me as odd. She almost never went to the West Side except for the theatre district in mid-town. I thought I was being replaced so I asked her point blank, "Is it a guy you're visiting?"

James stood up at that point and asked what her reaction was.

"She laughed and told me, It's just a friend who lives on West End Avenue. That caused my ears to perk up. That's why I remember her answer and the reference to West End Avenue. You know why I also remember that night so well?"

The detectives shook their heads. Dick said it was the day before his birthday, a biggie–his thirtieth. They had planned an evening out with drinks and dinner."

Cheri moved closer. "Did you see her at all that evening?"

"No, that's what gave me the idea she was cheating on me." He chuckled. "I mean, she was already cheating on her husband, so why not me, too?"

James took a pair of bifocals out of his breast pocket and walked around the table. "Did Kati strike you as an opportunist?"

"In what way?"

"Did you ever get the feeling that Kati married a rich, older man to advance her career."

"She never told me that," said Tom.

"But did you get that feeling? That's what I'm asking," said James.

"Yeah, Kati was a user. She used me to meet people, so guess I would call her an opportunist."

"You had an affair with her, correct?"

Dick laughed as he pulled off his leather jacket. "A short one."

"But in that short time," said James, "did you get the feeling she wanted a career in the theater more than anything in the world?"

"Definitely."

Cheri moved to Dick's left side and checked out the wedding ring on his finger. So, they were both married. How convenient. "Are you planning to move *Suffer Queen* to Broadway?" she asked.

Dick shrugged. "I don't know. We'd love to, but the producers have to raise the money first. One-woman shows don't make much money unless there's a name attached to it."

"Were the producers planning to have Kati star in the show?"

The director looked uncomfortable and took a long time before he answered. "No, we need a name. Also, her husband told me that he wasn't planning to invest any more money in the show."

James took off his glasses and put them on the desk. Cheri knew that was a nervous habit of his, putting them on, taking them off, although he didn't appear nervous. "Did you tell Kati that?" he asked.

Dick faced both detectives. "Yes, and she wasn't happy about her husband's decision." Cheri moved closer and picked up the questioning. "Do you think she wanted revenge on you?"

"I think she would've wanted revenge if the show moved to Broadway without her."

"And her husband?"

Dick pulled out a stick of gum and threw the wrapper in the trash. "She was livid at him. She probably wanted revenge against him, too, for not planning to invest any more money.

To tell you the truth, we might've kept her in the show if her husband promised to pour more money into it." Dick hesitated then said softly, "I'm not saying she isn't talented, but there are lots of young beautiful women in the theater. They come to New York from Hollywood for the challenge of a play on Broadway then fly back to the money-making jobs in movies."

Cheri crossed her arms in front of her and leaned across the desk. "Did Kati's husband buy her the role in *Suffer Queen*?"

Dick took his time answering. "There were equally talented actresses, but during auditions, her husband's donation definitely moved Kati up to first choice. We're a small theater and always in need of money."

Cheri let out a whoosh of air and walked around the room before stopping directly in front of Dick." Would you agree to be a witness for the prosecution when the time comes?"

He sat up straighter. "Not sure I can do that. I'm busy and it would take a lot of time."

Cheri moved in like a mother lion stalking her prey. "What if we can guarantee that you wouldn't have to testify in person. There are closed circuit cameras and Skype.

"Would that change things? We could do that for you. You'd be an important witness in the case."

Dick nodded. "I don't mean to be difficult, but if I'm in rehearsals, then yeah I would tell them what I told you without having to go to court. Either way, I would say that when I told her the producers want to move the play uptown, but without her because she wasn't enough of a name, she looked at me with so much anger, I was afraid of her at that moment."

"How would you describe the way she looked at you," said Cheri.

Dick took a deep breath. "She stared at me as if she was thinking I'll get even with you. Not long after that I ended our relationship. That really pissed her off. She was probably hoping I'd change the producers' minds."

Cheri checked the tape recorder then asked, "Can you think of anything else you want to tell us?"

Dick cleared his throat. "There is something else. When I met Kati before *Suffer Queen* she was up for a starring role in a play off-Broadway and told me, I'd kill for that role, but she didn't get the part. Went to somebody who had more of a name."

Cheri noticed James looking intently at Dick as he asked, "What's the point? Did the other actress die?"

Dick looked from one detective to the other. "No. But she got hit by a car, and they hired someone from television and Hollywood."

"Interesting," said Cheri, catching James's eye. He didn't look happy about what happened to the actress, but he didn't ask any more questions. It was probably coincidental about her getting hit by a car but she guessed what her partnr was thinking: Our Kati takes care of herself.

After a few more questions, the detectives thanked Dick, handed him a card and walked him to the door. "We'll be in touch," said Cheri.

After he left the interrogation room, Cheri let out a whoop. "Can you believe our luck?"

"Yeah," said James. "We're good."

"Dick lucked out, too. Or he might have been her second victim, especially if *Suffer Queen* moved to Broadway without her."

James nodded. "Now she'll be able to perform for a bigger audience, her fellow inmates."

"And she probably will," said Cheri. "Meanwhile, we'll have another case to look forward to soon. Hope it'll be as interesting as the Rabinowitz case."

The following evening, Cheri and James went to celebrate at their favorite Italian restaurant. After opening a bottle of French champagne, James proposed a toast in English and Spanish. Cheri added one in Brazilian Portugese.

"Are you disappointed the captain vetoed the trip to Rio?"

"A little," she said, holding the glass of champagne to her nose. She loved the bubbly smell almost as much as she loved the taste. "Here's to us." They clinked glasses and toasted again as the waiter set a plate of Italian bread and olive oil on the table. The overhead lights were low and there were very few people in the restaurant. Cheri realized it was early for New Yorkers to be having dinner. She was still a Montanan and preferred to eat early.

She inhaled deeply as her entree was placed in front of her and the smell of garlic wafted up from the food. When she leaned closer she also smelled thyme, one of her favorite herbs.

Just then, Dominic, the owner of the restaurant, walked over from a nearby table and admired their choice of food and champagne. "So, what are you two celebrating?"

"Remember the guy in the paper?" said James. "The stock-broker who was pushed off the balcony? We just arrested his wife. Well, one of his wives. He had three."

Dominick rested his hands on his bulging stomach. "Three wives? Hope he was rich." His stomach shook as he laughed. "Me? I'd rather fly to the moon in a rocket than marry again." He topped off their glasses of champagne. "Salud," he said, pointing to their food.

"Mangia, mangia," he added, looking at Cheri. "Eat, eat. You're too skinny." He winked as he turned and walked to another table. Cheri held up her glass of champagne and said, "We did it, without Rio and without Detective Melo."

She took a bite of her food, enjoying the mix of herbs and spices. "The veal is great, thanks for the suggestion."

"Glad you like it." She smiled back at him, noticing not for the first time how super he looked in a new blue and white striped shirt. "You know," she added, "I always trusted my instincts, but my hunch about Leslie was wrong."

"Hey, you're not perfect."

"I always thought I was."

"You're still perfect for me."

"Thanks. You're perfect for me, too."

He winked at her. "By the way, I heard from Leslie today. She has a good chance of recouping some of the money she invested in Ben's gold mine. Said it will take time, but it'll be worth the wait. She also invited us to a concert she's giving in April at the Metropolitan Museum of Art, said she'll send invitations."

"Impressive,' said Cheri, "I'm happy for her. But good thing she doesn't know how hard I tried to nail her or she wouldn't have invited me." She leaned forward and whispered, "She say anything about Jazz getting stabbed?"

James shook his head. "She didn't comment, but she's mucho relieved that he called the attorney about the class action suit. That'll get him off her back. No more texts, no more calls. And she's back to walking dogs at Bideawee."

"Good for her, but can't believe my hunch was so off base."

"Let it go," said James.

"I will," she told him. "As far as Jazz is concerned, better for all of us that his cousin Serge is sniffing dust. As for Kati, she is talented, could have made it as an actor without Ben's money." James tapped his forehead with his index finger.

He cupped his mouth and started coughing as if he had gotten a piece of meat stuck in his throat.

"You okay?"

He nodded then cleared his throat. "I'm fine." He leaned across the table. "The Rabinowitz case is closed. We can ask the captain for a week off." He took a deep breath. "I have an idea," he whispered. "Marry me and we'll go to Ipanema Beach in Rio on our honeymoon." He winked as he pulled a blue Tiffany box out of his pocket and lifted the lid, revealing a diamond ring."

"What? Are you serious?"

"Totally serious. We're good together, for business and pleasure." When she didn't respond he said, "Do you want to think it over?"

"I don't have to."

James rubbed his chin, a worried expression on his face. Just then his cell rang. He glanced at the number and said, "Damn, I have to take this call."

Cheri eyed the ring, simple yet tasteful, as she listened to his side of the conversation. She could tell it was work related but couldn't figure out what happened.

He kept repeating, "Uh-huh. Uh-huh... Bad timing," he told her. "A homicide. Not far from here. We have to get there ASAP."

She dropped her napkin on the table while James signaled to Dominick. The restaurant owner rushed over, a concerned expression on his face. "Is there a problem with the food?" he asked. "I'll bring another dish."

"No problem," said James. "I just got a call about a murder in the theatre district. We'll be back as soon as we can. You can nuke our food later."

Dominick winked at Cheri. "For you, I tell them to cook fresh. Come back when you're ready. Theater district, you said?"

James nodded.

"No need for investigation," said Dominick. "It was the understudy."

The detectives chuckled as they pulled on coats, scarves, hats, and gloves.

As they raced through the crowded streets to their car James told her, "One of the actors found a dead body backstage with puncture wounds, possibly also strangled. A fellow actor."

"The theater," she said, "Right up my alley."

He stopped and grabbed her hand. "You never gave me your answer."

"We have to hurry. The theater district is packed at this hour."

"I know," he said, as he maneuvered his way through the crowd. "But you can still give me your answer."

"What? I can't hear you over this noise."

"Your answer. Tell me your answer."

"I'll tell you in the car," she shouted.

About the Author

The author of four books for young people, published by Houghton Mifflin, Barefoot Books, and Scholastic (2) Edith Tarbescu is also a produced playwright.

Two of her ten-minute plays, "Mother's Day" and "Phone Play," were published in anthologies by Smith & Kraus. Her full-length play, "Molly's Boots" was one of the winners in the competition by or about Native Americans and was performed at the Edward Albee Theater Festival in Valdez, Alaska. A one-woman play, "Suffer Queen," about Rosie Ahearn Keene, of Dublin Ireland, was performed in New York and incluided performances at the Abingdon Theatre. She studied playwriting at the Yale School of Drama where, in addition to writing plays, she also acted on stage. Her various essays were published in newspapers and magazines including The Hartford Courant, Newsday, The Berkshire Eagle, The Christian Science Monitor, and The New York Times. A short story, titled "Belfast Blues," was published in the July, 2019 issue of Adelaide Magazine. She grew up in Brooklyn, New York then lived in Connecticut for many years before moving to Albuquerque, New Mexico twenty years ago where she collects Native American pottery and visits pueblos for feast days, etc. Her hobbies include photography, reading, and aerobics. She is currently at work on a memoir titled "Beyond Brooklyn."

To read more about Edith go to: www.edithtarbescu.com

Made in the USA
Las Vegas, NV
01 April 2021